THE ADVENTURERS GUILD

THE ADVENTURERS GUILD

ZACK LORAN CLARK

AND

NICK ELIOPULOS

DISNEY • HYPERION

Los Angeles   New York

Copyright © 2017 by Zack Loran Clark and Nick Eliopulos

All rights reserved. Published by Disney • Hyperion, an imprint of Disney Book Group. No part of this book may be reproduced or transmitted in any form or by any means, electronic or mechanical, including photocopying, recording, or by any information storage and retrieval system, without written permission from the publisher. For information address Disney • Hyperion, 125 West End Avenue, New York, New York 10023.

First Hardcover Edition, October 2017
First Paperback Edition, October 2018
3 5 7 9 10 8 6 4 2
FAC-026988-19011
Printed in the United States of America

This book is set in FCaslonTwelve/Monotype
Designed by Phil Caminiti
Map art by Virginia Allyn

Library of Congress Control Number for Hardcover: 2017000680
ISBN 978-1-368-00035-2

Visit www.DisneyBooks.com

SUSTAINABLE FORESTRY INITIATIVE Certified Sourcing
www.sfiprogram.org
SFI-00993

THIS LABEL APPLIES TO TEXT STOCK

Chapter One

Zed

Though the world had ended long before Zed was born, this was still the scariest day of his young life.

He stood in Freestone's marketplace—a vibrant hash of stalls and tents crushed between the city's wealthy intown and its outtown slums. Many of the shops were stacked on top of one another into colorful jumbles like painted blocks, piling as high as the city would allow.

The market itself seemed nervous that morning. At this early hour, the air usually thrummed with merchants greeting one another and the busy chatter of servants haggling with grocers.

Not today. Today the market was quiet. Only the sounds of hammers pounding in the distance echoed across the square.

Freestone was preparing for its Guildculling.

Brock, Zed's best friend, stood beside him. The two boys were staring at a large purple tent, on which a wooden sign hung above the entrance flap, with script carved in a careful hand.

Makiva's Fortunes and Charms

Old Makiva was a self-described mystic, though some called her a witch. She sold charms for everything. There were charms for weddings, and dog bites, and protection from bad omens. There were even charms for cleaner laundry.

Half the peasantry of Freestone had one of her talismans tucked away into a pocket or hanging under their shirts. They said plenty of the nobles did, too, though none of them admitted it openly.

One of Makiva's most popular items was the Guildculling charm—a lucky token meant to guide its bearer to their proper destiny. It was also one of her most expensive.

"I'll bet she's not really so scary," Brock whispered. "Jett says she's a fake. His mother bought a fresh-air charm to keep his father from breaking wind in the night, and now the smell is twice as bad. Besides, if Makiva were really magic, she'd be with the Silverglows."

At Zed's look, Brock winced.

"All I mean is," he continued carefully, "she won't curse you. Probably."

"Do you think I'm wasting the coin?" Zed asked. He pulled a small silver piece from his pocket and felt his ears warm at the thought of what his mother could do with the extra money.

Brock looked down at the silver, then back up at Zed. "If it gives you some peace, it's not wasted."

Zed smiled wanly. Brock never worried. But then, things tended to work out for him. His parents were both members of the Merchants Guild, one of the four High Guilds. They weren't nobles, exactly, but they weren't far off. And Brock was practically guaranteed a spot with the Merchants.

Brock was also the most generous person Zed had ever met. He had been the one to get Zed the silver piece, after weeks of complaining to his father that he needed new shoes for the Guildculling. He planned on telling his parents that the coin had been stolen.

As far back as Zed could remember, he'd been anticipating and dreading this day, when Freestone's children who came of age were claimed by one of the city's many craft unions. For most of Zed's friends, the event would be a formality, a rite of passage. Like Brock, they'd been learning their parents' trades since they were small, and they would now officially become apprentices in their families' guilds.

But there were always some surprises. Especially when it came to the High Guilds.

"It won't be long before people start arriving," Brock said, gazing around at the muted square. Beyond it, Freestone's high wall towered over the city, visible from every point within. "I expected there to be more already."

Zed nodded, pocketing the coin again. "In other words," he said, "hurry up." He took a deep breath, smiled at his friend, and strode forward, opening the tent flap with both hands.

He was immediately surprised by how dark it was inside. The tent was made of deep purple cloth—a garish color for a non-noble—but even so, he'd expected it to let more light in. Most traders kept their stalls neat and sunny, to better display their goods. This tent seemed designed to create a gloomy atmosphere.

As his eyes adjusted, Zed discovered he was surrounded by the strangest and most fantastic wares he'd ever seen in a shop, made all the more unnerving in the shadows. There was a basket filled with watches and clocks—all broken. Working timepieces were so rare that only nobles could afford them. He saw some that were made of metal and wood, though a few particularly bewildering examples appeared to be set into carved bones.

Bowls of incense smoldered in every corner. Their burning leaves and powders filled the top of the tent with a cloud of rotten-sweet smoke. The skeletons of small creatures lined the canopies. Most were of animals that Zed had never seen before.

But what truly filled the space were the charms. Everywhere Zed looked, tiny wooden tokens hung from bits of strand, dangling from hooks along the walls and lying in knots on the tables.

Most were suspended from the roof of the tent, hanging from the lavender clouds, just within reach of an outstretched hand. Zed was reminded of spiders that used filaments of sticky thread to ensnare their prey, yanking their unfortunate meals into hidden burrows.

The charms were all wooden, carved into small icons. Many were animals, though a few more abstract examples stood out among the bunch: a hook, a grinning skull, a hand with an eye in its palm.

The charm seller herself sat in the center of the space, behind a narrow divining table.

Before today, Zed had only ever seen the woman in glimpses. As a younger boy, he and his friends had once spent an entire evening staking out her tent from a distance, hoping to get a better look at Old Makiva when she retired from the market.

One by one, Zed's friends had been called home that night, until only he and Brock remained. But as the lamps in the stalls were all snuffed out, and the square fell into a yawning gloom, they too had finally given up their watch.

For all Zed knew, the mystic had never emerged from her tent.

She was younger than Zed had expected of a woman everyone called Old Makiva. Her dark brown skin was smooth and pretty.

Hundreds of years ago, Freestone had been a central trade city, filled with pilgrims, merchants, and dignitaries from all over the world. Such journeys were impossible now, but the city retained its diversity. No two of Zed's friends seemed to share the exact same heritage; they were a patchwork quilt of colors and patterns. His own fawn-colored skin and small features looked quite different from Brock's pale face and broad smile.

But Zed's background was still more complicated than most.

The charm seller lifted her eyes and watched him in silence for a long moment. Zed opened his mouth to say something, but found his earlier gumption had abandoned him, along with his voice.

He was about to retreat—fling the tent's flap aside and run—when the woman's eyes flicked to the wooden stool sitting opposite her. "You're the first this morning," she said, in a warm, not-at-all-frightening voice. "Good for you. Diligence is a kind of charm all its own."

Zed swallowed, but the lump remained in his throat. He approached the table and slowly took a seat.

As he did, he noticed that Old Makiva was in the process of carving a new charm from a piece of wood. The knife she used was curved and graceful looking, the metal gleaming green in the darkness somehow.

"You're here for a Guildculling charm," she said.

It wasn't a question, but Zed nodded anyway.

"I haven't seen an elf-blooded child in the culling in many years."

Zed felt his ears prickle at that, a sure signal that they were turning bright red. He'd been raised by his mother since birth, and, having inherited the majority of her features, he looked essentially human. But his high, peaked ears gave him away as elf-blooded—the only elf-blooded person in Freestone, as far as he knew. Most of the other kids had given up making fun of his ears years ago, though Zed still recognized the surprised look of an adult noticing them for the first time.

"So tell me, elf-blooded child," Makiva continued. "Which guild are you hoping for?"

"My mom's in the Servants Guild," Zed croaked. He cleared his throat. "She takes pride in her work, but says my best chance for a comfortable life is a skilled craft. She's put every bit of coin she could spare into teaching me to read and write."

The woman nodded, though she was no longer looking at Zed. Her eyes were on the charm she was carving, moving the knife fluidly between deft fingers. "So your mother hopes the Scribes will take you. But I've never met a boy your age who didn't dream of being claimed by one of the High Guilds." She flashed Zed a quick smile before returning her attention to her work. "What guild are *you* wishing for, Zed?"

Zed startled. He didn't remember telling the mystic his name. He licked his lips and spoke in an embarrassed whisper. "The Silverglows. I've got a bit of mana already, I think. I hear it takes most wizards a while to develop theirs. It's 'cause I'm a . . .

Well, I figured it must be from my father. So I wrote to them, to let them know about it, but I couldn't find anyone to sponsor or vouch for me. I never heard back."

Zed took a deep breath, slowly shaking his head. "I know I'm being foolish. If the Scribes claim me, it'll still be the luckiest thing that's ever happened to me. But joining the Mages Guild would change my mother's life. The money could buy her a real home, and the title . . ." Zed shifted in his seat. "Well, maybe people wouldn't look down on us so much if I were *Magus* Zed Kagari."

Makiva made a low noise of sympathy. "People, I'm afraid, have always found inventive ways of looking down, regardless of their elevation. But I don't believe it's foolish to dream. The Mages Guild—"

Suddenly the harsh noise of a horse's whinnying cut through the tent.

"Uh, pardon, Messere," Brock's voice called loudly from outside. "There's someone in there al—"

"Get out of my way," said a young voice, taut with contempt. "I'll tell you *once*."

Zed turned in his stool. There was a moment of quiet, followed by the reluctant *pit-pat* of Brock stepping aside.

The tent flap was thrown open, and in the blinding glare of the morning sun, Zed could just make out a suit of gleaming armor.

A noble's armor.

He scrambled to his feet and backed away against the far side of the tent, setting the charms there rattling. The noble stepped farther in, and Zed was surprised to see a boy his own age. He must have come for a Guildculling charm, too. But why? He wouldn't need luck. The nobles always made it into the best guilds.

Zed quickly glanced out the open flap before it billowed closed. Brock shot him a panicked expression, and then the tent fell again into darkness.

The noble boy peered around the space with a look of disgust, pausing on Zed for only as long as he did any of the other curios that surrounded them. He was olive-skinned and handsome and strong, everything the girls in Zed's quarter expected a noble would be. He also looked mean, which was what Zed expected them to be.

Makiva spoke first. "Hello, young Messere," she said. "I'm afraid I'm with another customer right now. Perhaps you wouldn't mind waiting outside?"

The boy's sneer deepened. He shot a hostile look at Zed. Zed bowed his head immediately, as his mother had taught him. "It's no trouble, Messere! You can have my spot."

"What's wrong with your ears?" the young lord asked, in a tone that betrayed a blatant *lack* of curiosity.

Zed's ears grew hot, then his face. When the silence stretched from a pause into a moment, he realized the noble actually expected a response.

"I'm . . . elf . . ." Zed was too flustered to trust himself to speak further. If Brock were here, he'd have a snappy response ready. But servants' sons didn't get away with snappy responses.

"The boy has kindly offered you his seat, Messere," Makiva said, indicating with her hand. "Zed, would you like to wait outside for now?"

"This won't take long," the noble said, rolling his eyes. "I'll be gone before he finally chokes out that sentence." He glanced at the stool he'd been offered before nudging it away with his foot. Apparently he preferred to stand.

Makiva leaned back. She set the charm she'd been carving down on the table, but kept her knife in hand. "So," she said. "What guild are you hoping for, my lord?"

The noble stared at her for a moment with a single eyebrow raised. He swept his hand over the grand suit of armor he was currently wearing. "The Bakers Guild, clearly."

"The knights it is, then," Makiva sighed. The woman stood with a groan. She reached up and began pawing at the charms hanging from the ceiling, which clicked together with a sound like a rainy evening. "But I don't know why you'd need a charm from me. By the way you wear that armor, young Lord Micah Guerra"—Makiva announced the boy's name almost absently— "I'd expect you were an *obvious* choice for the Stone Sons."

Zed shuffled uncomfortably on his feet. He'd heard of the Guerras, of course, but knew very little about them. The nobles lived in the center of the city, in Freestone's stately intown. It was a district preoccupied with expansive family lines and shifting titles.

Zed's mother served at an elegant manor, but the two of them lived together in the bustle of the outtown tenement houses. They may as well have lived in a different city altogether. Zed himself had only ever seen the nobles' rooftops from afar.

The young lord swiveled his shoulders beneath their pauldrons. "So you *can* see through this muck after all."

"Any first- or second-born noble is all but guaranteed a spot in the more prestigious guilds," Makiva continued, searching through her charms, which jounced in waves above their heads. "As a boy, you're permitted to compete for a place among the knights. But, failing that, you'd still be welcomed by the Stewards Guild, to govern our fair city."

Makiva put a hand to her neck, cracking it from side to side. "But that's only the first two children, isn't it?"

Lord Micah Guerra narrowed his eyes. "Are you honestly *still* talking?"

Makiva nodded demurely. "Apologies, Messere."

Zed realized what the mystic had been hinting at now. If a family in Freestone had more than two children, the third-born and beyond were automatically claimed by the Golden Way Temple—the Healers Guild. The Golden Way was one of the four High Guilds, with the Mages, Knights, and Merchants. The healers were revered by Freestone, but they were also a monastic order. Guild members took a sacred vow to live by the

Golden Way, as monks and nuns. They renounced their names and titles—and could never have families of their own.

This was one of the ways that Freestone controlled its growing population. The walls could only hold so many and still protect them from the Dangers outside.

If Micah Guerra was one of those unlucky third children, then he would join the temple as a novice today—*unless* the Knights Guild or Mages Guild claimed him first. The two had priority.

"Ah!" Makiva chirruped with delight. "Here we are." She yanked a strand of twine from the ceiling and the charm came loose, then she handed it over to Guerra.

The young lord eyed the carving suspiciously. "It's . . . What is it?"

"It's called a badger," Makiva said. "They lived outside the wall once. Perhaps they still do. Surprisingly nasty when provoked, but very dedicated to family. That will be three silver, if you please."

Zed started to sweat when he heard the price. Brock had sworn it would be one silver.

Micah Guerra pulled three gleaming coins from a pouch at his waist and tossed them onto the divining table. Then he swept out of the tent without another word, his eyes on his wooden charm.

As the tent flap closed, Zed felt the breath he'd been holding burst out. His shoulders slumped.

"Well, that was . . . bracing," Makiva said. She sat down on her pillowed seat behind the divining table, then held out a hand to the stool Lord Guerra had pushed away. "Where were we?" she asked, as she resumed her carving.

"I can't remember a thing before the lord entered," Zed replied with a nervous laugh. He found his ears still burned as he set the stool right. Zed hesitated, hovering over the table uncertainly. "Only," he began, "the thing is, I should probably go. Three silver is more than I've got."

"The young messere got the special noble rate," the mystic said with a wink. "I have no doubt that you and I can come to an agreement of our own." She waved again at the stool, her gaze insistent. Zed sat down with a grateful smile. "Since you were interrupted," Makiva continued, "and quite rudely, I might add—I am going to offer you a challenge, Zed."

Zed frowned. "What sort of challenge?"

Makiva waved her dagger in a wide arc around the tent. "If you can pick out which charm is yours, you can have it for free."

Zed's mouth fell open. He looked up and gazed across a sea of wooden tokens, all hanging from bits of twine. There must have been hundreds of them in the murky tent. Perhaps more.

"And what if I can't?" he asked nervously. In the stories, a witch's challenge always came with a dire cost for losing.

"Oh, it's nothing. A trifle, really." Makiva's voice fell to a whisper. "You must only . . . give me a piece of your soul."

Zed gasped, his eyes falling back to the charm seller.

The mystic burst into a fit of laughter, resting the dagger on her stomach—a little dangerously, Zed thought.

"Peasants are so easy to scare," she said. "No, no. If you guess incorrectly, then you'll just have to pay the full price. *One* silver piece. But you get only one guess."

Zed nodded, breaking into a nervous grin. He glanced at the ceiling again for a long moment, thinking. There were as many charms here as there were stars. Picking one out was impossible. Finally he looked back down at Makiva.

"Is that it?" he said, pointing to the charm in the mystic's hand—the one she was currently carving.

The woman looked up from her work, and her mouth spread into a wide smile.

"Why, yes, it is," she said softly. She set the charm down on the table and pushed it across to him.

Zed couldn't believe it. It had been a wild guess. He picked up the charm and held it close to his face. A small creature was carved from the wood, its bushy tail wrapped around its body. A loop had been whittled into the top of the charm, so a length of twine or string could be pulled through.

"This one is called a fox," the charm seller said. "Clever and agile, with vivid red fur. Foxes are nervous but playful little creatures. A bit like you, I think. People once believed they had magical gifts."

Zed looked up at Makiva. "It's lovely," he said. "Are you sure?"

The charm seller nodded. "We'll say the generous young Lord Guerra paid *for* you."

Zed tucked the charm into his trousers. He must have been grinning like a loon. "Thank you so much," he said.

"I have something else for you," Makiva added, searching beneath the tablecloth. "An extra prize for your clever guess." She withdrew her hand and held it out over the table, her fingers clasped tightly around something inside. Slowly, she unfurled her palm.

Resting there was a length of silvery chain. Even in the dim space, the cord glistened with a light all its own—more jewel than metal. Every link was a tiny work of art, joined together into a spiraling string of masterpieces.

"It's . . ." Zed started. But to call it beautiful wouldn't do the thing justice. There was something about the chain that spoke to him. It was unlike anything he'd ever seen, and yet it filled him with a familiar sense of yearning.

His eyes rose from the glittering cord to Makiva. "It must be worth a fortune."

"It's priceless, in fact," Makiva said. "Though I'm sure the Merchants Guild would give it their best try. You remind me of its last owner, Zed. How long ago was it that the elves sent rangers to our city?"

"It was . . . it was twelve years ago," Zed answered softly.

"So it was," Makiva agreed with a slow smile.

There were no elves in Freestone. No full-blooded elves,

anyway. They had their own city—Llethanyl—with their own walls and customs and guilds, or whatever elves called them.

Zed glanced once more at the chain, cupped in the charm seller's dark hand like the moon reflected in a midnight pool.

"I can't take this," he said. "It's too much."

Makiva smiled a bit coyly. "You're the one person in this city who *should* have it, I think. The chain is made of a metal called mythril—a favorite of the elves. It's less delicate than it looks, I promise. But if it will convince you, then I'll accept a delayed payment. Once you've made your way, we can speak again."

Zed considered the offer. "Thank you," he said, taking the cord from Makiva's outstretched hand. He slipped the end through the loop in the fox charm and was pleased with how the wooden pendant looked on such a fine chain.

Outside, the first bell struck from the Golden Way Temple, signaling the official start of the morning.

"I should get going," Zed said. "My mom'll worry if she can't find me in the square. And I'm sure you've got more people waiting."

Makiva sighed in mock exasperation. "I'm sure. Good-bye, Zed. Keep your chin up today and your ears held high."

Zed laughed and nodded, then swept out of the tent to go find his destiny.

Chapter Two
Brock

Brock had promised his father that he'd stay out of trouble on this of all mornings. As his parents never tired of reminding him, the Guildculling was the most important day of a young person's life. He'd worked hard to prove himself worthy of the Merchants Guild—lost countless summer days to sorting applications from fur traders, leatherworkers, and smiths. Worse were the long nights spent solving math problems by candlelight, until the ache in his eyes matched the ache in his fingers. Yet even after all that, there were no guarantees.

So after breakfast his father had held out a silver coin, and when Brock reached for it his father had gripped his hand, pressing the silver to Brock's palm and holding tight.

"No fights," he'd said. "No trouble. No mischief."

Brock had pointed at himself with his free hand as if to say, *Who, me?*

"Ah, yes. The portrait of the dutiful son." His father glowered. "I want to hear you say it: No mischief." He shrugged. "Or no coin."

Brock had been learning from merchant lords long enough to recognize a bad deal when he heard one. But then he thought of his best friend, Zed, and the promise he'd made him.

He resolved to stop making promises. Right after this one.

"No mischief," he told his father. "You have a deal."

Now, standing outside the charm seller's tent, that promise weighed on him like an iron breastplate. Because someone needed to teach little Lord Micah Guerra a lesson.

Brock listened at the tent's flap long enough to confirm his initial impression of the noble's character. Then, when it was clear that Micah would step outside at any moment, Brock slid over to the larger boy's horse and grabbed its reins.

The horse regarded him impassively, and Brock, seeing his reflection in the beast's big brown eyes, took the opportunity to straighten out his tunic. "Play along, would you? There's a carrot in it for you."

"Oy!" called Micah's bullish voice. "Hands off my horse."

"I beg pardon, Messere," Brock said, smiling shyly and averting his eyes. "He looked fit to bolt. I thought to hold him until you returned."

"A broken horse doesn't 'bolt,' you idiot."

Brock swallowed his retort. He kept his mouth shut and focused on the role he was playing: submissive and timid. He held the reins up and kept his eyes down. As he'd expected, Micah wasn't content to simply accept the reins from him. He took the opportunity to shove his shoulder against Brock as well.

It hurt. In fact, it felt like being run into by an anvil.

Even so, Brock smiled with satisfaction as he watched the noble saddle up and trot away to the sound of the morning bell.

Zed appeared some moments later, stepping from the tent. His ears were bright pink, which meant that the woman had been particularly nice to him . . . or particularly mean. Or that he'd said or done something to embarrass himself, or perhaps simply that he was remembering something embarrassing that had happened years before. Zed was horrible at hiding his emotions and had no talent for bluffing; he'd make a terrible merchant.

Brock hoped fiercely that he'd make a decent mage.

"How'd it go in there?" he asked.

Zed held up his new charm. "It's even better than I'd hoped. It's called a fox."

The charm itself looked like a bushy-tailed dog. What

really drew Brock's eye was the glistening chain, not silver but something like it. "Aw, you got an accessory for yours? No fair." Brock opened his palm to show the charm he'd lifted off of Micah Guerra. "All I got was this ugly thing."

Zed gasped. "Brock, you didn't!" But then he laughed, which Brock took as encouragement.

"What do you think?" he asked. "Am I Stone Sons material now?"

"If the Stone Sons want you, we'll know that thing's magic—extremely powerful magic."

"Aw, I don't know." Brock flexed his paltry bicep. "I've won a fight or two."

Zed rolled his eyes. "You've outrun a fight or two. It's not the same thing."

"Well, it isn't losing. But seriously." Brock frowned at the wooden carving. "Is there anything to these? Can you sense mana coming off them?"

"Not exactly," Zed said. He took a tentative sniff at his wooden fox. "Supposedly magic smells minty."

Brock licked his own charm. "Mine is more wood than mint, I think. But also more wood than woodland creature, which I'm happy for."

"Gross," said Zed. "Oh! I almost forgot." He produced a silver coin. "You can get those shoes after all."

Brock grinned. "Charmed the charm seller, eh?" He slapped

his friend on the back. "I know just the thing to spend this silver on."

"It's shoes, right?" said Zed warily. "I'm pretty sure it's supposed to be shoes."

"Not shoes. I'll be right back." And Brock dashed across the square, noting that the space was already filling with spectators. On the easternmost side, beneath the rising sun, members of the Works Guild were setting up the stage as a prim steward looked on. "Save me a spot!" he called back over his shoulder.

Brock burst into one of the newer tents on the square—the pale green tent of the town's very first perfumer. Brock's father had been the one to approve the man's license, and he'd told Brock all about the strange alchemy the man practiced, mixing oils and herbs and powders to trick the nose and summon scents unbidden from the air.

"Can you make a man smell of mint?" Brock asked.

The perfumer bowed his head in greeting. "Indeed I can, Messere," the man said. "I have the materials at hand."

"Excellent," Brock said, playing a new role now—that of a young man with money to spare. "I'd like my friend to absolutely reek of mint within five minutes."

It wasn't that Brock had no faith in the fox charm. But there was the luck you got, and the luck you made, and a smart man bet only on the latter.

He watched the perfumer at work—first with mortar and

pestle, then fire and glass—and he felt a dawning sense of awe. The man's actions were careful and precise, but quick, and it was immediately obvious to Brock that he had been honing his craft a long time.

Brock leaned over and sniffed as the mixture began to bubble in its flask.

"It doesn't smell right."

"Not yet," the man said. "But you'll see." He steepled his fingers, never taking his eyes off his project. "I have to trick the contents into becoming something new. Here." He withdrew a stoppered vial from his pocket and handed it across the counter to Brock. "Smell."

Brock took the vial and considered the liquid within, a dull yellow the shade of an especially weak tea. But when he unstoppered the vial and took a sniff, he was reminded of something else entirely.

"It smells like breakfast," he said. His mouth flooded with saliva. "Like the best breakfast I ever had."

The perfumer smiled. "Maple and cinnamon. Or the illusion of them, anyway." His eyes flicked to Brock for a brief moment. "You definitely don't want to drink that, whatever your senses are telling you."

"Amazing," Brock said, and he meant it. This was what he loved most about the merchant quarter, where intown and outtown met and those from all walks of life mingled freely. Each time he thought he'd seen everything the city had to offer, some artisan came up with something entirely new. And once Brock had taken his place in the Merchants Guild, he'd have a hand in ensuring that the best of them—the true artists in their midst—found the success they deserved.

After all, a perfumer's wares would never be as in demand as wheat or salt or wool. But Brock had the unshakable sense that Freestone would be a bleaker place without perfumers and glassworkers and even strange old Makiva and her wooden charms.

He watched the boiling mixture as intently as the perfumer did, wondering if there would be some outward sign of change to herald its completion. He paid no attention to the sound of the tent flap opening behind him.

But he took immediate notice of the sound of his father's frustrated sigh.

"There you are," Brock's father said.

Brock paled, turning slowly. He felt his stomach tighten, the excitement of the previous minute swept away in an instant, already forgotten.

"Father. I can explain."

Brock steeled himself for a lecture, but his father smiled and placed a hand on his shoulder. "Here's my little rogue, never where he's supposed to be," he said with an insincere smile. His grip was the grip of a drowning man, slick with sweat.

Something was wrong.

Two figures followed his father into the tent. The first was a plump, pale man with thin lips, dressed in black finery from head to toe. One pace behind him was a woman, a full head taller than him, in the drab gray uniform of the Servants Guild.

Brock recognized the man immediately. Everyone in Freestone knew Lord Borace Quilby by sight. Not only was he the head of the Merchants Guild—rumor had it he was richer than the king himself.

But the first to speak was the perfumer. "It—it's an honor to have you in my humble shop," he said, bowing his head much lower than he had for Brock.

"Thank you," Quilby said. "Your hospitality is greatly appreciated and will be remembered. Now, we would be all the more grateful if you would leave us for a moment."

"Of—of course," the merchant said, and he walked to the tent's flap, head still bowed, not sparing a glance for the concoction he had watched so intently before. "I'll stand outside and ensure you're not disturbed," he said before ducking out. Brock almost thought he seemed to be addressing the woman, although she was clearly Quilby's servant.

He considered her once more. Drab from head to toe, except for an immaculate brooch at her chest in the shape of a spider's web.

"Brock," his father said, turning to stand beside him, "this is Lord Quilby, guildmaster of the Merchants Guild. Lord Quilby, I present my son, Brock Dunderfel."

Brock's rearing kicked in then, and he dropped smoothly to one knee. "Lord Quilby," he said.

"Up, up, my boy," Quilby insisted, and Brock rose to greet his appraising look. "If these knees weren't so old, I should be the one bowing to you. I've heard such things about you. Such a promising applicant!"

For once Brock wished he blushed as easily as Zed. He suspected a blush would be endearing at the moment, proof of some humility. But Brock didn't feel especially humble on this point. He *was* a promising applicant; it was a simple truth.

He gave a polite smile, though. "Thank you, my lord."

Quilby's tongue darted, moistening his small gash of a mouth. "Yes, well. I'm quite glad to have tracked you down before the ceremony. It's very rare, you understand—quite against protocol for a guild to announce its intentions beforehand. Not least because the knights or mages might yet swoop in to claim you. Isn't that right?"

Brock shrugged playfully. "I don't have any natural talent for magic. As for being knighted, well, I'm told that lifting a sword is a requirement."

Quilby squirmed a bit, as if unsure how to respond to levity, and Brock sensed his father tensing up at his side.

"What I mean to say, my lord," added Brock, "is that I believe I was born to join the Merchants Guild. I've worked very hard for this day, following the honorable example of my parents. It's all I've ever wanted." He clasped his hands before him, and caught the faintest hint of mint wafting his way from the glassworks at his back.

"Good, good," Quilby said. He turned partially toward the woman standing at his shoulder and gave her a small smile. "Young Messere Dunderfel, in truth it is not the knights nor the mages that concern me this day, but another guild entirely. Tell me, what do you know of the Sea of Stars?"

"The Adventurers Guild?" Brock fought the urge to shrug again. "I know very little."

"Aye," said Quilby. "And therein lies the problem." He licked his thin lips once more, just a flash of tongue, like a frog after a fly. "Young Messere, here is what you should know about the so-called Adventurers Guild. It is made up of the fey-brained and fiend-touched. Nobody knows precisely how many they number, but they are heavily armed. The guild's leader has proven quite intractable, putting her own concerns above the laws of king and nature, to the point that many believe the guild now endangers the very community it was formed to protect." The tongue darted, pink on white. "They also have a habit in recent years of drafting the most promising apprentices from other guilds."

"Drafting . . . ?" Brock said, drawing out the word, taking the opportunity to break eye contact with Quilby and glance at the woman. She was watching him, but her expression gave away nothing.

"By ancient writ, and in recognition of the danger the guild faces in the name of Freestone, the Sea of Stars has the authority to forcibly recruit one apprentice each year from any other guild. Traditionally it is a right they don't exercise—they've long been content to fill their ranks with criminals, outcasts, and orphans. But that has changed under the leadership of the Basilisk."

Brock almost startled to hear the name. Alabasel Frond was the guildmistress of the Adventurers Guild, and he had thought that her nickname was whispered only among the town's youths. Apparently adults used it behind her back, as well. It was a reference to her flinty gaze, which, like the gaze of the basilisk, supposedly had the power to turn a person to stone. But Brock suspected that in the woman's case it had less to do with any sort of magic and more to do with her ruined face.

He'd seen her, just once, from across the marketplace, and his eyes had gone immediately to the series of oddly shaped scars running down one cheek, all the way from her iron-colored hair to her neckline. The scars looked like winking stars, or plus signs. Rumor had it that they were the result of a run-in with some monstrous Danger that had caught her in its grip, wrapping one long tentacle around her head as its savage barbs found purchase in her skin.

He couldn't imagine the pain she'd have felt pulling free of that embrace.

"Six months ago," Quilby continued, "they drafted a

promising young mage just as she was settling into her hard-earned place in the Mages Guild. The two previous years, they took Stone Sons in the early days of their apprenticeships."

Brock felt his father's hand again on his shoulder, and he realized he'd been rocking on his heels. All the adults were looking at him expectantly.

"You're afraid they'll take an apprentice from the merchants?" he asked.

"Quite the opposite," said Quilby.

Brock's eyes narrowed. "So you . . . *want* them to take an apprentice from the merchants?"

"A particularly promising apprentice, yes."

Quilby smiled, and Brock felt the color drain from his cheeks. "No way."

"Son," said his father, "Lord Quilby has been spreading rumors for weeks now. Making sure certain people hear about . . . a very promising young recruit. . . ."

"You want *me*—"

"Lord Quilby needs a man on the inside," said the woman, and Brock could swear the temperature in the tent fell when she spoke. "We think that man could be you."

"I don't understand," Brock said. "Does the Adventurers Guild need an accountant? Because my talents—"

"Your talents go beyond bookkeeping," said Quilby. "Come, Messere, now is not the time to begin feigning humility. We need a young man with eyes sharp enough to see the things Frond would keep hidden, and wise enough to do so with discretion."

"You need a spy, you mean."

"Just so," said Quilby. He tapped the side of his nose purposefully, then produced a small circular token from his breast pocket.

Brock sought his father's eyes. When he found them, he pleaded silently for help. But his father only nodded gravely, then pushed Brock's shoulder toward Quilby. "Go on, son."

Brock took one step, then another. Inside, he felt the dull thrum of panic. But on the outside, his movements were measured and calm. He had seen this ceremony enough times to know what was happening and how he was meant to act. He stood before Quilby, arms rigid at his side, and he lifted his gaze to meet the merchant lord's.

The Guildculling was meant to take place under the open sky, before the public. It was supposed to be the moment Brock was finally recognized, before king and commoner, as the worthy heir to his parents and their lofty station in Freestone.

Instead, he was getting this back-alley shadow play. He suddenly had a feeling he'd proven himself worthy of all the wrong things.

"Brock Dunderfel," Quilby began, fairly quivering, "I hereby claim you for the Merchants Guild."

"Thank—"

"And," Quilby continued, adding to the familiar ritual, "I claim you for the Merchants Guild's Shadow."

Brock had no idea what Quilby meant by that. It wasn't part of any ceremony he'd ever witnessed. He waited a moment, to be sure the man had finished. The perfumer's mixture, left to boil unattended, filled his nose with the acrid smell of burnt chemicals. "Thank you," he finally said, his mouth dry. "I humbly accept."

Quilby handed over the token, and it was official—Brock was a member of the Merchants Guild. Just as he'd always expected. And yet this had gone nothing like he'd thought it would.

"Now," said Quilby, as Brock swayed on his feet, "whatever happens out there—whatever other tokens you accept upon that stage or in the days to come—you are first and foremost one of us. Don't forget it, but . . ." Quilby tapped his nose again. *Keep it secret.*

Brock realized with a dawning dread that he'd just made another promise. Perhaps the most difficult promise he'd ever made.

He looked down at the piece of bronze in his hand. It bore the familiar sigil of the Merchants Guild.

On the reverse was the image of a spiderweb.

Chapter Three

Zed

Zed's mother peered down at him with a suspicious expression.

"Gone an hour, and you're already a mess," she said briskly. She licked her thumb and scrubbed at a smudge on Zed's face. "Did you even comb your hair?"

She was outfitted in her guild's gray tunic dress and servant's smock. The noblewoman who employed her had given her the morning off, but she would need to return to her duties once the Guildculling was over.

"It looks dumb when I do," Zed grumbled.

"And half wild when you don't," she replied. "We'll settle for dumb."

Zed rolled his eyes and glanced away as his mother fussed over a cowlick.

A crowd had formed around the stage as the Works Guild finished their preparations. The square looked incredibly grand today, with the many banners of all the city's guilds floating over the stage, like colorful blossoms in a giant's garden. The display twisted a knot in Zed's stomach.

The square's large amphitheater was the focal point of Freestone's community life. Nearly every royal proclamation was made here, along with the city's weddings, Guildcullings, and even executions. Zed often wondered what it would be like to walk that stage alone toward his death, the crowd cheering and hissing as he shuffled to meet his fate.

Though the square's appearance changed from event to event, four immortal figures always remained the same. The statues of the Champions of Freestone rose from tall plinths, circling the square's great fountain, which separated the merchant tents from the stage.

Ser Jerra Freestone, the Paladin.

Magus Zahira Silverglow, the Enchantress.

Mother Aedra, Priestess of the Golden Way.

Dox Eural, the Assassin.

The heroes watched silently over all that happened in the square. Long ago they had been great friends and adventurers. After they saved the city during the Day of Dangers, each had founded one of the four High Guilds.

All except for Foster.

Zed's eyes drifted to the empty pedestal in the fountain that represented the fifth of the friends, his likeness banned forever from the city of Freestone.

Foster Pendleton: the Warlock. The Traitor. The Father of Monsters.

Foster the half-elf.

Life wasn't always easy for an elf-blooded boy, in a city whose most famous example was the man who'd destroyed the world.

Freestoners generally blamed the elven half of Foster's heritage, of course. Llethanyl's unchecked zeal for magic was legendary. The elves, Zed had learned secondhand, blamed human foolishness.

Still, the two cities maintained a sisterhood of sorts, even if it was a strained one. Every six years, either Freestone or Llethanyl sent adventurers across the Broken Roads to trade and to renew the friendship between their two peoples. Zed's own father had been one among many—a whole party that had come and gone in a fortnight. His mother talked about the visit as if it were a dream.

When Zed was six, his mother had paid a week's wages to have a letter written to the Sea of Stars, pleading with them to inquire about Zed's father during their upcoming visit with the elves. Besides that he was a ranger and a mage of some sort, all she knew of him was his name: Zerend. She'd given the same name to their son.

But by the time the adventurers had left for their journey, she'd still received no reply.

So it came as a surprise when a message arrived several weeks later, sealed with the stamp of the Adventurers Guild. It was a letter of condolence; Zerend had died soon after his visit to Freestone.

Zed had never seen his mother withdraw so completely. Days passed before she spoke a single word to him . . . to anyone. Her guild had nearly dismissed her.

"Your ears are turning red," Zed's mother said softly, drawing him from the unpleasant memory. He could hear a catch in her voice.

Zed looked down at his feet. His mother worried about him constantly, maybe even more than Zed himself did. Sometimes he would find her just staring at him—watching him with a look of such pure misery it set his ears tingling.

"Oh, Zed." His mother wrapped her arms around him. "Listen, whatever happens today—*whoever* claims you—just know that I'm already so proud of you."

"What if . . . what if no one does?" he asked. It was a worry he could barely manage to speak aloud. What if no guild wanted to take on the first elf-blooded child to appear in generations?

To be guildless was rare, but not unheard of. Those few who fell between the cracks and went unclaimed in the Guildculling were pitied and reviled by the rest of Freestone. Usually they were forced to live as beggars . . . or worse.

Of all the executions that took place in the square, the vast majority were of guildless criminals. Zed had even heard rumors the past few months of guildless beggars simply . . . disappearing. As if they'd never existed.

Zed's mother was silent as she held him to her. Finally, she let out a quiet breath and said, "Then I'll claim you for my own guild. We'll call ourselves the Best Guild, just to show them."

Zed snorted into her smock.

The second bell of the morning rang from the Golden Way Temple, echoing throughout the square.

"I have to go," Zed said, pulling away.

His mother kissed his forehead. "Any of them would be lucky to have you. Just as I've been lucky."

Zed could feel his eyes starting to burn. He nodded quickly, wiping at them, and turned around. He plunged through the crowd to the front of the amphitheater, where the other participants were filing in.

The young nobles were all seated near the stage—Zed recognized Micah Guerra frantically searching the pouch at his hip, likely for a small wooden badger that wasn't there. Seated beside him, a girl with olive-colored skin who looked remarkably like Micah shushed him.

The rest of the children all congregated behind the nobles in nervous, fidgeting clusters, dressed in the best clothes they had. Zed didn't need to look around to know that his best was among the worst.

He searched the crowd for Brock, remembering that his friend had asked him to save him a spot. It wasn't like Brock to cut it this close. What was taking so long?

There were just under a hundred participants in all. Most were human, though a small pack of brawny dwarven children hung together near the edge, about a foot shorter than the rest. They were the descendants of the dwarven merchants and smiths caught in Freestone during the Day of Dangers, cut off from the ancient city of their own people.

Zed caught the eye of one of them—his friend Jett—and the two exchanged a nervous grin. Like most of the dwarven boys his age, Jett was already shaving, though in recent weeks he'd decided instead to try for a beard. So far he'd managed impressive whiskers and a healthy patch of stubble on his chin.

"Not much of a spot," chirped a voice behind Zed. He jumped and turned to find Brock smiling at him.

"Did you find what you were looking for?" Zed asked, shaking away his nerves. He looked down—Brock had on the same shoes from that morning.

Brock shrugged off the scrutinizing look Zed was giving him. "I was a little distracted."

"By what?"

"My father."

Zed gasped. "You didn't get into trouble, did you?"

His friend glanced up at the stage with a faraway look. "I

don't know. Maybe." When he noticed Zed's worried expression, he smiled. "It'll be fine. I never stay in trouble for long."

The guildmasters had gathered on the stage, each one standing before their guild's banner. Most of the symbols on the banners were fairly straightforward—the smiths' banner depicted a hammer and anvil, the scribes' a feather quill.

The guildmasters from the four High Guilds were given extra berth, and their banners towered over the rest.

Horns sounded throughout the square. Zed felt his stomach clench with nervousness.

The Guildculling had begun.

Forta, the city crier, moved to the front of the stage, dressed in her Stewards Guild colors. All at once the square quieted.

"Oyez, oyez!" Forta called, her rich voice filling the square just as fully as any horns. A few straggling conversations came up short. The Mages Guild always cast a charm to augment the crier's voice for well-attended occasions.

"Today is the Freestone Guildculling," the crier announced. "Today, you sons and daughters of Freestone will become sovereign citizens of our city—one of the few lights that still dot the darkness."

Zed knew what was next. He'd heard the story time after time, year after year. And yet it never failed to move him.

"Two hundred and twenty-three years ago," Forta began, "Freestone awoke to a new world. Before that day, the lands of

Terryn were vibrant. Travelers walked the long roads from city to city in safety. Farmers tilled fields of grain as wide and open as the sky."

The crier paused, and Zed tried to picture it: farmsteads larger than the meager plots that fit within Freestone's walls, and great quilts of wheat that stretched all the way to the sea. How could a world possibly eat that much grain?

"It was an age of exploration and adventure," Forta called. "It was an age of friendship—when humans, dwarves, and elves all worked *together* for a better world.

"Then there came the day that all changed: the Day of Dangers."

As if on cue, a cloud drifted over the sun. Zed's arms broke out into goose bumps as the square was cast in shade.

"Monsters—hungry, unnatural beasts once consigned to their own hideous planes of existence—appeared from nowhere. They fell upon the lands of Terryn like a plague. They hunted the roads and blighted the farms. They butchered *every person* that they found, whether human, elf, or dwarf; man, woman, or child.

"Monsters destroyed our world." Here Forta paused, casting a long look over the square. "All in the span of a single day.

"Only those few cities that could protect themselves survived," she said. The crier's voice grew softer, though it still echoed magically throughout the square. "We were among the lucky. We were protected—by our wall . . ." The crier raised her hands, indicating the high barrier that surrounded Freestone.

As if they needed the reminder; the wall was visible from every part of the city. The only thing Zed had ever seen beyond it was sky overhead.

"By our wards . . ." Forta continued, nodding to Silverglow Tower, the tallest structure in the city. The obelisk loomed high in the city's center, where the wizards maintained the city's magical protections.

"And," Forta finished, "by our champions." She brought her hands together slowly, pointing to the statues of the four Champions of Freestone. "It is because of them that we survive to this day, despite the machinations of Foster the Traitor. And it is through their creation of the four High Guilds that Freestone still stands as one of the last bastions of civilization in all of Terryn."

The entire square burst into cheers and applause. Zed and Brock cheered as well, Zed pumping his fist high into the air. Forta gave the crowd a satisfied look, lingering for a moment in the applause.

Finally, she raised her hands to call for silence. "Let us now begin, as we always have, with the claims of the High Guilds. First I call the guildmaster of the Knights Guild, Ser Castor Brent."

A tall man dressed in gleaming armor strode forward from beneath a brown banner depicting a shield made of interlocking stones. The crowd immediately went wild again—stomping their feet and chanting "Stone Sons."

The Knights Guild had been founded by Jerra Freestone, easily the most beloved of the Champions. The second son of the royal family, he went on to become the most accoladed warrior in the city's history. During the Day of Dangers, he led the knights that barricaded the gates against the monster horde, until Zahira Silverglow and her mages could finish erecting their magical wards.

Ser Brent nodded gravely, then raised his hand to quiet the crowd once more.

"The Knights Guild claims six boys as squires this year," he called in a booming voice. Zed saw Micah Guerra sit up a bit straighter in his seat. The girl beside him crossed her arms, her mouth pulling into a tight frown.

The guildmaster read from a sheet of parchment. "Wil Merle, Niko Medina, Dav Levitan, Scot Blar, Trevis Berklund, and Ed Dorty. Squires, please come accept your Knights Guild tokens. You will report to the barracks at first bell tomorrow morning." Now the knight finally cracked a smile. "The last one to arrive has latrine duty."

Laughter filled the square, and the six boys chosen received hoots and swats on the head as they climbed up to the stage. Ser Brent handed each new squire a token, emblazoned with the Knights Guild emblem, to show that they had been claimed.

Zed glanced at Micah Guerra. The boy's mouth was wide open in an expression of undisguised shock. The girl beside him touched his arm, but Micah yanked it away from her angrily.

"What about me?!"

Zed would hardly have believed it if he hadn't seen Micah with his own eyes. The young noble leaped to his feet and pointed an accusing finger at the guildmaster.

Ser Brent's smile immediately fell. He raised his eyebrows in a look that could only be interpreted as a warning.

Hushed whispers filled the square as people realized what was going on. Micah was contesting the claim. Zed had never heard of this happening before.

"Pardon, Lord Guerra," Forta said, stepping forward. "But the ceremony must contin—"

"I am the best candidate you had!" Micah shouted, ignoring the crier. "Wil can barely lift his shield! Ed isn't even a *noble*!"

Finally noticing the whole stage gawping down at him in horror, Micah seemed to falter. "Please," he said less heatedly, lowering his hand. "Please, you don't understand!"

Ser Brent crossed his thick arms and stared down at Micah with a stern frown.

"I think I do understand you," he said. "The day you ran practice drills, I watched you trip another participant who'd finished well behind you. You mocked him as he left the field. Your whole life I've seen you torture those weaker than you, Messere Guerra. But a knight's charge is *to* the weak. We are guardians. We serve the people of this city, no less than any other guild represented on this stage. I understand you, and that is exactly why you will never be a knight of Freestone."

Micah's face pinched in anguish. "Please . . ." he said one final time.

"Wil's strength will come with training," Ser Brent continued, ignoring the plea. "And when Ed becomes a full knight, he'll have earned his nobility. You, Messere, have a different skill to learn. Perhaps one of the other fine guilds here will be gracious enough to teach it to you."

As Ser Brent moved back to his guild's banner, the square exploded once again into excited whispers. Such a breach of etiquette during a Guildculling was unprecedented, and few had ever seen a noble—even a young one—humiliated so openly.

Micah drooped back into his seat without another word, crouching tightly into himself. He looked like he'd been punched in the stomach.

"Wow," Brock whispered. "I almost feel bad for the guy."

All Zed could do was nod dumbly. Though he'd immediately disliked Micah Guerra, as a fellow participant in the Guildculling he couldn't help but empathize.

And the Silverglows were next.

Forta cleared her throat to calm the crowd, then held a hand out to the next banner, on which a moon was depicted over a gray field. The Mages Guild emblems were all enchanted, so that the moon changed phases to match the real one. It hung now as a thick crescent.

Beneath it stood the guildmistress of the Mages Guild, a

woman Zed recognized as Archmagus Dafonil Grima. He'd watched her every year, enraptured, as she announced her guild's claims. They always made the fewest of any—never more than one or two children a year. Wizards were a very rare sort.

Archmagus Grima glided forward, inclining her head to the crier.

Immediately the whispers stopped as the crowd waited for her to speak. If the Stone Sons inspired, the Silverglows awed. Few in Freestone were quite sure what to think of the mages. Rumors abounded about the sorts of animals you might get turned into if you crossed one. The guild's main charge was to maintain the wards that protected the city, though just how they did this was a closely guarded secret. They were beneficent but remote—living secluded lives in Silverglow Tower. Strange lights and noises sometimes exploded from the spire, not to mention the smells.

Zed nervously tucked a hand into his collar, searching for the fox charm. He felt the cool touch of metal as his fingers made contact with the elven chain Makiva had given him. After some more wiggling he found the wooden charm and rubbed it with his thumb, making a silent wish.

"The Mages Guild would like to claim two children as apprentice wizards," Grima said cooly. Her voice was as velvety as her shimmering cloak. Zed could have imagined it, but he thought the archmagus caught his eye as she spoke.

"We claim Andrew Howl and Teri Uchi."

Gasps and squeals sounded from the friends of Andrew and Teri. The crowd all clapped politely for the two and they moved to take their tokens.

Zed let out a breath. He had expected this. He'd prepared for it. But it still didn't make the moment any easier.

"They're fools, if you ask me," Brock whispered beside him. "Terrifying, powerful, please-don't-tell-anyone-I-said-this fools."

Zed tried out a laugh. It sounded as fake as it felt.

He forced himself to look back up at the stage, and was surprised to see that the archmagus was still standing at the front after handing out her tokens. She waited patiently for the crowd to quiet.

With a mischievous look, Grima finally raised her hand. "Additionally," she said, cutting through the noise. "We would like to claim Zerend Kagari as an apprentice *sorcerer.*"

Zed wasn't sure whether the crowd had gone silent in surprise, or if he'd just been momentarily struck deaf.

His name. She'd said his name.

He was going to join the Mages Guild—not as a wizard, but a sorcerer. What was the difference? It didn't matter! He was going to be a magus, with the title and everything!

Zed slowly realized that Brock was shouting his name beside him. Brock grabbed his shoulder and pushed him forward. Zed's face split into a huge grin as he walked to the stage, awash in the sounds of applause. People were *clapping*—for *him.*

He felt a tingling rush of heat surge into his cheeks and ears, but he didn't care if he was blushing. This was the greatest moment of his life.

Archmagus Grima nodded at him, a smile playing coyly at the corners of her mouth. She handed Zed his token, on which a crescent moon glowed magically with pale light.

Zed turned around and searched the crowd for his mother. He found her with her hands pressed over her mouth, tears of happiness streaming down her cheeks.

Zed didn't think it was possible, but he actually grinned wider.

As he returned to his spot and the archmagus to her banner, the clapping slowly diminished. Forta moved to the front and introduced Mother Brenner, the guildmistress of the Healers Guild. The woman stood beneath a white silk banner depicting a golden sun. Apparently, before the Day of Dangers, healing had been a costly thing, and many died because they couldn't afford care. Nowadays the Golden Way Temple offered free healing to any who needed it—even to the guildless. Mother Brenner was beloved. Formerly a noble herself, she was often a voice for mercy or prudence during the city's more tumultuous times.

Zed could barely concentrate through his own relief and happiness, but when he heard Micah Guerra's name called among the new novices of the Golden Way, tucked curtly between Lea Eovard and Zak Lews, he glanced to the front. The young noble's expression was pure misery.

No, Zed realized, *not a noble anymore.* Once he took his oaths, he'd be Brother Micah. He'd no longer have even a surname.

After the new novices received their tokens, the Merchants Guild made their claims. Their banner was a black field with three interlocking loops: copper, silver, and gold.

The Merchants Guild had been established by Dox Eural. Before he was a Champion of Freestone, Dox had been a thief and spy, the most notorious member of the band of heroes.

It was on the Day of Dangers that he finally proved his loyalty to the city.

In the two centuries that followed, the details of what happened that day vacillated somewhere between history and legend. Foster Pendleton, in a bid to enhance his magical prowess, performed a forbidden ritual outside the bounds of the city. He hoped to open a gateway to another plane and bargain for power with the entity that lived there.

Instead, Foster weakened the boundaries between *all* the planes—allowing foul creatures from other worlds to pass into Terryn. The monsters rampaged, consuming whole cities in the span of hours.

While the other three Champions defended their home, Dox set out alone into the mayhem to confront his former best friend. He found Foster still locked in his calamitous ritual, blind to all the suffering he had caused.

The only way to halt the ritual was for the warlock to die.

And so, with a heavy heart, Dox killed his wayward friend. For that act, he would be known as the Assassin.

When Dox returned to Freestone, he realized he had been too late. He stopped more monsters from entering Terryn, but those that had crossed over would remain forever. And so Dox gave up his guileful ways and formed the Merchants Guild, to help establish lawful commerce for a stranded city on the brink of chaos.

The merchants' guildmaster, Lord Quilby, stepped spiritedly to the front of the stage. Zed forced himself to concentrate for just a bit longer. This was Brock's moment. Quilby lowered himself into a steep bow, then read through a list of names prepared on fine parchment.

Brock Dunderfel was the very first.

Zed cheered for Brock, who smiled bashfully. The other participants around them all slapped his back and shoulders in congratulations.

Brock climbed the stage with his fellow new merchants to receive his token, then returned to Zed's side with a nod. Zed had expected his friend to bask in the applause a bit more, but Brock must have known better than to gloat. He could always read a crowd.

When Quilby returned to his place on the stage, Forta stepped forward.

"Now I welcome the leader of a guild whose function is vital to the continued life of our city. Alabasel Frond will make the claims for the Adventurers Guild."

The square became intensely quiet as Frond—the Basilisk—ambled to the front of the stage from beneath her guild's deep blue banner, sprinkled with white stars.

The guildmistress wore a sword slung brazenly across her back in a curved scabbard, as if she were a knighted Stone Son instead of a glorified goon. Her fingers tapped restlessly at several sharp metal points that were banded into her belt. She was the only woman Zed had ever seen carry weapons openly in public. Zed's mother claimed she looked ridiculous, armed and armored like a man.

Zed thought she was terrifying.

The Sea of Stars was not a High Guild in name, but it had powers and responsibilities no other could declare. After the four High Guilds were formed, the Champions of Freestone realized that their city would not survive unless some brave souls agreed to search the monster-ridden wastes for resources. And so together they formed a fifth guild, one whose office was to explore the wilds—and to hunt the Dangers that lurked there.

Few ever asked to join the Adventurers Guild. They were the only citizens of Freestone who left the safety of the city's walls, and their members often died young. Indeed, Frond herself was a mess of improbable scars, a living warning of what waited outside.

Although the task of exploring the lands of Terryn was vital, it was a thankless one. Many considered the members of the guild tainted by the very creatures they fought. Common gossip told of monsters that left lasting afflictions: plagues that could spread with a touch, or blights of the mind that turned the clever into raving fools.

But the Adventurers Guild had privileges in the Guildculling that made up for its unpopularity. Anyone who volunteered to join would be accepted automatically, for instance, regardless of gender, station, or creed—or even if they were in another guild. A person could avoid guildlessness in this way, though for most the prospect didn't seem much better.

Then there was the draft.

Alabasel Frond cleared her throat, surveying the crowd with flinty eyes. Zed dropped his gaze as she passed over him.

"We'll take two this year," the guildmistress said in a gravelly alto. "Dwarfson Jett Thunder-Hammer and Liza Guerra, the noble brat's sister." Then she spat right on the stage.

Zed and Brock both turned to look at Jett, whose face had paled in horror. The other dwarves around him grumbled in solidarity, but none protested in the way Micah had done.

Not even Micah, for his own sister. The girl seated beside him stared up at Frond with shaky resolve. Zed couldn't guess what the Adventurers Guild would want with a pampered noble who'd probably never held a weapon in her life.

Slowly, Jett and Liza moved to the stage, where Frond waited with a frown. She flicked her tokens to the two, not bothering with any ceremony. To their credit, both caught them. Farther back, Zed could see the guildmasters of the Stewards and Smiths Guilds each crossing a name from their lists of claims.

When the two new adventurers had retreated, the guild-mistress looked over the crowd once more.

"Anyone else want to volunteer?" she asked the remaining participants.

The crowd hummed softly as it turned its attention away from Frond, speculating at the guild's strange selections. Zed watched Jett as he returned to his place with the other dwarves. He'd never seen a dwarf cry, but for once he believed it might be possible.

"In that case I'll take the sorcerer, too," Frond said. "The elf-blooded boy. I'm invoking the draft."

Zed's body realized what had happened before he did. Every hair on his arms stood on end.

"*No*," Brock whispered. "No, that's not possible."

There was a beat of windless silence more thunderous than any horn Zed had ever heard. Then a flood of whispers sussed through the quiet. All around him, eyes found Zed. For the second time that morning, he was the focus of attention for the entire square—and this time he felt the weight of every single gaze.

As the foundations for everything Zed had ever wanted

crumbled away beneath him, he realized that he would become legendary today, maybe even more so than Micah Guerra. Zed was the elf-blooded boy who'd nearly gotten away with it. Power, nobility, and prestige had all been within his grasp . . . and then fate had corrected its mistake.

"Don't go," Brock hissed in his ear. "Don't take the token."

"I don't have a choice." The words came automatically, as if to underscore the point.

"It's a death sentence!" Brock said.

A death sentence. Zed thought of his mother. Zed's father had died outside those walls. Would she grieve Zed as she had him? Who would watch out for her then?

He began a second grueling walk to the stage. As he moved, the crowd of participants parted for him, quicker than before. He raised his face as he got closer and found Alabasel Frond staring mirthlessly at him. He scowled right back at her.

When he was a foot from the stage, the Basilisk flicked her thumb and Zed's token arced through the air. He missed the catch and it landed in a clot of mud. Zed bent to pick it up, his face burning, and that was when he heard Brock's voice.

"I'll enlist!" his friend shouted. "I want to join the Adventurers Guild!"

Zed shot up, shouting "No!" but his voice was lost in the outburst of gasps and chatter that followed. Brock pushed his way forward until he stood beside Zed, staring defiantly up at the guildmistress.

"Brock, don't, please!" Zed said. "*You* have a future!" His eyes found Lord Quilby upon the stage. The guildmaster of the Merchants Guild watched the proceedings impassively, though Zed could see the man was sweating. His tongue flicked quickly over his thin lips.

Brock ignored him, eyes on the Basilisk. "Did you hear me, Guildmistress? I said I volunteer."

Frond's mouth spread into a toxic smile. "Oh, I heard you, merchant's son. I suppose I should consider this my lucky day." Her smile tightened into a sneer. "What rare selflessness. It warms the heart." The woman's grin vanished at the same moment she flipped a token through the air.

Brock caught it one-handed.

"Apprentices," Frond barked. "You will report to the guildhall with your belongings at first bell." As she turned from the stage and moved back to her banner, the Basilisk added, "Early or late, you will *all* have latrine duty."

Chapter Four
Brock

B rock found it difficult to pack that evening. He couldn't
shake the thought that he was deciding what to wear to
his own funeral.

In the end, he kept it simple. Two pairs of trousers.
A few tunics and undershirts and a doublet. There wouldn't be
any need for dress clothes where he was going.

He looked around his room, feeling sorry for himself and
a bit afraid. Then he wondered what Zed was feeling at that
moment, and his own misery wilted, burned back by the anger
he felt on behalf of his friend. Brock found a sort of comfort in
anger. All the better if it were righteous and on behalf of another.

With nothing left to do, he headed downstairs for dinner.

Most structures in Freestone were several stories tall. Outtown, closer to the wall, families lived stacked on top of one another. The narrow buildings were packed so close together that from the outside it was difficult to tell where one structure ended and another began. By contrast, Brock's family, like many families intown, had an entire three-story manor to themselves.

His father met him on the narrow staircase.

"You handled yourself well out there, boy," he said in a low voice, and Brock felt a little pride at that. "A bit ostentatious, but it got the job done."

Brock's momentary happiness soured. "Yeah, well, lucky the Stars take anyone, even if they're *ostentatious*," he said, and his father shushed him.

"Your mother," he whispered, inclining his head downstairs toward the dining room.

"You haven't told her?" Brock hissed.

"That I put you up to this? She wouldn't understand. And there's little in this world more frightening than a woman defending her child." At Brock's dark look, his father continued, "Brock, I'm sick about this entire situation, believe me. This isn't what I wanted for you. But you don't say no to Borace Quilby."

"*You* don't say no to him, anyway," Brock grumbled.

Brock's father was not an affectionate man. He was stingy with his praise and usually offered only a handshake at birthdays and holidays. So Brock was startled when his father pulled him into a tight hug. "You keep your head down," he said. "You don't take any risks, you learn everything you can, and then we'll get you out of there."

Before Brock could even process what was happening, his father had released him, nodded gruffly, and walked away. Brock took a moment to compose himself before following downstairs.

Where his mother awaited him with daggers in her eyes.

"Brock Lilyorchid Dunderfel, what were you thinking?"

His father took his seat at the head of the dining room table, where servants had set out silver trays heaped with Brock's favorite foods: potatoes and chicken and little flatbreads covered in cheese. He showed no interest in interjecting on his son's behalf.

"I'm going to fix this," she said, shifting from fury to grim determination in a heartbeat. "Brock, you leave everything to me. I'll go down there to that guildhall and I'll tell that awful woman that you made a mistake. Or I—I'll petition the king himself."

She clasped Brock against her in an embrace, and all at once the traumas of the day washed over him anew. His knees felt weak, but his mom held him, so he knew he wouldn't fall. For a moment he wondered whether she couldn't really get him out of this. *She* would stand up to Quilby. She would do anything to keep him safe.

And then she said, "It's all that wretched elf boy's fault. I told you to stay away from him. I did everything I could. . . ."

Brock pulled away from her then. His knees were fine; he could stand on his own. He looked from his mother, dabbing her eyes theatrically, to his father, slathering a roll with butter, and he took great satisfaction when he said, "Actually, Mother, funny story, but it was all Father's idea."

Brock's father nearly choked on his bread.

✳

The banner of the Adventurers Guild hung heavy in the still morning air. It was meant to evoke the night sky—a "sea of stars"—but seeing it hang limply in the shadows, Brock couldn't make out a single point of white against the dark fabric. It looked like a funeral shroud strung up to dry.

Still, he was certain he had the right place. Everyone in Freestone knew the large, ramshackle wooden structure that the adventurers called home. It was built right up against the town wall, almost leaning against it, as if it were just another pile of stone and not the town's last line of defense against untold Dangers. Children believed the guildhall was a cursed place, and they dared one another to walk past its darkened windows. Adults knew for a fact that it was cursed, and they gave it a wide berth.

Brock did not approach the building yet, but stood and watched it from the shadows of a stable a ways down the dirt road. He'd arrived well before dawn, and in all the time it took the sky to gradually lighten, no one entered or exited the guildhall. The milkmaid with her bottles and the postal boy weighed down with parcels and leaflets each made their early-morning rounds without approaching the place.

Now, with the sun just peeking above the wall, a girl strode down the road, passing Brock without seeing him. Her gaze was stuck upon the slack flag above the guildhall's entrance. Brock recognized something of his own emotions in the steeliness of her eyes and the rigidness of her jaw. With her dark hair pulled back into a tight ponytail and yesterday's painted rouge gone from her cheeks, it took Brock a moment to recognize her. She was the young noble, Liza Guerra. His fellow apprentice.

He was considering calling out to her when he saw Zed come around the corner. Even from a distance, the boy looked miserable. His skin was pallid, his shoulders were hunched. If Brock didn't know better, he would have said that even his ears were drooping.

Brock stepped from the stable's awning and gave a little wave. But rather than cheering Zed up, the sight of Brock made him shrink even more. There was no mistaking the guilt clouding his expression.

"Tell me the truth," Brock said lightly, falling into step beside his friend. "You didn't sleep a wink, did you?"

Zed frowned and shook his head. "You?"

"Like a baby," Brock answered. "A baby who wakes wailing to a full diaper after dreams of sharp, gnashing teeth."

Zed's eyes fell to the ground. "Brock, you didn't have to . . . I'll never be able to—"

"Stop," Brock said. "We stick together." He felt a rush of guilt as Zed looked at him like he'd done something heroic. "I didn't have the constitution for the Merchants Guild anyway," he said. "You spend a day cross-referencing crop-rotation ledgers in the royal archive, then you can talk to me about Dangers." Zed rolled his eyes, but at least that got them off the ground.

Brock fingered the hidden inner pocket at his hip, where he'd stashed his Merchants Guild token—the one with the strange pattern of webbing on one side. This way it was out of sight, but impossible for him to forget as it pressed up against him.

He inclined his head toward Liza, who now stood before the guildhall, watching them approach. "So what's her story?" he said under his breath. She struck a formidable pose, with her chin held high and her fists at her hips, immaculately dressed in brand-new hunting leathers, with two shining daggers sheathed at her thighs. But Brock thought she looked less like an adventurer and more like a thespian portraying one onstage.

"Don't ask me," Zed answered. "She and I don't exactly run in the same circles."

"That," said Brock, slapping his arm around Zed's shoulders, "is about to change."

The girl nodded a greeting as they joined her, but she didn't relax her pose. Brock saw her eyes go to Zed's ears. "You're the sorcerer," she said to him.

"His name is Zed, actually," Brock said.

"Uh, glad to meet you," Zed said. He went predictably pink and started a curtsy, but Brock caught his arm. "Nuh-uh," he said, pulling him up. "We're all equals now. Isn't that right?" He held Liza's eyes like a challenge.

"That's right," she said, not blinking. "So let each be judged solely by their actions." She gave Zed a small curtsy. "Glad to meet you, Messere."

Brock tried to hide his surprise. He'd never seen a noble curtsy to a commoner before—especially not a commoner with pointy ears.

"Glad to meet you!" Zed blurted, apparently forgetting he'd said so already.

Brock smirked. "I'm glad everybody's so glad," he said.

There was a great racket of clanging metal, and Jett came barreling around the corner, a huge pack slung over his shoulders. He tottered up to them, red in the face and huffing. "Sorry to cut it so close," he said. "Short legs."

"Surely you're used to them by now?" Brock said. "They're not getting shorter?"

"It looks like you came prepared, though," Liza said. She tilted her head around him to look at the various implements hanging from his pack. "Is that a masterwork mallet with a bronze-inlaid stone handle? Nice."

Jett stared at the girl, opened his mouth to speak, and then began coughing uncontrollably. Brock went to slap him on the back, but he couldn't reach it for all the gear.

And then the door to the guildhall burst open, just as the first morning bell began to chime in the distance and a wave of warm, sour air rolled out into the chill morning. In the doorway stood Alabasel Frond, the puckered scars along her face glistening in the dawn. "Well," she said stonily. "Look at what the wyvern dragged in." And she stepped back into the gloom of the entryway.

Zed looked at Brock. Brock looked at Jett. Liza threw her shoulders back and stepped forward.

The boys followed her.

The hall was a close, dark space that reminded Brock of a tavern—a lowborn tavern his parents would never set foot in. The air was musty, and all the windows were covered with heavy drapes that let in little light and kept in the stench of unwashed women and men. The hearth was cold, the long wooden table at the room's center was mostly obscured by filthy dishes, and an unsettling statue stood at the far end of the room—a figure of a boy, one hand clenched in a fist, the other held out before him as if warning them all to stay away.

Their new guildmates had gathered to watch their arrival. Some glared, leaning back against the walls; others sat at the table and picked meat from the bones of yesterday's meal, seemingly uninterested. Brock remembered Quilby's complaint of the day before: Between the guild's alleged mortality rate and the fact that the their ranks were occasionally bolstered by the guildless outside of the formal Guildculling, no one in Freestone seemed to know just how many adventurers there were at any given moment.

Brock counted off two dozen men and women, and filed that information away for later.

At the merchants' hall this morning, there would be a magnificent five-course feast, with gifts exchanged and speeches of welcome from all the city's most successful and respected citizens. Here, Alabasel Frond brought them to attention by spitting a wad of mucus in the general direction of a battered spittoon.

Brock angled his shoulder so that Liza was forced to make room for him at the front of their group. He could sense Zed trembling just behind him, either out of fear or anger at the woman who had snatched his dream away. He slipped his arm back to grip his friend's hand.

"Adventurers die," the woman said without preamble, then allowed a silence to settle for several long, uncomfortable seconds. Brock's throat was dry, and he fought to keep his face impassive as her eyes swept across them. "They die horrible and useless deaths," she continued at last. "Let the fair folk of Freestone call us whatever they like. 'Adventurers,' if it eases their conscience. But make no mistake: You are *soldiers*. Do you know the difference?"

Her eyes again swept over the group. Brock was unsure

whether she expected an answer or merely paused for effect, but Liza spoke up: "Discipline," she said.

The muscles of Alabasel's scarred face tightened in a sour smile. "Discipline, yes. You will know a chain of command. You will follow orders at all times, in all things. But the key difference is this: Soldiers die, too. But they die with purpose. Their deaths mean something."

"So much to look forward to." Brock said it without really intending to, but he wasn't sorry. He didn't much care for the woman's scare tactics.

And he wasn't planning on being here long enough to get himself killed, meaningfully or not.

Alabasel regarded him coldly, and he felt the look mirrored in Liza's sideways glance, but the other guild members gave no indication they were even paying attention, instead murmuring to one another or else looking on indifferently from their benches. All except for one girl, standing by the hearth, who wrung her hands as she watched them. She didn't look much older than the apprentices, and she wore a silver charm around her neck—a crescent moon. Brock marked her immediately as the young wizard who had been drafted the previous year.

"Tell me, Apprentice Dunderfel," Frond said, bringing Brock's attention back to her steely eyes. "What does this guild's sigil represent?"

Brock wasn't entirely sure what to make of the question. "A sea of stars?"

"But why? What do the stars stand for?"

Brock had never really thought of it, but the longer he groped for an answer, the longer Frond would fix him with her uncanny stare. "Us?" he suggested. "The bright new recruits lighting the way to glory."

A bearded man at the table chuckled into his flagon.

"A pretty sentiment," Frond said, and she pulled several objects from her belt—flat, metallic circles with protruding blades. Throwing stars. "And like most pretty things, false." She turned on her heel, tore a starred banner from the wall, and draped it across the table, knocking over a pewter stein without a care. The mutterings inside the hall came to an abrupt stop.

"Freestone," she said, and she stabbed one of her throwing stars into one star of the flag, pinning it to the table. "Llethanyl," she said, and stabbed a second star in the same manner. "Dragnacht. Vloegstan. Everglen." She stabbed the three remaining stars. "Points of light in the darkness." She looked back up at them. "So far as we know, that's all that's left. Every other city, town, or cottage—every other person—fallen to Dangers. Swallowed whole."

Zed's sweaty hand slipped from Brock's grip.

"We keep it from getting worse," Frond added. "Glory be cursed." And she walked away.

"Um," Brock said in a low voice. "Do we follow her, or . . . ?"

Liza huffed and stepped away from the group, following in Frond's wake. Brock looked back at his friends, shrugged, and joined her as she wove through the crowded space, slipping past the men and women who now watched them in silence. Brock sensed their scrutiny, and he suddenly felt awkward, unsure what to do with his hands. Behind him he could hear Jett's muttered apologies as he clashed and clanged his way through the crowd. The wizard girl looked right past Brock, and he knew her gaze was on Zed, while Brock caught the eye of a sneering man whose ruined bottom lip had been torn or cut and healed poorly.

Frond led them to the dark doorway at the very end of the hall, and as they passed the statue, Jett let out a low whistle. "Extraordinary work. Dwarven, no doubt."

Brock peered past the stone figure's outstretched arm and saw the look of terror on its face, and he agreed he'd seen nothing else like it. It surpassed even the carvings of the Four Champions in the town square.

"That was a recruit from a few years ago," Frond said. "Started out as a Stone Son, ironically enough."

"A *knight* carved this?" Jett said with undisguised awe.

"You misunderstand," Frond answered. "That *is* the recruit. He was petrified in the field. Took three men to drag him back."

Jett's jaw hung open, and Brock felt his stomach drop. He took an involuntary step closer to Zed as low chuckles came from the men seated nearby.

Feet dragging, they followed Frond through the doorway and down an uneven stairwell. "Barracks are upstairs," she told them. "But there's no sense getting comfortable until you've been initiated."

Brock didn't like the sound of that.

The stairs ended in a cavernous wood-paneled cellar. Despite being underground, the space was far brighter than the dining hall, lit with dozens of lanterns hanging from the rafters. Straw dummies were positioned throughout the room, as well as several mannequins loaded with armor. The long walls on each side were almost entirely obscured by mounted objects. On the left wall was every manner of weapon Brock had ever seen, and many besides that he'd never imagined. On the right, he saw a multitude of stuffed animal heads. He recognized a wolf and a grizzly bear from storybooks, but there were also other, far stranger things. Things he'd never want to bump into in the dark of night.

Two figures stood among the mannequins. One was a pale-skinned woman, short and curvy, with bands of gold running all along her ears and shining pauldrons strapped to her shoulders. The second was a man, tall and thin, in a heavy hooded robe that obscured his features. Brock could see dark brown skin and a sharp nose, and thin lips set in a salt-and-pepper beard. He wore a belt of interlocking metal rings strung with all manner of keys.

"Lotte is our quartermaster," Frond said, gesturing at the woman. "And Hexam is our archivist."

Lotte stepped forward and smiled handsomely. Her flowing blond ringlets were a marked contrast to Frond's close-cropped gray hair. Brock searched her face for scars and, finding none, wondered whether that made her unique among members of the guild. "Greetings, apprentices," she said. "You'll be spending a lot of time in this room in the months ahead."

While the woman continued a speech that felt much more rehearsed than anything Frond had said, Brock leaned toward Zed, who was fairly squirming in his boots.

"You all right?" he whispered.

"That smell," Zed answered. "What is that?"

Brock sniffed at the air. It was a bit mustier down here than it had been in the great hall, but he was already growing accustomed to it.

"Frond's armpits, I think," he whispered. Zed didn't seem put at ease.

"Choice and maintenance of weapon are among the most important skills you'll learn here," the quartermaster was saying. "You may start by choosing one item from our collection, which in addition to anything on your person now, is all you'll have access to during the test."

"Uh, what is the test?" Zed asked, actually raising his hand first.

Alabasel grinned at her colleagues as if sharing a private joke.

"Not knowing is part of it," Lotte answered.

"Good thing Jett brought his house with him," Brock said.

He flicked an iron pan with his finger. "Maybe it's a cooking challenge?"

Liza actually huffed in annoyance and, surprising no one, stepped forward to make her selection first. But Brock *was* surprised by her choice. She passed by swords and maces and a miniature lance to take up a large, gleaming shield that came to a point at the bottom. It was enameled dark blue, with five star-shaped patches of silver shining through the paint.

Jett went immediately for a large maul, which he hefted from its hooks with both hands.

"Honoring the ancestors?" Brock teased.

"I've been swinging a hammer since I was a pebble in my mam's boot," Jett said gruffly. "Just . . . never swung it at anything that moved."

Zed walked slowly along the wall, taking his time, looking at each object he passed. Brock thought his friend might be agonizing over the choice, but when he caught a glimpse of Zed's face, it was contemplative and calm. He zeroed in on a quarter-staff, considering it carefully. To Brock's eye, there was nothing exceptional about it—in fact, it looked like a student's training staff, lacking even the simple leather grip of a weightier staff mounted farther down the wall.

Brock tapped at the token sewn into his pants. What was he doing here? What was he meant to be seeing? He considered making an inventory of the weapons. Surely that was the sort of thing Quilby would want to know about? The armory was impressive enough, and would be dangerous in the wrong hands.

He eyed the animal heads again, trophies of past victories over the beasts beyond the city gates. It was a ghastly menagerie. There were lizards of every size and color; a compound-eyed insect with mandibles as big as his hands. And not just heads. There were wings and claws and jaws of serrated teeth mounted on plaques, and a long purple tentacle lined with suckers and barbs. The barbs reminded Brock immediately of the puckered scars along Alabasel Frond's face and neck.

"Dunderfel," Frond said sharply. "You're up."

Brock turned to see that Zed had taken the training staff. All eyes were on Brock; it was his turn to choose a weapon.

Frond's gaze flicked from him to the tentacle, and she scowled. That told Brock he was onto something.

He took the mounted tentacle from the wall, buckling a bit beneath its weight.

"What are you doing?" demanded the robed man, Hexam.

"Choosing my weapon. You said anything from the wall, right?"

"Don't be absurd," Frond said, seething, taking a step forward. "That can't possibly be of use."

"Then it must be of value, if it's on display here," Brock said. "So I'm guessing my odds of getting through this test intact are better as long as I've got this with me. Doesn't that make it a weapon?"

Frond clenched her jaw. "Suit yourself," she ground out. "But I think you'll be sorry." She pointed toward the arched doorway at the back of the room. "Walk all the way down the hall until you come to a door. Go through it, all together, and shut it behind you. I'll be along with instructions."

Brock breathed a little easier, knowing they'd be together for what came next. But as they shuffled out of the room, he felt a dull pain blooming in his lower back. He was already regretting the tentacle.

They walked along a hallway lined with closed doors and lit at regular intervals with hooded lanterns. When the trophy room was well behind them, Liza stepped to the side, allowing Zed and Jett to walk ahead of her. Brock had fallen to the rear as he struggled with his burden.

"Need any help?" she asked.

"Actually, if you'd—"

"Too bad," she said sharply. "Now listen. I've seen you twice in my life. And both times, you managed to make a complete spectacle of yourself, for no good reason I can see."

Heat rushed to Brock's cheeks. "Right, because your family didn't make any kind of scene at the Guildculling."

She flinched at the reminder, and Brock felt a momentary twinge of guilt, but she regained her composure immediately. "We're not talking about Micah. We're talking about you. And you need to start thinking about the consequences of your actions. Because you're part of a team now."

"Oh yeah?" Brock said, unable to keep the defensiveness from his voice. "So who died and made you team captain?"

She pursed her lips and gave his tentacle a pointed look. "I think you're about to." Then she flipped her ponytail into his face and hurried up the corridor, forcing him to struggle to catch up. His legs burned, his fingers ached, and he felt certain the ground was sloping gently upward.

"May I never see the monster they cut this from," he muttered, then regretted wasting the breath.

He caught up to the others as they stood contemplating a heavy metal door that blocked their way.

"What do you think we'll find in there?" Jett asked.

"My guess is it's something that'll want to hurt us," Zed said.

Brock tried to quip, but only wheezed.

Liza held up her shield and drew a blade with her free hand. "Stay behind me until I tell you otherwise."

Brock wanted to disagree on principle, but he found he couldn't argue with that plan. Instead he turned to Zed. "We stick together," he said. Zed eyed the tentacle skeptically. "It'll be fine. They obviously don't want to get their recruits killed on the first day."

"Not all of us, at least," Liza said. She kicked open the door, and the four of them charged ahead into bright daylight. The door slammed swiftly behind them. Brock held the tentacle out ahead of him like a lance, standing back-to-back with Zed as he waited for his vision to clear.

"We're outside," Zed said.

"Obviously," Brock said. "The sun is—"

"No, I mean we're *outside*. We're outside the wall!"

Brock blinked furiously, and he saw the great stone wall to one side, and on the other . . . *trees*.

"Apprentices!" called a familiar voice, and they all turned, looking up to the very top of the wall, where Alabasel Frond loomed over them.

"Here are your instructions: Survive the night." And with that, she ducked from view, leaving them to the forest and the strange, sinister sounds that came from it.

Chapter Five

Zed

Zed blinked as his eyes adjusted in the glare of the morning. Slowly, the muddy radiance became crisper, more detailed.

His first thought was: Green.

The world outside the wall was vivid green. Trees clumped together, as crowded as the stalls in the marketplace. Their branches fought for space like squabbling siblings. The morning light poured in from between them, casting flowing patterns into the fabric of lush grass just beneath.

It was quiet beyond the wall. Zed heard a sound like voices, a whole chorus of whispers, and he realized only slowly that it was the wind blowing through all those leaves.

His second thought was: We're going to die out here.

He took a retreating step, and his back hit the metal door that had been sealed shut behind them.

"She's kidding, right?" he said, trying and failing to restrain the high note of panic in his voice.

"Right," said Brock. "Frond. A real merry entertainer, that one."

"Hey!" Jett called back up at the parapet where the Basilisk had just been standing. "Hey, wait! What about food and water? How are we supposed to eat?"

The only answer he received was the squawking of a bird in the distance.

"This isn't a test," Zed said. "This is murder! We haven't even been trained!"

Liza frowned. She had been silently watching the tree line since Frond disappeared over the wall. "Be quiet," she said. "We don't know what's out there."

"I think that's his point," said Brock.

There was a squall of noise in one of the trees. Zed screamed, dropping the wooden training staff he'd selected from the weapons wall, and covered his head. A flock of birds emerged from within the tree's branches and gusted away.

"Will you *calm down*?" Liza growled. "If there *is* anything out here, it sure as Fie knows where we are now."

"Sorry," Zed said, reaching down to retrieve the staff. He

caught the tail end of a protective look Brock was giving him, as he turned to face Liza.

"I'm getting pretty sick of your team-leader act," Brock shot at her. "You think just because you've got fancy leathers and a couple of daggers that you're better than us?"

Liza scowled, but she didn't so much as turn her head in Brock's direction. "Better than you, at least. Whatever statement you were trying to make with that . . . thing . . . I hope it was worth it to you. It's got to be more useless than your friend's stick."

Brock hugged the tentacle tighter to his chest. "Now you're just being mean. Ser Feeler is very sensitive."

Jett snorted.

Zed turned his attention from the bickering. There was something strange about the air here, a quality he couldn't quite place. As a wind picked up and set the leaves around them fussing, he breathed in deeply and tasted a crispness come with it. A tingling sensation climbed across Zed's spine then—a restless, vivifying thrill.

"Does anyone else smell that?" he asked. "It's . . . minty."

Brock quirked an eyebrow, but for once, Liza didn't chastise him. Instead she nodded.

"It's probably the wards," she said. "The ones that the Mages Guild uses to repel the Dangers. Supposedly the magic smells of mint."

"I don't smell anything," said Jett.

"You're not a wizard," Liza said. "Or a sorcerer," she added, nodding at Zed. "My mother once hosted Magus Chhibber at one of her salons. She said it takes magic to sense magic."

"So if the wards repel monsters," Brock said thoughtfully, "we should be safe near the wall, right?"

Liza opened her mouth to reply, apparently in rebuke, but paused. "I suppose that makes sense," she said finally.

"Oh, thank you," Brock breathed, dropping the tentacle to the ground with a groan. "That thing was really starting to get heavy."

"Somehow I doubt the test is as simple as staying near the wall," Liza said. Still, she lowered her shield and relaxed her shoulders, rolling them around.

Jett eased off his enormous clanking knapsack, then leaned back and plopped down beside it. "They're probably just trying to scare us," he said breezily. "I heard the smith initiations involve enchanted buckets they got from the mages. The water inside is always ice-cold."

Zed also sat down, but kept his back firmly planted against the wall. He set the training staff in his lap, and looked out again into the tree line. Now that his heart had stopped beating so intensely, he was able to concentrate more on his surroundings.

Even the wall was greener on this side. Ivy clung to the stone like emerald veins in a great gray neck. Zed's eyes followed the wall along its curve until he saw the city gate, maybe a hundred yards away.

Even after all this time, the vestiges of the old road could still be seen leading away into the forest. The stone was cracked and covered with lichen, but once it must have been a wide, grand artery into the city, bringing life-giving resources and travelers of all kinds.

Birds sang in high, sweet voices—much louder out here than within the city walls—and everywhere the sunlight touched, motes of pollen and dander sparkled in the air, like magic dust in a fey story.

The forest loomed just behind it all, cool and stoic. It felt to Zed like a single dark figure, watching them with shrouded eyes. He avoided looking at it directly.

Hours passed in silence. Zed spent his first morning as an adventurer picking at grass and listening to the temple bells ringing from over the wall. Morning faded into midday one clang at a time, and before he knew it the sun was high overhead.

This close to the wall, he could sense the hum of the city, alive and bustling on the other side. Soon the smell of freshly baked bread floated over, taunting them.

"I'm *starving*," Jett said bleakly. "I thought they'd feed us, at least."

"Feed us to what?" Liza cracked. Catching herself in a joke, she turned quickly back to the tree line.

"Maybe we should eat the tentacle," Zed said. "That'd show them."

"Leave Ser Feeler out of this," Brock responded. He was standing, but had leaned back against the wall. The pose was casual, but his eyes scanned the woods just as intently as Liza's. The young Guerra, for her part, was still standing sentry. She'd stuck her daggers into the dirt at her feet, but kept the iron shield high on her arm.

"You don't suppose there's anything edible nearby?" Jett asked. "Berries or . . . I don't know, wild vegetables? What grows outside the wall?"

Brock grunted. "As if any of us—"

"Elfgrass grows around the city," Liza interrupted. "It's safe to eat. Also huntsman's lettuce."

All three boys turned to stare at her.

"What?" she said.

"Just surprised that a noble girl knows so much about wild plants," Brock said. "Tell me, which fork is the elfgrass fork? I always get them confused."

Liza scrunched her nose. "Well, excuse me for being prepared. At least one of us is."

"But how?" Zed asked. "I mean, how could you have known you'd be chosen for the Adventurers Guild?"

Liza glanced back at him and sighed. She hesitated a moment, then seemed to make up her mind about something.

"Brock isn't the only one who volunteered for this," she said. "I wrote to Frond in secret, weeks before the Guildculling, asking her to pick me for the Sea of Stars. Not even my parents knew. But *unlike* Brock, I didn't walk in completely unprepared."

Zed was surprised by his reaction to this news. He felt . . . angry. He glanced around to find Jett biting his lip awkwardly. Even Brock seemed momentarily stunned into silence.

"Why?" Zed asked finally, his voice barely louder than a whisper. "Why would you *volunteer* to join the most dangerous guild in Freestone?" Even to his own ear he sounded accusatory, but he couldn't shake away the anger. Her decision to volunteer felt like an insult to his own draft. Who would willingly choose this kind of life?

"What does it matter how I got here?" Liza said defensively. "I'm no different from the rest of you."

Brock snorted. "None of *us* arrived already outfitted with fancy leathers and gleaming weapons. How much did the Noble Lord Daddy have to spend to get *those* on a day's notice? Probably more than Zed's family sees in a year."

Liza's olive skin flushed to a brilliant pink. Zed guessed that he was a similar color.

"You don't know anything about me *or* my family," she said.

"Oh, that's where you're wrong," Brock continued, apparently on a roll. "You see, we met your brother in the market just yesterday morning, and he had no qualms about pushing past

Zed in line. As if he was nothing. Admit it, a week ago you'd just as soon have spat on Zed as shake his hand. Don't *you* tell *us* how we're the same."

"Brock . . ." Zed said. "It's all right."

"Listen to your friend," Liza growled. "You really need to shut it."

Brock threw his hands into air. "And the noble tells the commoners to quiet down! Well, that didn't take long. So much for everyone being judged equally." His eyes took on a hard gleam, and he lowered himself into an exaggerated curtsy. "I apologize if our baseborn ignorance is slowing you down, *Messere*. If only we'd known one of the illustrious Guerras had *chosen* to slum it with us on our first day as Freestone's human shields."

Liza's face had gone totally still. Zed expected her to attack Brock, and readied himself to pull her off. So he was surprised when instead a single thin tear fell from the corner of her eye, juddering toward her cheek. Liza wiped it away impatiently and turned on her heel.

"I'll go forage," she said. She was off before any of them could protest. In just moments she'd disappeared into the trees.

The three boys looked after her, mouths agape.

"She—she left," Zed said. "She left the wall."

"She'll be fine," Brock said grumpily. "She's so *prepared* and all."

"That was pretty harsh," said Jett. "Even if you were right."

Zed frowned, and glanced at his friend. "I know you were defending me, but—"

"Not just you," Brock said. He sighed. "Maybe me a bit, too."

Zed looked back at the forest, amazed at how quickly it had swallowed the girl's retreating form.

"So, uh, do you guys think I have a chance with her?" Jett asked, absently stroking the fuzz on his chin. "I felt like I was getting signals."

Zed coughed out a laugh, in spite of himself.

"She's all yours," said Brock.

A shrill, gibbering cry cut suddenly through the forest, punctuated by abrupt quiet.

It was not a human sound.

Zed and Jett leaped to their feet, grabbing their weapons.

"Oh, no . . ." Zed said. "What was that?"

"Liza!" Jett shouted into trees. "Are you all right?" There was no response.

"Her . . . her daggers," Brock stammered, eyes wide. "She forgot her daggers." He scrambled to grab the two blades poking up from the ground. In his hurry, he slipped, accidentally lobbing one of them over his shoulder. The dagger narrowly missed Jett, instead piercing the hide of the tentacle right beside him.

"Be *careful*!" Jett shouted.

Brock righted himself and yanked the dagger from the tentacle. Its blade was smudged with a green-black stain that clung to the metal. He rushed away without another word, plunging into the trees.

Zed hesitated, frowning down at the wimpy-looking staff in his hands. *Why* had he chosen such a useless weapon? Back in the guildhall he'd thought . . .

He shook his head. There was no time for this. He and Jett crashed forward, following Brock into the woods.

✳

The interior of the forest was darker and much cooler than the area outside. Trees were *everywhere*. The air was crisp here, filled with a briskness that made Zed feel light and energetic. He searched around and just caught sight of Brock's doublet flickering between the trees.

"This way!" he shouted at Jett, following his friend.

The two huffed as they scrambled forward. In the quiet of the woods, Zed could hear his own heart beating rapidly in his ears.

Finally he glimpsed a flash of brilliance. Liza's metal shield caught the light bleeding down through the branches like a signal fire. She held it with a skill that could only have been honed by practice.

Liza's eyes darted to the others. "About time!" she said. "Everyone, pull in! Make a *V* formation, so we look bigger."

In front of them stood three creatures unlike anything Zed had ever seen.

They walked on two legs, like men, but their bodies were

green and scaled like lizards. Each creature was a little taller than Jett, their bare feet ending in wicked talons. Their faces erupted into long, pointed snouts, from which rows of sharp teeth hung erratically, like gruesome icicles.

Strangely, they all wore clothing. The three were dressed in a patchwork of leather rags. Two held curved, jagged blades that seemed to have been carved from bone.

The third held a large femur, ornamented with a bloodred stone that was banded to the top in a grisly imitation of a mage's scepter. This one's scales were tinged with red.

Zed could hardly believe what he was seeing, but there was no doubting it. These were Dangers. Real live monsters stood before him.

Brock rushed behind Liza as she'd instructed, positioning the daggers in front of him. One blade's tip was still smudged green-black, where it had stabbed the tentacle.

"Don't be fooled by their size," Liza called. "These are kobolds. They're smart, and they're *vicious*."

At the sound of Liza's warning, the creature with the bone scepter rolled its jaundiced yellow eyes toward her. It cried out in a high, yipping voice—it sounded almost like a dog—and the other two followed suit, barking quick responses.

The noise sent a prickling sensation traveling along Zed's arms. The cries had the sharp, hungry quality of a baying pack of hounds, but Zed could also sense something else beneath it: a ferocious intelligence.

These *kobolds* were communicating.

The two beasts with swords surged forward, weapons raised. One lunged straight for Brock, but was intercepted by Liza, who girded herself and raised her shield high, blocking a blow from the creature's wicked-looking blade. She bashed it back with a quick biff from her shield.

The second, however, curved around her in a wide arc.

"They're trying to flank us!" Liza shouted. "Jett, can you actually lift that hammer?"

At the sound of his name, Jett seemed to come to. He heaved his maul into the air and charged forward, with a cry that must have been an attempt at a dwarven bellow. In seconds he had plowed straight into the scheming kobold. It howled as the hammer connected, and skidded to the ground in a heap a couple of yards away.

The kobold engaging with Liza answered the attack on its comrade with a furious yipping cry. It dove forward, pulling in its arms and legs, and rolled neatly behind her defensive line.

"No!" shouted Brock.

As the monster sprang up he was there, daggers ready to catch the sword.

Zed had never once seen Brock fight. Despite his sharp tongue, few kids were dumb enough to chase down a merchant's son—and the ones who *were* dumb enough usually found themselves being led straight into a Stone Son's armored chest. But desperation seemed to have brought out an intuitive talent in

Brock. He swiped the daggers, deflecting a blow meant for Liza with a grinding clash. Then he held the stained blade out, waving it around to fend off the kobold.

Zed, for his part, was petrified. He stood rooted to one spot, trying desperately to keep an eye on everything at once. His sweat-slicked hands clung to the training staff, held defensively in front of him.

"Fie, they're fast," Liza cursed in frustration, pivoting to face the retreating kobold. "Everyone, pull together!" she shouted. "Make a circle!"

The kobold that Jett had knocked to the ground rose up again, clicking its teeth. The dwarf sidled up to Liza, holding his maul high, ready to swing if the beast came near.

The two kobolds barked and lunged, but kept their distance, harrying the team while staying out of range of their weapons.

Then Zed felt it.

A familiar sensation washed over him, similar to the feeling he'd had in the presence of Freestone's magic wards. Except instead of mint, this was accompanied by a fetid burning smell that nearly made him gag.

He'd smelled it once before that day, in the guild's weapons hall.

Zed's eyes landed on the third kobold, the one holding the scepter. The red stone on top shivered with an awful radiance.

"Magic!" Zed shouted.

Liza turned just as the kobold raised its scepter into the air. The red stone flared with light.

Several things happened in the span of an instant. A loud pealing rang through the forest, higher than the highest bells in the Golden Way Temple. The air around the stone began to churn, darkening to a sickly green color. A nimbus of green fog swirled around the tip of the scepter like a storm cloud, and then, as the instant ended, the miasma surged out in a growing wave, straight at Liza.

The girl braced herself, digging her back foot into the dirt. "*Down!*" she cried.

Jett and Brock were still diving behind her as the spell hit Liza's shield. Putrid clouds broke over the iron, spewing out in all directions. The two kobold warriors leaped out of the way, but Zed wasn't as quick. A plume of the smog gushed over him.

Zed had the sense to hold his breath, but the miasma stung his eyes, making them water. He felt the strength draining from his limbs as it overtook him.

Zed coughed, and before he could stop himself, he'd gasped a lungful of the polluted air. His head swam and his stomach lurched as the world seemed to somersault around him. He fell to his knees, dropping the training staff.

He well and truly gagged now, and would have been sick right then, had he anything in his belly to throw up.

Through the dark fog, he could just make out his friends huddled together behind Liza's shield.

Then he saw the kobolds.

Both of the monstrous warriors faced him now, finally noticing the sheep that had strayed from its flock. They strode forward menacingly, silent within the gloom.

Zed couldn't stand. He wasn't even sure he could lift the staff. Whatever hex the kobold mage had cast, it had worked. He was defenseless.

The smell from before hit him again—rotten eggs set aflame. It wafted on a wave of something else. Zed remembered the odd charge to the air he'd felt around Freestone's walls.

He'd sensed the strangeness in the guildhall, too, just that morning. Lotte had been instructing the team to pick their weapons—warning them of how important the choice would be. Zed had panicked, staring at a wall full of instruments he had no idea how to use. Some he wasn't even sure he knew how to hold.

Then he'd felt it. It was a nagging, tingling sensation. A pull he couldn't explain, drawing him to . . .

. . . the staff.

His eyes now fell upon the wooden training staff right next to his hand.

It looked like a normal practice weapon. A little out of condition, actually.

But there was something else there. Something working

from within it that called to Zed, just as it had called to him that morning. All he had to do . . .

The kobolds were almost on him now. The nearest, only a foot away, raised its serrated blade.

Zed reached out and grabbed the staff, and in the moment of contact, whatever was inside it reached out and grabbed *him*. Something within Zed, a hidden font, shuddered and was set ablaze.

He raised the staff, and the air around it rippled. The wood grew warm under his hand, then hot. Still, Zed held on.

The kobolds hesitated, just long enough.

The staff exploded.

Fire was everywhere: in the air, on the ground, in Zed's hand. Tongues of flame licked hungrily from between his fingers, eating the poisonous cloud like starving things. The kobolds screeched as they were caught within the blast. Zed saw the dark smudges of their bodies thrown through the air.

Flame was all around him, but he didn't feel it. Instead he felt . . . great. Strong. Confident. The staff pulsed contentedly in his grip.

And then it all faded.

The flames guttered out, dying just as quickly as they were born. The wooden staff cracked in half in Zed's hand, splintering into two distinct pieces. He looked down at them and saw that the ends had been singed black. Zed raised his eyes.

In fact, *everything* around him was black. He was sitting in the center of a smoldering ring. The ground within the circle was charred and burning. Smoke streamed from the edges.

The two kobolds that had been hit by the blast were smoking lumps, tossed several feet away. Only Zed himself was left untouched by the flame.

He found Brock's gaze. He, Jett, and Liza were watching him with wide eyes and open mouths.

"Zed?" Brock called unsurely.

Liza found herself first. She glanced back at the kobold mage. The creature let out a furious shriek and raised its scepter into the air again.

"It's trying to cast!" Liza yelled. She threw herself forward, pressing her shoulder into the back of the shield. Girl met beast with a metallic *clang!* Girl won.

As it was bashed backward, the kobold dropped its scepter. Jett stepped forward to the instrument, raised his maul high in the air, and brought it down hard upon the red stone. There was only a flicker of bloody light as the rock was pulverized.

The kobold, clever enough to realize it had lost, leaped to its feet and pounded a howling retreat into the trees. Zed tried to follow it with his eyes, but lost the green scales in the forest soon enough.

The four apprentices stood alone in the woods, breathing raggedly.

Then Liza turned around to face the others. It was the first time Zed had seen her smile.

"That," she huffed, "was *amazing*!"

✳

By the time night descended, Zed and the others had eaten their fill of wild greens.

He sat now against Freestone's great wall, quietly watching the forest line. The glow of the city's torches spilled over the wall, providing them with some dim light to see by.

Night seemed to give the forest a new voice. Strange calls sounded from within the trees—jabbering shrieks and low, mournful howls.

Zed was too tired to be afraid anymore. Whatever he'd done with the staff had drained him, leaving him more exhausted than he'd ever been in his life. He knew what mana was: the force that wizards used to power their spells. He'd even tapped into his own mana once, after reading a layman's pamphlet on magic that Brock had bought for him. It felt just like the leaflet had described—a reservoir of . . . *something* that existed inside of him. Something that was only his.

Now that reservoir felt totally empty. The staff had used it up.

Jett had been the one to explain what happened.

"Enchanted weapon," he said nonchalantly on the walk back

to the wall. "My father works on them sometimes. The staff had a charged spell inside, ready to be used by a mage. There are a few different kinds, actually. Da says dwarven runes are the best, but no one in Freestone actually knows how to make them anymore."

"Did you know the staff was . . . enchanted when you picked it?" Brock asked Zed.

Zed had shrugged. "No. Something felt strange about it, but I wasn't sure what. Honestly, I almost went for a spear instead. I only grabbed the staff at the last second."

"Good thing you did," Liza said cheerily.

Zed had been so pleased by the praise that he didn't tell them the staff felt . . . different from the magic at the wall. The smell of it was all wrong.

"Look at the stars," Brock said, calling Zed back from his thoughts. Brock pointed up above the tree line, where a whole blanket of twinkling lights glittered, stretching on as far as Zed could see. "It almost seems like there's more of them from out here."

"There are," Liza said faintly. "The light in the city makes them harder to see from inside the walls. Stars need darkness to shine."

Zed inhaled deeply, taking in the scent of the forest and the minty smell of the wards. For hours now he'd just been quietly admiring the trees, awash in the almost liquid sounds of the wind moving through leaves.

Mom, he thought. *I'm outside the wall. I'm outside and it's . . . wonderful. Did you know there's a plant called elfgrass? It grows all around the city.*

Zed turned and caught Brock frowning down at the two daggers laid in front of him. Liza had told him to keep them for the time being. She couldn't use them while holding her shield, anyway. One dagger still had a blade stained by the tentacle; the viscous green-black smear clung stubbornly to the metal. Brock had tried to wipe the gunk away hours ago, but the substance, whatever it was, had dissolved the fabric of his jerkin into a waxy film. They left it alone after that.

"So, um . . ." Brock ventured quietly. "I'm sorry, Liza." His eyes rose and found the girl. "About what I said today."

Liza continued staring outward, but her face softened.

"Me, too," she said after a moment. "Because the truth is that maybe I did come here expecting to take charge. My family has always believed that we—that *they*—are society's betters. That it's our duty to lead the commoners, and keep them in their place. Micah, especially, feels that way." She winced, glancing over at Zed. "I hope he wasn't too cruel to you yesterday."

Zed frowned. "Brock was there, too."

"Micah told me about visiting Old Makiva for a charm. He never mentioned seeing a snotty merchant kid. . . . Just a boy with pointed ears."

"Oh," Zed said, heat prickling his ear tips.

"Is it hard for you? Are most people cruel, like my brother?"

"Not *to* me," Zed said. "Usually, if I stay quiet, most people don't really notice me at all. Or my ears."

"But there's always someone like Micah just around the corner," Liza said with a sigh. "Someone lucky enough to be both cruel *and* perceptive." She frowned out into the woods. "People expect nobles to be charming, trained in courtly niceties. But the funny thing is, the more noble you are, the less nice you have to be. It's others who have to be nice to *you*. Micah's mistake was not realizing how vulnerable he truly was. He's our family's third-born, after my brother and me. Micah and I are twins, but I'm older. By seconds. Our parents treated it like it didn't matter, but it did. Micah never learned to be nice, because he thought our name protected him. Now he's mean *and* nameless."

"Did he ever bully you?" Zed asked.

Liza snorted. "He tried to, now and then." She smiled at Zed. "I'm not exactly a pushover."

"More like a pusher-overer," Brock agreed. "I'm sure that kobold thought so."

Liza smirked at Brock, but when she turned back to the forest, her face was thoughtful. "All my life I've wanted to be a knight," she said. "Micah and I sparred endlessly, ever since we were young. I'm every bit as good as him, but in the end it didn't matter—not to my parents, and not to the Stone Sons. I'm a girl, and that means I can never be a knight." She frowned, and gave a little shrug. "That's why I asked Frond to join. The Adventurers Guild doesn't care about who you are or where you come from. It was . . . It seemed like the only place I could be who I am."

"Sure," Brock said quietly. "I get that."

The night clicked and cooed and rattled as Zed took this in. Had he ever truly considered the Stone Sons' decree against women knights? Before Liza, he hadn't known any girls who dreamed of being warriors. There was the Basilisk, of course, but Frond had always seemed to prove the wrongness of it; people averted their eyes where the misfit adventurers were concerned.

And yet Liza had just guided them through battle like a dashing captain in a chivalric tale. Zed had never met a more knightly figure. He felt ashamed of his earlier anger.

"I don't know if it's 'cause you're a noble," Jett started, "but after what I saw out there, there isn't anyone I'd rather have leading me against a pack of walking, barking lizards. But for us . . ." Jett paused, unsure whether to continue. Liza turned to him, her expression neutral.

"My parents are both smiths," Jett said. "I've always wanted to work the forge like my da—to make great things." He waved a hand toward Zed and Brock. "We had dreams, too," he said. "Dreams *we* prepared for, just like you prepared for this. And we were close to getting those dreams. Then they were taken from us." He lowered his hand and clasped the handle of his maul, wringing it nervously. "It'll take some time to get used to our new lots," he said. "Just . . . be patient with us."

Liza was silent for a moment, then smiled. "Fair enough."

Jett's eyes found Brock's, then Zed's. "But it's not all gloom and doom, either. Being adventurers means we'll see things that our parents only ever dreamed of. We could visit the cities of our people, Zed. That's got to be worth something to you. It's a chance I never thought I'd have."

Zed nodded, chastened. How many times had he imagined visiting Llethanyl? How many nights had he fallen asleep dreaming of the silver spires of an elven capital twisting into the sky?

"If you're going to see these places," Liza said, "then you'll have to live long enough to do it. So let's look out for each other. We're a team, right?"

Jett glanced back at her, color rising in his cheeks. "Definitely," he said dreamily.

"Lovely speech, Jett," said Brock. "I do believe those are the most words I've heard you put together in a single stretch."

"*Definitely*," Zed gushed, imitating the dwarf. All four apprentices burst out laughing, even Jett.

Zed looked to the forest, grinning tiredly.

And saw a pale white face staring back at him.

He gasped and leaped to his feet. The others followed his gaze and rose in turn, grabbing at their gear.

The strange visage watched them from the trees, wreathed in shadow so that it seemed to be floating in midair. Zed couldn't tell whether it was male or female. In the darkness its skin looked white as an eggshell, and its lips were a bloody, fiery red. Its expression was completely placid—almost masklike.

Then there were the eyes.

Where the eyes should have been, two dark hollows stared out.

"What is it?" Zed asked nervously.

"I—I don't know," Liza said. "I think it's a Danger."

Jett took a step back. "It can't come near the wall, right?" he said. "The wards will keep it away."

Slowly, languidly, the pale face rose higher and inched its way forward. That was when Zed finally saw its body.

Though the creature's face looked somewhat human, that was where its humanity ended. The pale mask grew out into a long serpentine body, jet-black and covered in scales. It had the form of a snake—the largest, thickest snake that Zed had ever seen. It was easily twice as tall as any of them. A halo of oily black hair fell from the top of its head as it moved, shrouding the monster's empty eye sockets.

Its mouth opened—wider than any human mouth could or should—and from the recesses of its throat, a pink forked tongue emerged, tasting the air.

"Stay back and stay calm," Liza ordered. "Close to the wall!"

The creature's head twisted in midair, turning completely upside down.

"*Naga!*" a voice screamed out from somewhere nearby.

The air shook with a loud, cavernous noise. A horn was blaring from somewhere above them, in a note so heavy Zed felt it in his stomach.

The forest suddenly came alive with human figures. People melted from the trees, descended from the wall. The door into the guildhall burst open right beside Zed, and Alabasel Frond was there in an instant, her hands full of the sharp stars she'd stuck into the flag that morning.

"Back!" Frond shouted at the kids, almost as forcefully as the horn. But they were already pressed as far against the wall as they could go.

Zed realized the figures appearing around them were the members of the Sea of Stars. The truth slowly dawned on him then. The guild members had been there the whole time, watching them from the wall, and even outside the wards, hidden high within the trees.

The monster snapped its head back around. Its serene white face took in the arriving figures. Then its mouth yawned open again—and it screamed.

The noise was two sounds at once. First, a bloodcurdling human shriek cut through the forest. It was a scream that could only mean one thing: murder. Below it, rising from deeper within the monster, another sound joined the first in a dismal harmony. A loud, wet hiss rose up from the creature's throat—the warning of a cat backed into a corner.

The creature's head reared back, and it struck.

There was a flash of bright light, and the minty scent of magic, overwhelming Zed's senses.

The air was suddenly filled with small glittering particles.

With *writing*, Zed realized. Symbols carved themselves onto an invisible plane, written in light instead of ink. They were everywhere, and with them came a susurrus of strange whispers. A hundred different voices buzzed like insects, speaking words Zed couldn't understand.

The symbols were brightest where the monster's face made contact with the wards. The writing there acted like a second wall, holding the creature at bay.

A chill swept through Zed's whole body. He was actually witnessing the magic of the wards firsthand. They were beautiful. *This* was the power of the Mages Guild. The power that protected Freestone. A power he'd almost been a part of.

The naga reared back and let out another terrifying double scream.

It can't get us here, Zed thought gratefully. We're safe.

The monster turned its head, contemplating the glimmering barrier. Then the dark sockets of its eyes began to burn with an eerie light of their own.

"The naga's using magic!" Frond called up. "Hexam, we could use you about now."

From the top of the wall, voices began blustering orders. Zed looked up to see a pair of hands extend over the lip of the stone and begin to glow. Ribbons of light unfurled out from them, snaking toward the naga.

When they reached the creature, however, the ribbons began to fray. In the Danger's presence the tendrils burned away like paper set aflame, right back up to the hands that had cast them. Zed could hear screams of alarm from atop the wall.

"It's dispelling the magic!" the archivist's voice yelled down. "It's eating through my mana!"

"Fie," Frond cursed under her breath. She turned her gaze sharply to the naga. "All right, folks, let's get it—"

Another nightmarish scream. The monster threw itself at the barrier. There was a sick moment of resistance as the wards bent inward. Then the lustrous symbols began to burn away, just as the tendrils had. A dark hole formed in the wards, first the size of an apple, then a pumpkin, and then a cart's wheel.

Zed waited for the hole to close. The spell would right itself soon. The wards were the constant work of the Silverglows and had protected the city for over two hundred years. Their magic was like a living thing; it was the flesh that coated the city's tough stone skeleton.

The hole grew wider.

Zed licked his lips. His eyes darted nervously to Frond. The guildmistress's mouth hung open, and she stared at the growing breach with unmistakable alarm.

It was only then that he realized something had gone very wrong.

"*Attack!*" Frond screamed, even as she was flicking her pointed stars at the naga in a flurry of impossibly quick movements. They climbed up the creature's neck like footprints, the last striking it in the cheek.

Arrows rained down from the forest trees like shooting stars, most glancing off the creature's scales.

The naga shrieked and reared back. The archers were high above them in the trees, so its fiery eyes searched for a target it *could* strike through the rapidly growing hole in the wards.

Zed watched as it found Brock, who was standing and gaping at it in horror.

"Brock!" Zed yelled, lurching forward.

But the monster was faster. Worlds faster. Its face split open and fangs appeared from within the mask. There was a blur of action too quick to see, and then the naga was back, as if it had never moved.

But its fangs were bloody.

Zed gasped. Brock was on the ground, pushing himself back up. His eyes were wide and he was saying something. Saying it over and over.

"No, no, no, no . . ."

Jett stood over him—right where Brock had been just a moment earlier—his body totally rigid. The dwarf had saved Brock from the naga's strike by shoving him aside.

But then Jett looked down at his own leg, where two large punctures began to bleed. For a moment he appeared calm, almost thoughtful, watching contemplatively as a bloodstain blossomed on his pant leg. Then he teetered and fell to the side.

"*Kill it!*" Frond screamed. Having exhausted her stars, she pulled her gleaming curved blade from her back and threw herself forward, past the wards and into the path of the monster. Zed and Liza rushed over to Jett, whose gaze was clouding in shock.

"Help us!" Liza yelled, waving to the open guildhall door. Lotte had emerged from the door. She took one look at Jett and her eyes widened with distress.

The quartermaster rushed forward, ripping the sleeve off her own tunic shirt as she went.

"Raise him, *now*! Keep the bite below his heart!" Lotte shouted. "We have to get him to a healer immediately."

Zed nodded dumbly. He grabbed Jett under one arm while Liza held the other. Together they hefted the dwarf up as Lotte tied the cloth into a knot just above the wounds. The three dragged him toward the doorway.

"I think . . ." Jett mumbled. "I think it bit me."

As they carried the dwarf beyond the threshold of the door, Zed turned to search for Brock. He saw his friend was now standing, but still remained outside, staring down at the daggers on the ground. Beyond him, the senior guild members were all fighting the Danger.

"Brock!" Zed called. "Come on! Get inside!"

But Brock didn't seem to hear him. Instead, he picked up the blades. Brock raised the dagger with the stained tip. Then he turned to the monster and ran past the crumbling wards, plunging the knife into the snake's scaled belly.

Chapter Six

Brock

"It doesn't even hurt," Brock insisted as a young man spread ointment upon his cracked and bleeding hands. He was sitting on a cot in a small room off the basement hallway. "I'm fine."

"The hurt will come when the shock fades," Frond said from the doorway. Lotte was at her side. "Which is why we don't recommend stabbing creatures that have acidic blood."

Brock glared at her. "Well, my first plan was to stay on this side of the wall and never encounter a giant snake-beast wearing your mother's face, but I had to improvise." He pulled his hands away from the physician, who had begun to wrap them in a cloth bandage. "I'm fine. Fie! Focus on Jett!"

Frond crossed her arms. "Your friend is receiving the very best care we can provide."

"Curse it, Frond," Lotte said. "It's not enough and you know it. We need the Golden Way."

"Healing is useless until we counteract the venom. We're best equipped to do that here. . . ."

Lotte was a head shorter than Frond, but she stepped right up to the guildmistress and scowled menacingly.

Frond pinched the bridge of her nose and sighed. "However, once that's done, feel free to take the dwarfson to Brenner and her cult of glowing dimwits."

"We can't carry him across town!" Lotte cried.

"I wouldn't recommend it," the physician said. He wilted beneath Frond's scornful look. "Is what I would say if anybody asked me, but they didn't."

Frond ran her tongue across her teeth. "Fine," she said at last. She held up a finger. "One healer, and they stay upstairs."

Lotte spun around immediately and grabbed a passing adventurer through the open door. "Send for a healer," she said. "And have the boy moved up to my bedroom for now."

"I'll bring him up myself," Frond said.

The adventurer paused, looking from Frond to Lotte and back again.

"Well, get going!" Frond barked at him, waving him on and storming out after him.

Brock wasn't sorry to see her go.

Lotte put a hand on his arm. Her touch was light, but there was dried blood under her fingernails. Her torn shirtsleeve, which she'd used as a tourniquet, was a disquieting reminder of where that blood had come from. "You did well out there, Brock. I'm sorry things got so out of control. Now let Hank patch you up." She inclined her head toward the young physician. "I'll see your friend is taken care of."

Brock realized he'd been puffing out his chest. He exhaled, letting some of the tension out of his shoulders. "Thanks," he said.

"You're welcome," Lotte said, and the simple nicety was almost enough to reduce Brock to tears. She pulled a small object from her pocket, tarnished gold and pearl, and considered it in silence for a moment.

"Is that . . . You have a timepiece?" Brock asked.

"I do," she said, tucking it away again. "A memento from a different life. You're from intown, aren't you?"

Brock nodded. "My parents are both with the Merchants Guild."

"Well, I know firsthand what an adjustment this is, but you'll get used to things here. Just try not to rile Frond up too much. Leave that to me, yeah?"

She winked, stepped briskly from the room, and began shouting orders as soon as she'd turned the corner.

Once his hands were bandaged, Brock stepped out into the long hallway that led, in one direction, beyond the wall, and he shivered. The metal door at the end of the tunnel felt like scant protection against the Dangers he'd now seen with his own eyes . . . and the hundreds he could scarcely imagine. He turned and walked the other way, following the path as it sloped downward. Lotte had already vanished, and the men and women who ran up and down the hallway didn't spare him a glance.

Might as well take a look around, he figured. It could be some time before he had another opportunity like this.

He passed several doors, turning their knobs as he went, finding them locked.

Until he found one that wasn't, and the door swung open to reveal a ghastly sight.

Hexam—the "archivist," Frond had called him—stood with his back to the door. The sleeves of his robe were pulled back, and his arms were covered in green-black goo to the elbows. In one hand he held a small knife, dangerously sharp and wet with that same goo. His other hand held flesh—a black organ of some sort—which he was attempting to pull free from the dead body splayed open on the slab before him.

It was the body of the naga, its forked tongue hanging limply from its slack fanged jaw. Its false face was split down the middle and hanging open so that half of its features faced the far wall and the other half of its humanlike mask stared blankly ahead at Brock.

He recoiled in horror, unsure whether the fact that the

creature was dead made it any less frightening than it had been before.

"In or out!" cried the archivist. "You'll let the cold escape."

Brock slammed the door shut, and realized only after the fact that he'd opted for "in." It was, in fact, cold in the room. Unnaturally so—Brock knew magic had to be at work, and then he realized that was all the more obvious for the fact that the room was lit by a soft, diffuse light for which he could see no source. Zed would want to hear about this place, and Brock wondered if the guild couldn't teach his friend a fair amount of magic after all. The entire room—floor and walls and ceiling—was set with tiles, a sharp contrast to the dirt and planks that gave sad, slanted form to the rest of the guildhall. Shelves crowded with glass bottles and jars lined the walls, and Brock was reminded of the trophy room—although these keepsakes were even more macabre: there were fragments of bone and eyeballs suspended in sealed jars interspersed with containers of colorful powders and liquids and oozes. The naga's slab sat against the far wall, with a small table to the right and a lectern to the left.

There was a wet snapping sound as Hexam pulled the black organ free from the body of the snake-beast.

"What are you *doing*?" Brock asked. Overcome with curiosity, he crept forward, one shuffling foot at a time.

"Looking for buried treasure," answered the man. "Bring a jar!"

Brock grabbed an empty and open jar with both bandaged hands, swung it toward Hexam, and the man dropped the organ into it with a wet plop.

Brock's stomach quailed.

"Don't faint on me, boy. That kidney's worth more than three of you."

"I'm not. I won't." Brock stuck out his chin. "I'm the one who killed this thing, you know."

Hexam raised an eyebrow and turned to regard him for the first time. His hood was pulled back, revealing his sharp, dark eyes. His hair and beard were both trimmed short, jet-black with a smattering of white, and his skin was a rich shade of brown. "I think technically it was the smear of lurker's alkali on your blade that killed it. How are your hands?"

"They're holding a monster's kidney," he said. "Can I put this thing down?"

The man tilted his head toward the small table, on which Brock saw a variety of gleaming metal tools, like weapons in miniature. There was a dagger not much larger than a man's finger, a hooked instrument like a tiny scythe, and the daintiest shears Brock had ever seen. He set the still-open jar down among them.

"Anyway," he asked, "if its blood is so harmful, why are you rolling around in it?"

Hexam gestured vaguely at the jars on the wall to his left. "Secretions from the gastric mill of the karkinos. Slather a thick coat of it on a man's skin, and any known acid is neutralized before it can do damage." He stuck both hands into the large opening cut into the naga's snakelike trunk and began rooting through its innards. "Doesn't help terribly much with the smell, though."

Brock wandered over to the other side of the room, where a book stood open upon the lectern. It was an old book, its pages frayed and stained and yellow with age. It was open to a detailed illustration of a naga, and Brock saw that the artist had taken great care to capture the beast in all its gruesome glory, drawing each scale upon its long serpentine form.

Brock read aloud from the small block of text written beside the illustration: "'The naga is a solitary hunter of fiendish origin. Paralyzes its prey with a fast-acting and potent venom, which is produced by glands in the throat. Natural spell-casting talent (sorcery). Corrosive blood. Scaled hide resistant to acid.'"

There was another wet snap, and Hexam grumbled. "Now hold on. Was that a kidney or a gallbladder, then?"

Brock turned the page and found a second naga illustration, but this one appeared to show the beast turned inside out, its bones and organs exposed in a bloodless and sterile approximation of the scene unfolding now within this very room. Brock's eyes went to the drawing of the monster's throat, where its venom glands were labeled in neat script.

"Can this help Jett somehow? He was bitten."

Hexam plopped an organ into another empty jar, his eyes

darting from kidney to gallbladder, puzzling out which was which. "Of course," he said. He turned to look at Brock, hands held up before him. "Whatever you've heard, we look after our own. I should have no fewer than three journeymen assisting here, but the first thing I did was extract this creature's venom glands and set them to work on the antitoxin. They're seeing to your friend now." He rubbed the slime between his fingers. "But in the meantime, we can't let this little beauty rot on us, can we?"

✳

Brock emerged from Hexam's chamber some time later, bone weary and numb with cold. It was the middle of the night, and he expected the guildhall to be silent by now. But though the underground hallway no longer buzzed with activity, there was a commotion coming from somewhere nearby.

He crept along the sloping passage until it ended at the trophy room with its morbid mementos. The sounds grew louder. He could make out shouting voices and clomping boots coming from above—the ground floor. Suddenly there was a great racket as something large and heavy came crashing down.

It sounded like the guildhall was under siege.

This time, Brock chose a proper weapon, tearing a short sword from its place on the wall, barely breaking his stride on the way to the spiral staircase that took him up, up. He thought of the wards giving way to the naga's assault; he remembered the undisguised panic the sight had instilled in warriors who were by all accounts above fear. Had something followed them back into the city?

Brock slammed open the door at the top of the stairs, and the chaos he saw left him breathless.

The entire guild stood crammed into the dining hall. Some of them held weapons aloft, catching the firelight against their blades while they swayed in song. Others wielded greasy drumsticks and flagons of sloshing liquid. There was a man playing a lute, though the music was drowned out by the din. A woman hung from the chandelier in the center of the room, spattering those beneath her with wax from the swaying fixture's candles.

It was a party. The Adventurers Guild was having a party.

"Brock!"

Somehow, over all the clamor, he heard Zed call out his name. Brock scanned the crowd for his friend—and saw a snub-nosed beast with razor-sharp tusks charging his way.

Brock screamed, dropping his sword as he leaped backward, flailing his arms. He couldn't get far, though—the crowd had already closed in around him, so that he slammed right into the unyielding press of bodies as the monster approached him.

Then the beast held up its hands—human hands. It tilted its head back, and Zed peered out from beneath its savage snout.

"Where have you been?" Zed asked.

"What are you *wearing*?" Brock countered.

"It's an animal skin—they called it a boar," Zed said matter-of-factly. "Are you all right? How are your hands?"

Brock huffed. "The next person who asks about my hands is gonna get them!"

Zed looked at him quizzically.

"As fists, I mean," Brock said. "As in, I'm going to punch the next person—forget it. *Why* are you wearing an animal skin on your head?"

Zed shrugged. "It's a tradition. We're being initiated!" There was a frantic gleam in his eye, and he seemed . . . twitchy.

"Are you feeling all right?" Brock asked.

"Here he is!" shouted a man, and suddenly a heavy hand slapped Brock's back. It was a friendly gesture, but the force of it nearly took Brock off his feet.

"Get this young adventurer a mantle!" shouted the man.

"Get him some food!" cried another.

"Food for the naga slayer!" the first man hollered.

"Naga slayer!" the men chanted together. "Na! Ga! Slay! Er!"

"Oh, please don't let that stick," Brock said.

Someone shoved a massive chicken leg into his left hand, and a heavy flagon into his right, all while men and women reached out from the crowd to slap and batter at him playfully.

"You *have* to try that drink," Zed said.

"What is it?" he asked, sniffing at it suspiciously.

"It's not anything bad. They make it right here in the guildhall!"

That only made Brock more suspicious. He peered into the flagon. The drink was a rich amber color, somewhat syrupy but frothing with bubbles. He took a tentative sip and was startled by the intensity of the flavor.

"It's so sweet!" he said.

"That's thanks to the beebread," said a boy at his shoulder, probably no more than a few years older than Brock, pale-skinned with long blond braids. "Harvested from the hives of the scorpion bees of Kraken Cove by yours truly." The boy smiled, revealing a set of crooked teeth the same yellow color as his hair.

"Right," said the boy beside him, dark-skinned and sleepy-looking. He wore a three-horned helmet of metal and bone. "And who harvested the stingers from your sore and sorry hide? Longest day of my life." He nodded at Brock in greeting. "Nice job out there today. For a new kid, I mean. Brock, right? I'm Syd. This sack of hammers is Fife. Near everything he says is a lie."

"Right, right." Fife tapped his chin. "Unless *that's* a lie, of course."

"It's not," Syd said flatly.

"Here's a truth: I've never taken down a naga." Fife's voice was heavy with regret. "A grimspider, yes. A devouring hood. Two amphibimen, and more kobolds than I can count . . ."

"So, five or six kobolds then?" Brock said.

A shadow passed over Fife's face, and for a moment Brock

feared he'd misjudged the moment, but then Fife broke out in wheezing laughter.

"A mouth on this one, I think," Syd said.

"Mouth," Fife said, nodding at Brock, "and ears," he added, gesturing at Zed. "Put 'em together and you've got half a decent apprentice."

Fife saluted comically and walked away. Syd lingered a moment more. "Watch out for each other, okay?" Then he turned to follow after Fife, tri-horned helmet bobbing through the crowd.

"They seemed nice!" Zed chirped from beneath his boar.

Don't get too attached, Brock wanted to say. *We're not going to be here long enough to make friends.*

Brock sipped again at the drink and then sniffed at the greasy meat, and his stomach gurgled. All he could think of was Hexam slicing away at the dead creature in the basement.

"Are you gonna . . . ?" Zed said.

"Be my guest," Brock answered, and he held out the drumstick. But Zed took the flagon instead and, two-handed, tipped its contents into his mouth, gulping it down.

"So good," he said, and then he gave a little belch, which the men around them acknowledged with a cheer. "I'll get you some more!" he said, and before Brock could stop him, he darted through the crowd.

Brock found a mostly empty plate on the table to his side and dropped his drumstick on it, then turned back to find himself eye to eye with the hideous lizard skin sitting atop Liza's head.

"Gee-aaah!" he screamed, flinching. "Oh, come on!"

"Settle down!" Liza barked. "Where's Zed?"

"He went for more of that drink."

"The ambrosia? Blech." She stuck out her tongue. "That stuff is pure sugar."

"Oh, no," Brock said.

"What?"

"Zed . . . doesn't handle sugar well. I once smuggled him a few hard candies from one of my mother's parties, and he spent the next two hours dancing in place while excitedly alphabetizing his sock drawer."

"How do you alphabetize socks?"

"I still don't know!" Brock cried.

A tremendous crash sounded from across the room, and Brock saw the chandelier had torn free of the ceiling. There was a clattering noise as the woman who'd inadvertently pulled it down lifted herself to her knees and raised her arms to raucous applause.

"I don't want to alarm you," Brock said. "But I think these people may be out of their minds."

"I'm here!" Zed cried. "I'm back! Don't worry!" He handed Brock a flagon—it was empty.

Brock shot him a look, and Zed burped a pipsqueak burp. "Sorry."

"And it might be contagious," Brock told Liza.

"What's contagious?" asked Zed. "I feel really good, actually. Like, really good."

"How are your hands, by the way?" Liza asked Brock.

Zed's eyes went wide, and he looked hard at Brock as if daring him to follow through with his earlier threat.

Brock pointedly ignored Zed and his bulging eyes. "They're . . . a little tender, actually." He leaned in closer to them and lowered his voice. "Has it occurred to anyone else that what happened outside the wall was a complete disaster? What are we celebrating, exactly?"

"It's an annual tradition," Liza said. "The recruits survive a night outside, then return to a day of revelry."

"Not all of us."

"We wanted to stay with Jett," Zed said, suddenly somber. "But they ran us off. Told us they had it under control and we were just getting in the way. They said he needed to sleep it off. . . ."

"I think it's more serious than they were letting on," Brock said. "Hexam has people working on an antitoxin, and Lotte insisted on sending for a healer on top of that."

"That's good, though," said Liza. "The healers can handle just about anything. Maybe everything will be all right."

"Frond certainly wants to act like it. But what that thing did to the wards . . . Shouldn't we be raising the alarm?" Brock asked.

"And start a panic?" Liza said, putting her fists on her hips.

The lizard skin that was draped over her head and shoulders flopped about.

"It's impossible to take you seriously with that thing on your head."

"Oh, were you taking me seriously before?"

"I never actually saw any healers arrive," Zed interjected.

"There has to be a side entrance. I doubt Frond would want them to see all *this*." Brock scanned the crowd. Most of the men and women there towered above them, but one girl was their height—and looking right at them from across the room. "Follow me," he said.

"Where?" Liza demanded.

"To make friends!"

Brock led them through the crush of the crowd, putting on a friendly face and giving a little wave as he approached the girl, whom he recognized from their arrival at the guildhall. She had red curls and a silver crescent moon on a string around her neck.

"Hi!" Brock said lightly. "You look like someone who knows a thing or two about magic."

"Uh, I do?" said the girl. She smiled. "Thanks."

Brock smiled back. He'd had a feeling a former Mages Guild apprentice who still wore the guild's symbol would take that as a compliment. He introduced himself and Liza, leaving Zed for last.

"It's really good to meet you," the girl said, taking Zed's hand. "I'm Jayna. I've never met a sorcerer before!"

"Uh, me neither," Zed said brightly. "Other than me, of course. Not that I've . . . met me. That's not even possible!" He brought his fist to his mouth and started flexing his jaw, desperately suppressing a burp.

Brock sighed. "Maybe you can settle a dispute for us, Jayna," he said. "I was just telling my friends here that there's a room in the basement that's been made cold. You know . . . with magic." He raised an eyebrow. "But Liza here said that's not even possible."

"Hey!" Liza said, but she didn't contradict him.

"Sure it's possible," Jayna said with a shrug. "The trick is that it's taxing on the caster's mana. A sustained spell like that requires a focus. Magic gets stored inside, then released slowly to power the effect. It's complicated spellwork."

"But I bet you could do it," Brock said.

"Well, no." Jayna rolled her eyes. "Well, I could, I mean, I can generate cold, but I wouldn't be able to maintain a focus on my own, even if I could get my hands on a suitable gemstone." She turned to Zed. "I'm sorry you didn't get a chance to see the Mages guildhall. I was only there a few months, but I learned so much in that time."

"They must teach you magic here," Liza said. "Otherwise why recruit mages at all?"

Jayna nodded. "Hexam teaches me. But it's not a real priority for him, you can tell. When I do get instruction, it's very . . . combat oriented? You'll learn to attack with Icebite or Gestalt's

Rending Rime long before you learn how to ward a room."

"But Hexam would know how," Brock suggested.

"Hexam for sure. He'd be the only one here who could."

"Thanks, Jayna. You've been a real help. Now Liza here owes me a steak dinner."

Liza glowered at him. "I hope you like your steak rarely."

"Glad I could help," Jayna said, oblivious to the daggers in Liza's eyes. "Say, Zed." She reached out to touch his arm, hesitated, seemed to lose the words. Her eyes flicked to Brock and Liza. "Tomorrow is our weekly lesson with Hexam. Let's talk more in the morning. About magic. *Before* you talk to Hexam."

Zed nodded uncertainly, picking up on her hesitation. But she quickly bid them good night and retreated to the back of the hall.

"Strange girl," Zed said. "Right? She was strange?"

"I've lost perspective," Brock said, addressing the boar. "But I sure don't like the idea that only one person here could set up an *easy* ward." He held Zed's eyes. "What are the odds the wards that keep the city from being overrun by endless waves of other-worldly terrors are easy wards?"

Zed gulped.

"Frond knows what she's doing," Liza said, stepping between them. "I'm sure she's already sent word to the Mages Guild."

"Let's ask her, to be sure," he said. "Come on."

"Wait," Liza said. "Brock, wait a minute."

There was something in the way she said it—Brock found himself rooted to the spot.

"Don't go just yet," she said.

Brock searched her face. Her expression had gone very serious. Her eyes, deep brown with flecks of gold, bored into his, and she took his elbows in her hands.

"What—what is it?" he asked, suddenly breathless.

"I just need you to stand here just . . . one more moment . . ."

Out of nowhere, a weight slapped down upon Brock's head and shoulders, and rowdy laughter went up all around him. He knew right away he'd been draped with some monstrous animal hide. It reeked of wet fur.

Zed completely lost his composure, going bright red and doubling over as he cackled, his boar shaking with his laughter.

"I don't even want to know what it is," Brock said.

"Don't worry," Liza said lightly, patting his cheek. "It's a definite improvement."

✳

Sneaking away from the crowd took some time. They were stopped every few feet by men and women wanting to introduce themselves, and most of them made a point to slap, smack, punch, or shove them. Brock began to think he'd be far more bruised and battered by the party celebrating their battle than by the battle itself.

Eventually they made their way to the far end of the dining

hall and into the staircase they'd gone down before. This time, Brock intended to go up, but he paused upon the landing when he heard a loud thumping coming from a barred door at ground level. The three apprentices looked at one another as the thumping paused and then sounded out again, louder than before.

"Is someone locked in that closet?" Zed asked.

"There's only one way to find out," said Brock.

"There are a lot of ways to find out," Zed countered. "We could ask someone about it tomorrow, for example."

"Where's the fun in that?" Liza said, and she removed the bar and swung open the door.

It wasn't a closet at all, but a door to the outside. The woman who stood there, fist raised to knock again, wasn't immediately recognizable to Brock. She was old, her wrinkled face screwed up with annoyance, and her cloak was shapeless and drab.

But when she saw them standing on the threshold, her fist became an open hand of greeting, her annoyance dropped away, and Brock knew her the moment her wide smile beamed down on them.

"Mother Brenner," Liza gasped.

The guildmistress of the Golden Way dipped her head graciously. Mother Brenner wore no jewelry or cosmetics, and Brock had scarcely seen plainer dress. Yet everything about her bearing was noble, and her bright blue eyes and flawless white teeth lit up her face more than any decoration could.

Brock felt the scrutiny of those blue eyes as they swept over him, and he quickly slipped the animal mantle from his head and dropped it to the floor.

"I recognize you three," she said warmly. "Even under these charming . . . hats." She caressed Liza's lizard mantle as if it were a cat, then brought her hand down to lift Liza's chin. "I hear you've been through a terrible ordeal already."

Liza nodded.

"Are . . . are you here for Jett?" Zed asked. "He was injured. . . ."

"I sent my best healer to help Jett," Mother Brenner answered. "He should be with your friend now. I . . . am here for Alabasel Frond. May I enter?"

Brock was keenly aware of the rude and raucous sounds of the party at their backs. He remembered Frond's insistence that only one healer be allowed on the premises. He wasn't sure how to answer the Luminous Mother.

He regretted it straightaway, but it happened unconsciously: He turned to Liza to see what they should do.

Liza hesitated for a moment, nodded, and then stepped out of the way. "Of course, Mother Brenner," she said.

"Thank you, child," the guildmistress said, and then she swept past them and up the stairs.

Zed made a funny face at Brock and Liza, baring his teeth, half embarrassment and half eager anticipation, and he turned on his heel and followed her. Liza barred the door, and she and Brock went up after him, taking the stairs two at a time.

The staircase led to a hall lined with doorways, each one opening onto a room just large enough to hold a bunk and a dresser. Zed and Liza both tossed their mantles into a random room as they passed. At the end of the hallway was a closed door.

When Mother Brenner opened it, a warm, golden radiance spilled out. She stepped into the light, and they followed.

The room was square and plain, slightly larger than those they'd passed, with space for a proper bed and a bookshelf. The only decoration was a large vellum map pinned to the wall. It showed forests, mountains, lakes—with great blank patches scattered throughout, like a bird's-eye view of the land, obscured by passing clouds. Freestone stood at the very center of the map; in the context of the larger landscape, it looked shockingly small.

Jett lay on the bed, unconscious, but with more color in his cheeks than he'd had the last time Brock had seen him. Above him stood Lotte and a man in a flowing white robe trimmed in gold. The healer stood stock-still, his hands pressed to Jett's shoulders and emitting the vivid honeyed light that gilded the entire room. He didn't look up when they entered, but Alabasel Frond did.

"I told you to stay out," Frond barked, and it took Brock a long moment to register that she wasn't speaking to them but to Mother Brenner. He shouldn't have been surprised that her utter lack of civility would extend to the Luminous Mother, yet somehow he *was* surprised.

But Brenner was unfazed. "I like to keep a close watch on my people, Frond," she said. Her voice was calm but firm. "Pollux here is my responsibility. If any harm should befall him—well, the blame for that would rest uneasily on my shoulders."

Frond took a menacing step forward. "If you have something to say, Brenner, by all means spit it out."

"Let it be, Frond," Lotte said softly. "She's here. What harm can she do?"

Frond's gaze flicked to Brock and the rest, but she didn't say anything more, only leaned against the wall and turned back to watch the healer.

Brock had never seen a member of the Golden Way in action. His family had been blessed with good health, and the healers were not dispatched for the standard cuts and scrapes of an active childhood. By all accounts, the healing gift was a taxing one, and not without its dangers. It demanded a strict ascetic lifestyle and tremendous discipline, and it was employed only in serious circumstances.

He considered the healer at work, and he saw now the signs of strain written upon the man's face. Sweat dotted his brow, but his hands were steady, and the bright glow that came from them never faltered. Brock thought of gauntlets fresh from the blacksmith's furnace, the way they glowed orange with the memory of fire, and he marveled at the thought of such light without heat.

"It's beautiful," Liza said, holding up her own hand as if to catch the golden glow.

"Is it working?" Zed whispered.

Mother Brenner steepled her fingers. "Pollux is doing an excellent job."

"Is it magic?" Brock asked.

She inclined her head in consideration. "In truth, no. Strictly speaking, magic comes from"—she waved her hands in the air—"outside. Pollux is drawing upon his own life force—his anima—and adding it to your friend's own."

"And anima is totally different from mana?" Brock asked. "So you wouldn't be able to use it to fix the wards around the city?"

Mother Brenner startled, and Alabasel Frond sprung from the wall. "Brock!" she barked.

"Sorry," Brock said, affecting a sheepish shrug. "Was that a secret?"

"Frond, what is he talking about?" the Mother asked, and there was ice in her tone.

Frond stood in stony silence.

"Lotte?" Brenner tried.

Lotte shot a glance Frond's way, a moment of hesitation before she bowed her head in respect. "We're not exactly sure what happened, Mother. But the monster that did this to Jett seemed to create . . . or exploit . . . a weakness in the wards."

"*When* did this happen?"

"Only some hours ago," Lotte answered.

"Hours!" Brenner cried, her voice warbling with outrage. But she took a breath and her noble bearing settled over her again. "Alabasel," she said. "I'm disappointed in you. We allow you a certain amount of autonomy, but this—"

"You *allow*?" Frond growled.

"You should have notified the king's council at once."

"What happens outside the walls is of little interest to anyone but us," Frond said. "As your *High Guilds* have made very clear in the past. We're looking into it."

"It's bad enough you put your greenest apprentices in harm's way. You have no right to gamble with the lives of every single—"

Pollux cried out as if suddenly in pain, and the golden light extinguished as he pitched forward. Lotte sprang to her feet and caught the healer, who was limp in her arms.

"What happened?" asked Liza.

Mother Brenner crossed the room and touched Pollux's cheek. "He's fine. He used up everything he had, but he'll be all right with some rest." She turned to regard Jett, and there was trepidation in her gaze. She placed a palm against his brow, and it emitted a soft, subtle glow.

When she lifted her hand again, she closed her eyes as if overcome with grief. She stood, entirely ignoring the adults and crossing the room to stand before Brock and Zed and Liza. She touched Liza's shoulder gently.

Brock felt his mouth go dry and his stomach constrict. A high-pitched voice asked what was wrong, and he wasn't sure if it had come from Zed or Liza.

"Your friend will live," Mother Brenner said. She smiled so sadly as she said it that Brock wanted to make a joke about it, wanted to laugh at the gulf between her words and her expression, but his laughter died in his throat.

"He will live," she repeated. "But I fear he will never walk again."

Chapter Seven

Zed

"Ow," Zed said to no one. He was standing in an empty hallway, leaning beside a thick wooden door.

It was the morning after the initiation party, and Zed had a headache. His teeth ached from the accumulation of so much sugar. His mouth was thick and tacky, and his tongue tasted bad.

The guildhall was mostly empty this morning. Zed had seen only Lotte up, and the encounter was as brief as it was unsettling. The quartermaster had been standing at the end of the apprentice quarters' hallway, staring hard at the door to Jett's room. When Zed closed his own door, Lotte had glanced up at him. She wore a grave and guilty expression that twisted a knot in Zed's chest. Then she nodded, opened the door, and disappeared silently inside.

Jett.

The whole thing felt unreal. Never walk again? Just yesterday the dwarf had been tromping around, easily lugging a pack that was nearly twice his size. How could things go so wrong so quickly?

"Hey." Jayna approached from the far end of the hall. Her red curls were in disarray, but Zed had a sense that he looked far worse. "How are you feeling?" she asked.

Zed tried to groan, but burped instead. "Too much ambrosia," he said sheepishly.

Jayna smirked. "Well, it's good that you like it, I suppose. There's nothing better around here for rejuvenating your magic. Once you start casting real spells, your appetite will triple. Using mana takes a lot of energy."

The girl paused and her face became serious. She reached up and began fiddling with the silver moon hanging from her neck.

"But that's not what I meant," Jayna said. "How are you feeling . . . about your friend?"

Zed sighed and gazed at his feet. "You heard?"

"Liza told me this morning."

"Liza's already awake?" Zed asked, blinking back up at her.

Jayna leaned a bit closer. "She's been hitting practice dummies in the yard for at least an hour now," she said, her voice hushed with either terror or admiration.

The girl bit her lip. "What Frond said yesterday morning was true. People die around here. But for what it's worth, the guild-mistress doesn't give up on anyone. That statue in the receiving hall? The boy who got turned to stone? Frond said it took three men to carry him back, remember? What she didn't say was that before those three men arrived, she'd dragged him through the woods for two days. *Alone.* All to get him safely home."

"Did you know him?" Zed asked. "If he was petrified last year..."

Jayna frowned. "Yes," she said. "I knew him." She coughed, and Zed decided to let the subject lie.

He glanced at the door that towered beside them and reached for the handle. "Should we go in?"

Jayna grabbed his wrist.

"Not yet," she said. Her face was bright with a sudden intensity. The girl leaned in, and her voice fell to a whisper. "Just listen. I didn't want to say this in front of your friends, but there's something you should know about Hexam. The man is dangerous."

Zed's stomach dropped. "What do you mean?"

"If you'd truly joined the Mages Guild, they would have taught you about the different kinds of spells. About *forbidden magic*. It's incredibly important that you *never*—"

"Jayna, what are you tittering about out here?" Hexam's irritated voice blared from right above them. "Oh, for the love of mandrakes, get up off the floor, you two. And stop that screaming."

The master archivist hefted Zed and Jayna from the shrieking tangle they'd made of themselves following his sudden appearance. He was surprisingly strong for someone so wiry. As he set them on their feet, strange colored lights blinked out from within his chamber.

Hexam grunted. "Is it Feyday already? Then I suppose you want a lesson. Very well, come in." He turned and stepped back inside.

Jayna pressed her finger to her lips. *Say nothing.* Then she followed the archivist over the threshold.

The office was a dimly lit room that reminded Zed more of Old Makiva's tent than the rest of the ramshackle guildhall. Like the trophy room, it was packed full of monstrous remains. Claws, teeth, and other sharp body parts that Zed didn't have names for lined the walls, carefully installed on ornate plaques. There was a large display table covered with nothing but skulls, each labeled and arranged by size. The largest of them—a titanic yellow oval with two curling tusks—took up a quarter of the broad tabletop. Brock *had* to see this place.

The room was lit by a constellation of glowing orbs that hung from the ceiling. Each was a different color and size, and they all pulsated at disparate rhythms, dimming and then flaring gently back to life. The colors in the room shifted with them, sometimes green, or blue, or burgundy.

Magic. Zed felt a thrill of excitement that was laced with dread. Jayna's unfinished warning still hung in the air.

Hexam sat at his desk, his belt of keys jangling, and waved a hand in the direction of two guest chairs. Jayna took the seat on the right. Zed followed, sitting at the left.

"Jayna," Hexam began. "Remind me what your last assignment was."

"You had me memorize the Wizard's Shield spell."

"And did you?"

Jayna nodded, her red curls suddenly indigo as the light in the room shifted.

Hexam rubbed at his beard. "We'll test your Shield later. If it's adequate, then I think we can move on to something more complicated."

The archivist's gaze turned to Zed. His lips pulled into a tight frown. "I don't suppose I'd be lucky enough that you received *some* magical education before today?"

Zed hesitated, then shook his head.

"I didn't think so. Then let's start at the beginning. Jayna, instruct us—what is magic?"

The girl sat up a little straighter. Despite her warning about Hexam being dangerous, Jayna still seemed eager for his approval. "Magic is the use of mana to create any number of physical or numinous effects."

"What is mana, and where does it come from?"

"Mana is an invisible and supernatural force possessed by all spell-casting creatures. It is developed by establishing a controlled connection to the plane of Fey."

"Half right," Hexam grunted. "The Silverglows aren't listening in on us, Jayna. And you aren't doing yourself any favors by ignoring the truth. Now: What is the difference between wizards like yourself and a sorcerer like our pointy-eared friend here?"

Jayna faltered. "I . . . I only know a little, Magus."

Hexam sighed and leaned back in his chair. "I'm not a magus anymore, Jayna. And no, I don't suppose the Silverglows would have taught you that in your first few months."

He turned his gaze to Zed, then back to the girl. "Then this lesson is for both of you. The difference between wizardry and sorcery is one of science versus art. Of nurture . . . versus *nature*. A sorcerer's mana is innate. They are born with it, and this forever shapes how they use their magic.

"Wizards memorize their spells, which are developed through careful experimentation. If performed accurately, each spell is distinct and its effects are certain, as wizards benefit from the breadth of study and experience of those who came before them. But a sorcerer approaches magic like a singer approaches a tune. Many of their spells have no formal names, and the effects can tend to be . . . disorganized. Their magic can be honed with practice, but they will only ever become as powerful—or their range as extensive—as their talent allows. Some are forever amateurs. Some are virtuosos."

His chair creaked as he leaned forward. "Tell me, Zed. What drew you to the staff you picked for your initiation?"

Zed's ears flushed. It was the first time Hexam had said his name. He hadn't been sure the man even knew it. "It . . . smelled weird," he admitted. "Like rotten eggs. But more than that, I felt something strange coming from it. A pull."

Jayna let out a yelp. "Oh, no . . ." she moaned.

Hexam shot the girl a glare. "Be quiet, or you'll leave here without a new spell." The archivist turned back to Zed. "That smell is called sulfur. I believe that you may have a natural gift for sensing magic, Zed. Wizards must perform a Descry Mana spell to do so, and it's complicated spellwork, even for me—with many rare and expensive ingredients. Historically, high concentrations of mana have been said to have a . . . scent to them. Most say it smells minty. That's wizard magic, culled from a connection to the plane of Fey. But there is another kind. Of the six planes beyond our own, *two* are close enough to have developed true magical traditions. Mana can also be drawn from Fie—the infernal plane. This is the magic of witches and warlocks."

Zed experienced a sudden sensation like falling. His stomach lurched, and the blood all rushed to his head. Dark magic was illegal in Freestone, ever since Foster's betrayal. Anyone convicted of being a witch or warlock was executed. He turned to Jayna, but the girl avoided his eye. She wouldn't so much as glance at him.

"Wizards can't use this kind of magic," Hexam continued. "The two types of mana do not mix well. But a sorcerer, whose power comes from neither plane . . ."

There was a clatter as Zed abruptly stood, knocking his chair over. "But I didn't *know*!" he pleaded. "It's not my fault! The staff was right there on the wall—nobody warned me!"

"Oh, for crying—*sit down*!" Hexam shouted. The sheer volume of his order jolted Zed out of his panic. "You're not in any trouble, lad."

As Zed righted his chair, the archivist cast a sidelong look at Jayna. "This is your doing, I expect."

The girl narrowed her eyes. "Dark magic is forbidden for a reason," she said. Her voice was stern and imperious. "It's erratic and addictive and dangerous. It corrupts all who—"

"You are *excused*, Apprentice Jayna. Use the next few days to practice your Shield."

Jayna glared at Hexam for a long beat, then stood with a chirp of frustration. She still wouldn't meet Zed's eye as she hurried to the door. When she threw it open, however, there was a figure hunched on the other side. Zed recognized him from the party: Fife. The boy nearly fell over, his ear had been pressed so firmly against the door.

Fife righted himself with an embarrassed smile. "Ah. Sorry to, uh, intrude, Hexam."

"What do you want, Fife?"

"Frond needs the new apprentice. All the new apprentices, actually. The ones who can walk, anyway."

"We're in the middle of a lesson," Hexam said impatiently. "Can it wait?"

"Well, no . . ." Fife said. "They've been called by the king himself, you see. He's holding a council on what happened outside the wall."

Now Jayna finally looked back at Zed. Her eyes were wide.

"Fie," Hexam cursed. "Alabasel will be in a fine mood after this one. All right, you can take him." He cleared his throat. "Out you go, Jayna."

The girl hurried past Fife without another word.

"Zed, before you leave . . ." Hexam stood from his desk and walked over to a wide bookshelf filled with ancient-looking manuals. "Jayna was right about a few things. Fiendish magic *is* dangerous, just as any blade can be dangerous. And it *can* be corrupting, as much as coin, or a title, or a fine suit of armor."

The archivist selected a book from the shelf whose leather binding was so tawny it appeared bloodred. Until the light changed, and it was green. He carried it over to Zed and set it on the desk in front of him. The title, *Bonds of Blood and Fire*, was imprinted neatly into the leather.

"We in the Adventurers Guild are given leniencies that others aren't," Hexam said. His voice was soft, almost wistful. "Because we are called on to risk so much for this city. Risk is our lives, I'm afraid—and it is our duty. And that's all I'll say on the matter for today."

The sun was high as Zed made his way through the market, flanked by Brock and Liza. Frond walked far in front, moving briskly through the crowd toward the palace road.

"Nice gloves," Liza said to Brock.

Zed glanced down. Brock was wearing a pair of leather gloves that came up past his wrists.

"I'm willing to suffer for fashion," Brock said with a shrug. "And I probably shouldn't bleed on the king's rug. I meant to ask Mother Brenner if there was anything she could do, but after Jett . . ." He glared forward at Frond's back. "I'll heal, anyway."

"What do you think the king wants with *us*?" Zed asked nervously. The events of this morning were still bouncing around inside his head. He'd stashed Hexam's book under his bed before they headed out, but even having it there made him nervous. If what Hexam had said was true, then Zed had used dark magic—*illegal* magic—to fight off the kobolds. What if news of this had reached the king?

"We were closest to the wards when the naga broke through," Liza said. "He probably wants us to tell him what we saw."

"Well, I've seen plenty, and I've got plenty to tell him," Brock said. He glanced over at Liza. "You must have met the king in court. What's His Majesty like in person?"

Liza frowned. "Stern."

"Coming from you . . ."

"Oh, you'll have plenty coming from me, if you keep that up." Liza smiled prettily and cracked her knuckles.

"Why did I stand between you two?" Zed wondered aloud.

"My father says that the crown of Freestone grows heavier by the year," Liza continued. "To lead one of the last surviving cities in the world . . . the pressure on the king must be immense."

"Speaking of immense pressure," Brock said. "How's your stomach, Zed? Get into any more of that ambrosia today?"

Zed's insides lurched. "I think I'm off sugar for a while."

"I've heard that before." Brock smiled. "Just stay away from my socks."

As they made their way down the palace road, the crowd began to thin. When the noise of the market had finally died away, replaced by only a crisp quiet, Zed suddenly realized . . . He had crossed the boundary to intown. Large, stately homes fringed the clean, even cobbles.

It was the first time Zed had ever entered the central district. Freestone's peasantry weren't generally welcome here, aside from sanctioned members of the Servants Guild like his mother. Loiterers were quickly encouraged by the Stone Sons to be on their way.

While Brock and Liza continued to speculate about the king, their demeanors playful, Zed fell slowly out of step. His eyes darted around, taking in the peaceful houses and spacious streets. It was a place almost as foreign as the world outside

Freestone's walls—and yet he'd always lived just on the other side of the market.

Up ahead, Brock and Liza seemed to have come alive with their new surroundings, their footsteps echoing blithely. Even with their scrapes and bruises, the two fairly radiated confidence and gentility.

In contrast, Zed became aware of his own shoulders pulling inward, instinctively shrinking as small as possible. And he hated himself for it.

Mom, he thought. *Is this how you feel every day?* The notion filled him with a desolate, heartsick feeling.

Zed took a deep breath. He threw back his shoulders and hurried forward to catch up with his friends.

Frond kept the same quick pace the whole way, never once looking back at the three apprentices. Eventually, even the houses disappeared from the street, replaced by a steep climb to the castle itself. Then, before Zed knew it, the palace gate stood before them.

It was a monstrous, gorgeous thing. Golden as the sun and reeking of magical protections, it towered over even the strapping knights who stood sentry out front. The two Stone Sons remained perfectly still until Frond was just before the gate. Then one held out a plate-gloved hand.

The guildmistress stopped.

"State your name," one of the knights demanded, as Zed and the others caught up.

Frond grinned her lewdest grin yet at the man. Then she hawked and spat onto the ground.

An uncomfortable moment of silence followed. Apparently that was the only answer the knight was getting.

An exasperated noise echoed from within the helmet of the second guard. "Just let her through. Oy, Rafi!" he called up at the parapet beside the gate, where the face of a young squire was watching from above. The boy disappeared over the ledge.

A few moments later, the gate began to rattle and creak.

Frond waited until the bars had parted wide enough for one, then swept forward into the palace grounds. Zed and the others followed awkwardly, slipping through the gate one at a time.

"Poor scuds," Zed heard one of the knights mutter on their way past.

"The girl's a noble, no less . . ." the other replied.

Zed's ears burned as they hurried after their guildmistress.

The palace grounds were lovely. Flowering bushes framed the entire enormous estate in spectacular colors, and a few large trees even dotted the yard, a rare sight outside the timber lots. Members of the Knights Guild patrolled the grounds. Their metal armor gleamed in the midday light, making them look every bit the radiant warriors from the romantic tales.

Zed took in as much of the view as he could, but Frond continued without pause. Soon they arrived at the door to the palace, where a trim young man in a fine uniform stood waiting for them.

"Welcome, Guildmistress Frond." The young man fell into a deep bow. Zed had never seen anyone treat the Basilisk with such courtesy. Frond scowled impatiently at him.

"His Majesty is waiting for you in the council room," he continued. He turned to Zed and the others. "My name is Peter Magniole. I'm his majesty's seneschal."

"It's good to see you, Peter," Liza said with a small smile.

"And you, Messere Guerra. I'm . . . glad to see that you're in good health."

"Enough," Frond grunted.

Peter paused a moment, then cleared his throat. "Please follow me." He opened the palace door and motioned them inside.

"It's so good to see you, Peter," Brock whispered sourly.

Zed restrained a chuckle. Then, as he passed through the doors, he gasped aloud.

The inside of the palace was the most beautiful place Zed had ever laid eyes on. Rivers of multicolored light poured from stained glass in the ceiling. Statues of the Four Champions lined the great hall, each more exquisitely detailed than the last—and certainly more so than the ones in the market.

At the far end of the room a single throne loomed before a great, wide window, illuminated from behind. Zed realized that any who addressed the king there would have a hard time staring directly at him, which was perhaps the point of the design.

Zed had never felt so out of place before, even among the rank and rowdy adventurers. His clothes were plain, if not ragged. He'd barely had time to scrub his face before they'd headed out, and his hair was still a mess from the previous night. He felt like a living blemish scurrying across the pristine hall.

Frond looked even stranger. Her dark leathers were scuffed and scalded, but the many weapons she wore appeared sharp and pristine. And her scars . . .

Zed had almost become used to them in the past day. But here in the palace, surrounded by such unmarred beauty, each puckered blemish seemed especially red and vivid.

Peter led them down the hall to a clean white door. He opened it and stood aside, motioning for them to enter. "The king's council is very eager to speak with you," he said.

Frond hesitated for the briefest of moments, tapping her fingers against the points of her throwing stars. Was she steeling herself?

Then she stepped inside.

"Something tells me I'm going to enjoy this," Brock whispered as they followed her in.

✳

Compared to the palace entrance hall, the council chamber was more subdued. Which made it only the second most opulent room that Zed had ever been inside.

A thick slab of a table took up most of the space. It looked as if it had been cut from a single gigantic piece of wood, but the idea of a tree that large made Zed's head spin.

Unlike the painted plaster in the receiving hall, the walls of this room were all stone brick, giving the chamber an austere and chilly atmosphere. Curtains decorated in rich brown brocades were pulled closed over a dozen windows. The main sources of light were torch lamps and an enormous metal chandelier that hung over the table. The entrance hall was all splendid grandeur, but this was clearly a place of serious business.

To underscore that point, the five most important figures in Freestone all sat together at the far end of the table, staring directly at Zed and the others as they entered.

Frond led the way in, then paused at the foot of the table. Closest to her (which was not close at all) were the Luminous Mother Brenner and Lord Borace Quilby. Beyond them, Ser Castor Brent sat at the right hand of the king, and Archmagus Dafonil Grima at his left.

His Royal Majesty, King Gariland Freestone himself, waited at the table's apex. His chair was raised a full head above the others. As the king of Freestone, he was the de facto guildmaster of the Stewards Guild, though he didn't usually participate in public life as such.

Zed had only ever seen the king twice in person, when the children of his younger sister, the princess, went through their Guildcullings. Those years had been especially nervous ceremonies, with stiff pronouncements and muted applause.

This was by far the closest Zed had ever come to him—and frankly, it was the closest he ever wanted to come. His face was all sharp edges, including the grimace he now directed at Frond. Zed could see what Liza had meant about the king being stern. Even his crown was a severe loop of heavy-looking metal.

"Alabasel," King Freestone said.

"Your Majesty," Frond returned. Zed couldn't see her expression. "I hear you have some questions."

The king chuckled. It was not a cheery sound. "I hardly know where to begin. Perhaps I'll start with the least disquieting of the things I've heard, and work my way up from there. One of your apprentices was attacked during his initiation into your guild. Is this true?"

Frond shifted her weight from one foot to the other. "It is," she said. Zed ground his teeth to hear her speak so brusquely about Jett's injury.

"I am aware that the members of your guild undertake great dangers for the sake of our city, Guildmistress," the king said slowly. "But surely even you can agree that mangling apprentices on their *very first day* is a troubling practice."

"More than troubling," Ser Brent spoke up, his voice a growl. "Unconscionable."

"And imagine the outcry if it had been the young Messere Guerra," Lord Quilby added. "Instead of a dwarfson."

Zed bristled at the insinuation. He glanced at Liza, whose eyes were narrowed on Quilby.

"It's an affront to chivalry that we allowed her recruitment at all," Brent said. "The battlefield is no place for a gir—"

King Freestone raised his right hand and the knight immediately cut off.

"Alabasel," the king said. "Perhaps you would like to comment on this sad accident."

Frond nodded. "The initiation was the same as it's always been. The apprentices were watched by the guild, with bows ready to fire if needed, which they weren't. The apprentices handled themselves well, and that night were positioned inside the wards when the beast attacked. They . . . should have been safe."

"On that much we can agree," the king said icily. "I'd like to hear from the brave apprentices who witnessed the attack on their friend." Freestone's gaze turned from Frond to Zed and the others. "Perhaps you have something you'd like to share."

Zed's ears grew hot. His *face* grew hot. *Oh, no.* They were expected to talk? What should he say? Should he speak now? Why were the guildmasters all staring at them?

"Your Majesty," Brock said. He moved forward fluidly, until he was standing right beside Frond. "We have only our gratitude. Without the help of the Luminous Mother and her healers, Jett likely would not have survived."

Zed noticed a flutter of movement from the far corner. When he caught sight of the source, he fought to contain his surprise. There was *another person* in the room! A woman dressed in the gray smock of the Servants Guild stood away from the rest, listening silently from her nook and tapping a finger to her nose. Had she always been there?

The woman watched Brock with a blank expression, but made no effort to hide that she was staring. Zed's mother would never have been so brazen. Were all the palace servants this impudent? Everyone else in the room ignored her.

"It's Brother Pollux who deserves the credit," Mother Brenner replied humbly. "He did everything he could for that boy. I've never seen a monk pour so much of himself into a healing."

"Please offer him our thanks," Brock said. "I only wish that the Golden Way had been able to intercede sooner. Perhaps Jett . . ." He let the thought float there.

Frond was silent, but Zed could read the tension in her body. She didn't like the direction this was heading.

The king made a thoughtful noise. "Alabasel, why *didn't* you call on the healers earlier?"

The guildmistress clenched her fists. "We had a physician working on him, Your Majesty," she said. "Our own guild is very familiar with the toxins of the Dangers. I . . . thank the Mother for her help, but I do not believe the result would have been different were the Golden Way not summoned."

Mother Brenner stiffened at this slight. If the table hadn't already been against Frond, it certainly was now.

"And yet you did call them," the king said.

Frond nodded. "I wanted to give my apprentice every chance."

The king turned his attention to Brock. "Thank you for sharing your thoughts with us, Messere . . ."

"Brock Dunderfel," Lord Quilby answered for him, his eyes beaming with pride. The guildmaster of merchants licked his lips, then sighed woefully. "He was our first choice of apprentices this year. He gallantly volunteered for the Adventurers Guild when his young friend here was drafted from the mages."

"A brave and selfless act," the king said. "Those who risk their lives for the people of this city are truly the paragons of Freestone." The king's eyes fell once again on Frond. "I will try to remember that."

Frond was losing her patience. She bent into a churlish curtsy.

Brock took his former place beside Zed, looking as meek and demure as he was likely feeling satisfied.

"I suppose that leads us into what is unfortunately the more crucial issue," King Freestone began. "The city's wards have been punctured. I would know how, and how to fix them—*before* some enterprising monster slithers past Frond a second time."

Frond moved to speak, but the king raised his hand and brought her up short. "I believe we've heard enough from you for the moment," he said. "I am *hoping* the archmagus can shed some light on this very pressing problem."

Even from behind her, Zed could tell that Frond was scowling. Then, to his horror, she hawked up a wad of spit, and turned her head to the side to—

"Don't. You. *Dare.*" The king's eyes burned with fury. The assembled guildmasters all watched Frond with varying levels of shock and disgust.

Frond was totally still. The *room* was totally still. Then she swallowed the wad with a single noisy gulp.

King Freestone watched her a moment longer. Slowly, drawing on his composure, he turned to Grima. "Archmagus, please tell me you can *end* this council before anything drastic happens."

"I certainly hope so, Your Majesty," the wizard said. Of all the assembled guildmasters, the archmagus had yet to contribute. Considering the wards were the purview of the mages, Zed expected her to be a bit more nervous. But she was as aloof and composed as he'd ever seen her.

"From what I have heard," she said, "the Danger that attacked the city used a natural ability to dispel magic. Normally, the wards would be far too strong for something like that to work, but my mages have discovered something troubling. Our focus is degrading."

The adults at the table looked as if Grima had just spilled ambrosia on the king. Lord Quilby actually recoiled.

"Excuse me, Archmagus . . ." Liza asked. "What do you mean by our *focus*?"

Grima glanced patiently at Liza and the others. Zed felt a thrill when their eyes briefly met. "The wards to our city are created through the use of a focus for the spell. We maintain them by regularly adding our own magic to it. Normally, the focus *should* last for thousands of years without issue. But ours is weakening. No matter how much mana we add to it, the gem can't seem to contain it. If it becomes completely exhausted, the wards will expire."

The room was silent as the gravity of this statement sunk in.

Before the others could respond, Archmagus Grima held up a calming hand. "There is good news, however," she said. "My researchers have been poring over the problem, and discovered in an ancient text that there may be another suitable focus near the city." She laid her hands on the table. "Southeast of Freestone there was once a shrine inhabited by a sect of benign druids—nature priests. The druids are long extinct, but we believe that they had a focus similar to ours for their rituals . . . a large crystal. *It* may have survived."

"Do you know where this shrine is?" King Freestone asked.

The archmagus nodded. "We even found a map. The Scribes Guild will have a copy produced by sundown."

The king nodded approvingly. "I'm disappointed it took this tragedy for you to discover the weakness in the wards, Grima," he said. "But I appreciate your quick response."

"I cannot apologize enough," Grima said contritely. "Frond . . . is correct. Her apprentices should have been safe."

The king thought on this for a moment. He turned to Frond.

"Then there is a chance yet here to make things right. Or as right as they can be. Alabasel, I assume you can handle an expedition to this shrine."

Frond was silent a moment, her fingertips racing across the

points of her stars like a minstrel playing a lute. Then she seemed to catch herself, and curled her hand into a fist. "Your Majesty, may we speak privately for a moment?"

King Freestone watched her stonily. "You can say what you must here."

Frond looked around the room, then nodded. "I believe . . . something is happening here that we aren't seeing. Something malign."

The king let out a long sigh, which was echoed by the other guildmasters. Frond stood up straighter and narrowed her eyes.

"I've no patience for your paranoia today, Frond," the king said. "Perhaps it would have been better served protecting your apprentices. Don't speak of this again. Now go, collect this focus and return to us when you have it. No more secrets. No more hesitations. And I trust you can do this without injuring any more children?"

Frond answered the king with a single nod, perhaps not trusting herself to speak further. Then she turned on her heel and brushed past Zed, Brock, and Liza, out of the room.

Her expression was furious.

Chapter Eight

Brock

B rock was somber and silent on the walk back from the palace. He doubted whether anyone found that unusual, since he certainly had enough reason to sulk. As he and Zed and Liza hurried along in Frond's wake, the townspeople they passed gave them a wide berth, and though it was Frond's ruined face that caught their eyes, it was a reminder to each of the new adventurers that they were outsiders now.

But beyond that, Brock's mind was fixated on the servant woman in the council chamber. She had remained silent, but when she saw him watching her, she had repeated Quilby's gesture from days ago, tapping her nose as she smiled a small coy smile. It had made his skin crawl, and when he'd looked around at the others, he'd seen no indication that anyone else found her presence unusual.

He would have to sneak away today. The lower level of the guildhall was lined with locked doors, behind which could be any number of secrets juicy enough to satisfy Quilby. Once Frond had no more skeletons in her closet, Brock would have no further use as a spy.

He just hoped there weren't any actual skeletons behind those doors. . . .

But Brock's plans for the day were dashed when Lotte met them at the front door. She registered Frond's mood, stood well out of the guildmistress's way, and then pulled Brock and Zed aside.

"It's Jett," she told them. "He's awake, and he's asking for you."

✳

Jett had been moved to his own bedroom, identical to the tiny room Brock had been given, but darker. The candles were all extinguished, and heavy curtains blocked out the sun. Brock thought their friend must be sleeping again already, and to his shame he felt some momentary relief at the idea that they'd have to delay their visit.

He was all twisted up inside. Guilt and gratitude and pity churned together in his stomach, leaving him sour and miserable. He was supposed to be good at this sort of thing—his bravado and bluster allowed him to barrel through any situation, however awkward or scary or odd.

But now he stood frozen in the doorway. He kept second-guessing what he should say, how he should act. Was it better to put on a happy face, to tell jokes as if nothing had changed? Or would that be tactless, belittling to Jett and whatever he was going through?

While Brock hesitated, Zed stepped forward, hurrying right up to the narrow bed and throwing his arms around the dwarf.

"Careful!" Brock warned.

Jett scoffed. "What harm's he gonna do? He weighs less than the blankets."

Zed made an odd, strangled sound, as much a sob as a laugh.

"Aw, now," Jett said, clearly a little embarrassed. He patted Zed's back stiffly.

"We were so worried, Jett," Zed said, sitting back on the edge of the bed. He wiped at the corners of his eyes. "It's gloomy in here. Brock, would you open the curtains?"

"Sure," Brock said, and he moved from the threshold at last, grateful to have a task. As sunlight filled the small chamber, Brock felt a sudden rush of affection for his best friend. Here Brock was, trying so hard to figure out what he should appear to be feeling . . . while Zed had the courage to simply be himself.

"My mom always said sunlight can cure most ills," Zed said, and though Brock couldn't see his face from where he stood, he could hear his friend smiling. "But I'm pretty sure she's never even heard of a naga."

"Lucky her," Brock said. He meant it to be funny, but his voice sounded husky.

Jett's eyes found him, and they were somber.

"Jett, what you did out there—I owe you—I don't know how I'll ever repay—"

Jett made a rude sound. "You still sound like a merchant, Brock. They told me you killed the thing?"

Brock swallowed. Nodded.

"Then we're square. One adventurer to another."

Brock nodded again, slow and solemn.

"Wow!" Zed said excitedly, pointing at Jett's face. "Brock, look! In the sunlight you can really see Jett's facial hair coming in. That is gonna be some beard!"

Zed's laugh tinkled, and as Brock leaned close to peer at the fuzz above the young dwarf's lip, he thought he'd never seen such a smile as the one that lit up Jett's face.

✳

The guildhall was slow to rouse itself after the festivities of the night before. It was past noon before Brock and Zed began to hear the sounds of movement and voices from outside the bedroom, and when Hank the physician appeared with lunch for Jett and chased the boys off, they found the common area crowded with slow-moving, unwashed men and women all pitching in to clear away the worst of the mess.

Syd, the dark-skinned boy with the tri-horned helmet, approached them from across the room, taking long, languid steps. "Your friend is in the training yard," he said placidly. "She's beating up my friend. It's pretty funny."

The lack of emotion in his voice didn't make him seem especially amused, but he led them out the side door to the training yard.

Liza was there, hefting the shield she'd claimed from the wall downstairs along with a wooden training sword. She was battering away at Fife, whose own training sword lay at his feet as he clutched his shield with both hands.

"All right, Fife?" Syd called from the sidelines.

Fife peeked around the edge of his shield while Liza hammered away. "This is strategy! It's called the turtle maneuver. You'll—ow!" he cried, as Liza swiped at his exposed ear.

Syd rolled his hooded eyes at Brock and Zed. "I guess sometimes the best offense is a good defense. And sometimes the best defense isn't very good."

"Whose side are you on?" Fife cried.

"Hers," they all answered in unison.

Fife finally yielded, and only then did Liza show any sign of fatigue. She dropped the shield and rolled her shoulders, smiling at the new arrivals. "Who wants a go?"

"I should warn you," Fife said, wincing as he unwrapped his aching fingers from his shield's handle. "She's got a good arm."

"Not just for a girl?" she teased, apparently alluding to some earlier argument.

"Yeah," Fife said. "A girl minotaur."

"There's no such thing as a girl minotaur," Syd said flatly. He pointed to his helmet. "Horns."

While Fife puzzled that one out, the confusion written plainly across his face, Lotte appeared with a shield nearly identical to the one Liza had been using, but it shone with newness, its edges unmarred and unblemished.

"Try this," she said.

Liza lifted it, and she grinned.

"Better?" Lotte ask.

"It's perfect. The balance is much better."

"We didn't have anything quite in your size," Lotte said. "So I made one."

"You made this?" Liza said, smiling widely now. "For me? Just now?"

Lotte returned the smile. "Well, I had to keep occupied this morning while you all made nice with the king."

"I thought you were the quartermaster," Brock said.

"Quartermaster. Blacksmith. Sometimes I cook." Lotte took Liza's old shield from the ground. "We all have several roles here. We have to, since Frond insists we're to remain self-sufficient." She kicked Fife's forgotten training sword Brock's way. "Now pick up that sword and let me show you what *your* role is as an apprentice. Mostly, it's a lot of crying while I'm thrashing you."

※

Brock didn't cry, but only because he couldn't spare the water. Within minutes of starting to spar, he was covered in sweat. There were training swords of various sizes, and Brock found he had an inclination for the shortest daggerlike variety. It meant he had to be quick on his feet, but his arms gave out too quickly when he wielded anything larger.

They each went three rounds, with Zed making the poorest showing and Brock not terribly better. His muscles burned, and he was exhausted and certain they were nearing the end of the workout when Lotte said, "All right, I've got them warmed up for you."

And Brock turned to see Alabasel Frond entering the yard.

"Liza," Frond began. "You've trained with a shield before?"

"A, uh, a little," Liza answered, suddenly shy beneath Frond's scrutiny. "My elder brother, Fernando, and I are close. He taught me a little bit of everything. But it's been hard to find sparring partners since he moved out, so I've been practicing with blades more than shields."

"Show me," Frond said, and she drew her own impressive blade from the sheath at her back—no training sword, but actual steel. She pointed the curved sword at Liza and went through a series of slashes and jabs, but all at a fraction of normal speed, gauging Liza's blocks, making suggestions where she saw the girl's guard slip.

Zed went through a series of jerky motions beside Brock, like a marionette at the mercy of a hyperactive child.

"What are you doing exactly?" Brock asked.

"Stretching!" said Zed, who was apparently frantic at the prospect of going up against Frond. He pointed his elbows skyward and grimaced. "It's supposed to help."

"So is running away," Brock said.

And then Frond barked Brock's name, summoning him. He went over to her much more slowly than Liza had.

She considered the small training swords in his hands.

"Have you practiced much with daggers?"

Brock scoffed.

Frond waited.

Finally Brock said, "You're serious? Lady, I had a pretty average childhood, I think. Under what circumstances would I practice stabbing things?"

"Then punch me," she dared him, sheathing her sword.

"Excuse me?"

"You had an average childhood," she echoed. "Boys get into scraps, don't they? Show me how you fight."

Brock was at a complete loss. The truth was, now that he'd stabbed a naga, he had more experience stabbing than punching.

"You get one hit," Frond said. "So that I can evaluate your technique. Go on, now. Hit me."

"I . . ." Brock faltered, but he lifted his fists. "I guess my birthday wish came—"

Frond backhanded him across the face so swiftly he never saw it coming. All he knew was that one moment he was looking at her, the next he was on his back, and the moment after that, his cheek stung.

"You use your words as a shield in social situations," Frond told him. "But that shield will not serve you outside the wall."

Brock clambered slowly to his feet and dusted himself off. Frond took his wrists and lifted them, positioning his fists in front of his face. "This is a good defensive position when facing an upright terrestrial opponent."

"I'd hardly call you upri—"

She slammed him to the ground again.

"Dangers will not pause to respect your comic timing!"

Brock grumbled under his breath.

"And as for your *average childhood*," she said venomously, looming above him. "Every day you went not having to stab something was a day someone else took up a knife or a sword or a shield so that you wouldn't have to."

Brock's cheeks burned, and not just from being struck.

"Listen up," she said, turning to include Zed and Liza. "We leave at first light for the shrine, on the king's orders." She held up her hand to forestall any arguments, but Brock's head was spinning too much to produce one. "We'll be gone only a single day, and we will stay to a route I know well, so danger will be at a minimum. But keep your wits about you. And bring weapons." She looked over her shoulder at Brock. "You still get your free hit if you ever catch me with my guard down." Her mouth twisted into a fearsome grin. "But you won't."

She stormed off then, leaving Brock in the dirt and Liza and Zed staring at each other with huge eyes.

"Does this mean I don't have to spar with her?" Zed asked hopefully.

Liza shrugged. "I guess you get to live another day."

"Right," said Brock from the ground. "Because tomorrow, we're all dead meat."

✳

Brock, tired and sore, slept through dinner. He shuffled down from his bare room in time to claim the dregs of a lukewarm stew. Noticing that those adventurers still seated in the main hall were in the midst of a belching contest, he took his bowl of food downstairs.

The trophy wall in the basement made for unsettling company, but at least the room was quiet and didn't reek of burps. Too sore to sit, Brock paced as he ate, considering the gruesome menagerie before him. Someone had actually replaced Ser Feeler, now grass-stained and battered and bearing an unmistakable stab wound. Every one of the trophies represented a different species of creature that the guild had encountered. And Brock, whose education had been above average, couldn't identify more than a handful.

He'd heard of dragons, and basilisks, and a smattering of other monsters. But he didn't know anything much about them. Liza had recognized the kobolds but had clearly been unfamiliar with the naga.

He thought back to Hexam's book, the illustrated manuscript filled with such . . . disquieting detail about the snakelike creature. Did the Adventurers Guild possess the only real knowledge of these Dangers? Was that information somehow of use to Quilby?

Brock still wasn't sure what the merchant lord expected of him, but he resolved to get another look at Hexam's book at his first opportunity.

He heard footsteps on the stairs and turned to see Zed enter the room. Brock smiled, warm and genuine, and then was instantly annoyed when Liza followed on Zed's heels. He worried that it had looked like he was smiling at *her*.

But Liza smiled back, and Brock let it slide.

"Hey, Brock!" Zed said happily. "Liza's going to help me choose a weapon for tomorrow."

"Something easy to use," Liza said.

"And very, very light," Zed added. He rubbed his paltry bicep and winced under his own touch.

Brock remembered watching as his best friend had been

repeatedly trounced by Lotte earlier that day. His own muscles ached from his exertions, and his tailbone was sore. "I don't think we should go," he said.

"I don't think we really have a choice," Liza said, scanning the wall of weapons.

"But what's the point?" Brock complained.

"The focus, remember?" Liza prompted. "The shrine? Please tell me you were paying attention this morning, oh paragon of Freestone."

Brock stuck his tongue out at her back. "I mean why does she want *us* to go? Wouldn't you take anyone *but* the new kids on a mission of vital importance?"

"I'm sure she has her reasons," Liza said. She took a hunting knife from the wall and handed it hilt first to Zed. "Try this."

"Reasons, hmm." Brock counted off on his fingers. "She wants to kill us? Or she . . . Nope, that's all I can come up with."

"She wants to kill *you*, maybe," Liza said under her breath, and she watched as the knife slipped from Zed's hands, almost taking his thumb with it as he fumbled. She sighed. "Something with a sheath, perhaps?"

"I'm serious," Brock continued. "Didn't the king *just tell her* not to put us in harm's way?"

Liza shrugged. She took another knife from the wall, this one enclosed in a leather sleeve. "She said she knew the path. It's probably the best way to train us, so that we won't be in as much danger next time." She handed Zed the knife, then turned to face Brock. "Honestly I'm beginning to think it'll be safer out there with Frond than anywhere else without her. That woman is fierce."

Zed waved the knife around, keeping the sheath securely in place. "I sure wouldn't want to get on her bad side," he said.

"Well, if you see her good side," Brock grumbled, "be sure to point it out to me."

✳

Brock willed himself to remain outwardly calm as they walked the long hallway beneath the guildhall and the metal door at its end came into view. The door that led outside the city. His heart was racing, and his sweaty palms stung within their gloves, and all he could think about was how wrong things had gone the last time he'd stepped through that door.

The key difference, of course, was that Frond was crossing the threshold with them this time. Frond and Hexam, and Syd and Fife, all of whom acted as if they hadn't a care in the world.

"The shrine is a half day's march to the southeast," Frond told them as soon as they'd stepped out into the early-morning air. "We could get there and back before the sun sets . . . if not for the fact that we need time to find Grima's magical jewelry."

Zed gasped a little at Frond's lack of respect.

"Which means every moment we're at the shrine is a moment we'll be walking home in the dark," Hexam clarified.

They walked right into the tree line, Frond at the lead, and

Brock found himself literally dragging his feet, as if his body were preparing to stop and turn around on its own. But then Brock thought of the noise he was making with his long, shuffling footfalls, and he thought of the things that might hear them, and he focused on stepping lightly.

"You're walking funny," Zed whispered to him.

"Really? Maybe I should turn back and get that looked at," he replied.

"Why aren't we riding there?" Liza asked Frond. "We'd save hours."

Frond shook her head. "Horses spook too easily around Dangers."

"How silly of them," Brock mumbled, scanning the trees, flinching at the sound of the wind.

"In the Adventurers Guild we have a saying," Fife said. "Horses is for eating, not riding."

Zed and Liza shared a horrified look.

"We don't have that saying," Syd assured them, his three-horned helmet gleaming in the first rays of dawn. "That is something we neither say nor believe."

"Enough chatter," Frond said from the front of their line. "I want you two flanking them while Hexam brings up the rear."

The young men split apart and repositioned themselves, and Brock had to admit he breathed easier with armed and experienced warriors situated between him and the woods. Even Syd and Fife, who seemed unimpressive on the whole.

Only minutes into the hike, a soft rustling sound came from the undergrowth to one side of the path. Frond walked on as if unconcerned, but the apprentices all came up short.

Brock turned to the archivist at their backs. "Hexam," he hissed. "What was—"

That was when Zed screamed, a high-pitched, piercing shriek of undisguised terror. He leaped backward, crashing into Brock, who landed with a muted thud in a pile of wet and filthy leaves.

"Danger!" Zed cried, and he pointed into the tree line.

Liza raised her shield, and Brock groped about for his daggers while he scanned the area. It took several long moments before his eyes saw movement. There in the undergrowth was a small furry creature with a bushy tail. It was propped up on its hind legs, worrying at an acorn it held clutched in its tiny paws.

Syd and Fife burst into raucous laughter, and even Hexam chuckled. "It's just a squirrel," the archivist said.

Zed cowered theatrically. "Is it safe?" he said.

"Safe as can be," the man answered, clasping Brock's hand to haul him off the ground. "Perfectly natural. Honestly, what do they teach you children?"

The squirrel looked at them with bright eyes, pausing for a moment as if deciding whether to retreat. In the end, it stayed put, and resumed gnawing on its prize happily.

"It's . . . kind of cute," Liza said.

It was then that a throwing star flashed before them, taking the squirrel's head off in the blink of an eye.

Zed screamed again, and this time Brock and Liza joined him. Syd's and Fife's laughter came to an abrupt stop.

"Even natural animals can be corrupted," Frond said gruffly. Brock turned to her, his jaw hanging open, but her eyes were on the archivist. "We don't take any chances out here, Hexam. Not today."

Hexam nodded mutely, all the mirth gone from him. "Of course, Guildmistress," he said.

Zed and Liza frowned at each other while Brock wiped rotting leaves from his sodden breeches. He had a feeling it was going to be a long and distressing day.

They walked for hours without rest, many times the distance any of the apprentices had walked before at a single time. Freestone was a near-perfect circle, and though Brock had always thought of the city as a large place, it could be crossed from one end to the other and back again in a single afternoon.

As the day wore on without further incident, Brock's nervousness fell away. Eventually he found himself scanning the trees not in fear but in wonder. There were so many shades of green, it seemed absurd to call them all by the same name. Syd and Fife picked flowers all along the way, never stepping very far off the path but steadily filling little canvas sacks with blooms of brightest yellow and purple and red. He wondered if they had sweethearts back home, or whether they just used the things to cover up the sour stink of the guildhall.

In all the time they walked, Frond and Hexam never once consulted the map the archmagus had given them.

But Hexam's eyes kept drifting to Zed in a way that made Brock nervous.

And he wondered, not for the first time, why the Adventurers Guild had been so interested in having a sorcerer in their ranks.

✳

The sun was at its zenith when the forest path beneath their feet became hard.

"Stone," Liza said, and Brock saw that she was right. It was all cracked and worn now, mostly reclaimed by grass and broken by brush, but there had been a walkway of stone here once.

"We're here," Frond said.

They came around a bend, and the woods parted into a large natural clearing with a dome of forest canopy above, green light giving the entire space a dreamlike quality. At the center of the clearing, two massive trees stood twined around each other like great wooden braids. Up at the canopy, the branches were so enmeshed as to appear a single tree, but down near the verdant forest floor, the trunks parted enough to form a sort of natural doorway. The space between the trees was dark with shadow, but Brock could see the opening extended down into the earth.

"It's elven," Liza breathed. "The druids were elves."

Brock turned to see Zed thrumming with excitement. He clapped his friend's back. "Well, let's check it out!"

"Not so fast," Frond said. "The shrine is warded."

"But that's great news," Brock said.

"It would be," Frond answered. "If it were warded against Dangers."

"I don't follow."

Hexam stepped between Brock and Zed, placing a hand on each boy's shoulder. "The shrine is warded against *humans*."

Chapter Nine

Zed

"Humans?" Liza asked. "Why would the druids ward against *us*?"

Frond laid a hand on her hip, rattling the stars banded to her side. "Because before the Day of Dangers, *we* were the greatest threat to the druids. Don't let that pretty fable Forta spins for the Guildculling fool you, girl. There were roads before the monsters came, yes, but they weren't always crossed in friendship."

Hexam let his hands fall from Zed's and Brock's shoulders as he stepped forward. "In any case, before Foster's betrayal, the Dangers were still rare and remote. Those that did wander the world were the results of imprudent conjurings, or the occasional thinning of the planar gates as their alignments shifted. Back then, only professional monster hunters tended to cross paths with the benighted creatures."

"I don't understand," Zed said. "The Mages Guild has to maintain our wards. How could these have survived so long?"

Hexam coughed awkwardly. "Well, yes," he mumbled. "You see—"

"We don't know," said Frond.

"The power of the druids was tied to nature," Hexam added hastily. "And its secrets were lost with them."

"All except one," Fife said, his eyes locked nervously on the entrance. "The Red Tithe. Because the spirits of nature required a *sacrifice* for their power, didn't they? Every year, when the blood moon rose high in the sky, the boys and girls of Freestone were kept under heavy watch. Still . . . one child always went missing. It got so bad that mothers would bathe their infants in week-old garbage, just so they were less—"

"The druids didn't sacrifice humans," Syd interrupted.

Zed let out a squeak of relief, while Liza rolled her eyes.

Fife made an irritated noise. "Well they *might* have—for all you know."

"Probably to avenge all those poor horses," said Brock.

Syd glanced toward the scant trail leading back to the city. "Listen," he said, "as much as I'm enjoying the history lesson, the truth is we were lucky not running into any of those *bean-eyed* creatures Hex-man mentioned on the way here. But luck can change quick as an arrow when you're standing with a target on your back."

"How are we supposed to get in, though?" Liza asked. "If humans can't pass through the wards?" She was standing beside Frond and had addressed the question to her.

Zed realized that during the conversation, the girl had struck the same pose as their guildmistress. Her hand rested on her sword hip now, in a studied imitation of casualness.

Frond glanced to Hexam, who nodded silently.

"We don't," Frond said, her fingertips drumming against the points of her stars. "Not the humans among us, anyway."

Then she looked right at Zed.

It was like all the blood in his body rushed straight to his ears. *Frond* needed *him* for a mission? He just stood there, his mind tumbling helplessly between fear and pride.

"No," Brock answered for him. "Absolutely not."

A moment of uncomfortable silence passed among the group.

"Syd. Fife," Hexam said, turning to the journeymen. "Give us some eyes on the trees, will you? If we're going to wear a target, we may as well see the arrows coming."

Fife sighed. "Just when it was getting good. Come on, mate." The two turned and headed away into the woods, Fife galloping ahead while Syd plodded languidly behind him.

"This isn't up for discussion," Frond said, once they'd gone.

"You don't even know if it will work!" Brock answered

heatedly. "The wards may block him, too. Zed's *half human*. Which is more than I can say for you."

"Anyone with elven blood can pass through here," Hexam said. "I read the Silverglows' pages on the shrine. Foster himself visited it many times."

Zed felt the hairs rising along his arms. Foster the Warlock had been here. . . . He glanced toward the opening formed by the twining trees, trying to imagine what might wait within. The passage was shrouded by a layer of darkness as thick as any wall.

Brock shook his head, hands balled into fists at his sides. "The king *ordered* you to do this without hurting any more apprentices," he said. "How is Zed supposed to protect himself if there's a monster inside? He can't even cast any spells yet!"

"He cannot," Hexam agreed. "But *I* can. Zed will not be unprotected. Preservation spells and defensive charms are something of a specialty of mine."

"I'll do it," Zed said. Then his eyes widened in surprise at his own announcement.

"No, Zed, you don't have to," Brock said. "Not because *she* says so. The king—"

"We *need* that focus," Zed cut in. "The whole city needs it. People are counting on us, Brock, just like we counted on the Sea of Stars up until now. Frond . . . Frond is right."

Zed's gaze dropped to the ground. The hurt look on Brock's face at that last bit was more than he could meet eye to eye.

He felt a hand fall onto his shoulder. "It's Zed's choice," Liza said beside him. "And for what it's worth, I think he's being very brave."

"It's *never* been Zed's choice," Brock responded bitterly. "He's never had a chance for a real choice in his entire life. Frond made sure of that, and now she's dragged him here and made doubly sure he *can't* say no."

With that, he turned and stalked away from the group, to join Syd and Fife staring out into the woods.

"He'll cool off," Liza said with a frown.

Frond silently watched Brock as he strode away, her expression unreadable.

"One day he's going to take that shot, Alabasel," Hexam said.

The guildmistress nodded. "He won't be the first. Or the last." She turned her attention back to the group. "Grima told us the focus is a gem of some kind. It should be fairly obvious, but the druids would have kept it deep within the shrine. Once you remove it from its magic . . . focus . . . holder, the wards will dispel. If you run into trouble and can't get out, our only way in is by *you* breaking those wards."

Zed nodded. "What should I do if I see a Danger?"

"Absolutely nothing," said Hexam. The archivist raised his hands and Zed detected the sharp smell of magic almost immediately. His skin began to tingle, then a cool sensation washed over him like brisk rain—except his skin wasn't wet.

A moment later, lights flashed in his field of vision, like the facets of sparkling jewels. Zed blinked and the lights were gone, but the color had drained from the world, leaving everything around him tinged in gray.

"I've provided you with a bevy of magical protections," Hexam finally said, breathing heavily but keeping his arms raised. "A standard Arcane Armor, Rassuma's Congruous Cloak, Shadowsight, a third-level Addling Mirrors . . . No, don't try to talk. You'll find it's impossible, anyway, because of the Muffling Mantle. Now I am going to cast a very *fun* but very *fragile* spell: Invisibility. It's important that you move slowly with this one. Sudden movements—such as running, or attacking, or sneezing especially hard—will shake off the illusion. As long as you keep calm and don't bolt at the first sign of trouble, anything you encounter inside there should be unaware of . . . oh."

Hexam's legs buckled and he tilted dangerously to the side. Frond moved quickly to catch the wizard. After a moment, he found his strength and waved her away.

"Are you all right?" Liza asked.

"I haven't cast so much so quickly in years." The master archivist straightened himself. "Tonight I'll eat more than Syd and Fife combined, I think." He turned back to Zed. "Just be careful. And take your time."

"We'll be waiting for you out here," Frond added.

Zed nodded, hoping the gesture looked braver than he felt. Hexam raised his hands one more time and a layer of—something—seemed to fall over Zed. It was soft and sheer, though Zed could still see the world outside of it, as if through gauze.

Liza gasped. "He's gone," she said with awe.

Zed looked down at his own body. He could see himself beneath the magical layer. Apparently the spell only affected those outside its range.

With the others neither able to see nor hear him, Zed realized good-byes would be impossible. He took a deep, noiseless breath.

Good-bye, Zed, he told himself as he marched toward the shrine. *And good luck.*

✳

Zed had expected the darkness of the shrine to be overwhelming. From the outside it looked nearly solid, like a thick black pudding that would swallow him in one silent gulp.

He couldn't remember the names of any of the spells Hexam had listed except *Invisibility*, but one had clearly been cast to let him see through the shadows. Every stone and gnarled root was rendered in vivid, colorless detail. When the light from the tunnel's entrance cut away, Zed saw the new line of darkness as he did any other feature.

Downy moss clung to the corridor's earthen walls, and plants sprouted from nearly every visible crack. Motes of dust floated in the air, crisp in his charmed sight, but otherwise the tunnel leading in was surprisingly clean. The floor looked almost as if it had been swept, it was so unsullied by dirt or grime.

Zed moved slowly, as instructed. The shrine's tunnel was

totally silent. Even his own breath and footfalls had been magicked away. The absence of his usual noises felt thrilling and strange.

After a few minutes of careful progress, the path began to slope gently downward. Zed would have tried to sense for magic, but the reek of his own protections was overpowering.

Eventually Zed came to a split in the path, which was where he found the bones.

A pile of them as high as his knee lay right where the tunnels diverged. He stumbled to a halt as soon as he caught sight of them. Zed nearly turned and started running back the other way right then, but he remembered Hexam's warning . . . and his promise. Nothing could see him if he just kept calm.

He crept toward the bones.

They had been collected at the end of the path leading to the tunnel's entrance, keeping the passage between the two forks wide and clear. Zed would have to step carefully over the pile to move in either direction.

The bones themselves were spotless and white, as if they'd been picked clean and left bleaching in the sun. Most were from small birds and rodents, and Zed recognized the skulls of many rats among the jumble.

But what had killed them? Something so hungry that it hadn't left a single bit of meat or gristle behind.

Zed searched the branching tunnels for clues. With his

enhanced vision, he could easily see down either path, but both eventually angled away. He took a deep breath, closed his eyes, and listened.

Silence.

Then—a faint sound. The soft brush of movement, muffled and far away. It was coming from the right path.

So something *was* alive in here.

Zed opened his eyes. He stepped carefully over the bones, one leg at a time, then headed slowly down the left path. No need to rush right into danger, invisible or not.

The ground here was even cleaner than at the cave's entrance, polished down to the stone. Whatever creature lived within, it was apparently very tidy. Still, Zed hoped he wouldn't have to meet it.

Deeper the tunnel went, angling right, then left, then right again.

Zed was already feeling claustrophobic when he found the dead end. He tried to groan in frustration, but couldn't produce even a hiss through Hexam's magic.

But as he moved closer to the tunnel's end, the shadows soon resolved themselves into clear figures. People danced into Zed's view. The corridor finished at a great carved mural, rising half as tall again as Zed himself.

The carving had been partially eroded away, as if sanded down. Like the floor, it was scoured clean, but the image was still discernible. A host of thin figures stood around a great tree, whose branches twirled out into impossibly elegant spirals. The figures' hands were all raised joyfully.

And every one of them had long, pointed ears.

Zed ran a hand gently over the carving, his eyes wide. He traced his finger over one of the figure's sharp ears, and his own began to prickle with heat. The mural made him feel charged and fascinated and ... and sad all at once.

Elves had once lived so close to Freestone. Less than a day's journey away. Had any of them thought to make it to the city when the Dangers struck? Perhaps by then it was already too late. Freestone had to shut its doors against the world in order to survive.

Zed suddenly imagined Foster the Traitor once standing in this same spot, staring at this same relief. He drew his hand away from the mural, and held it to his chest.

He turned around and glanced nervously back the way he'd come. The focus wasn't here. He would have to take the right path after all, and face whatever creature was there. Zed took a deep breath. He cast one last longing look at the elven mural, then began retracing his steps.

He'd just rounded the first corner when he heard the noise: a scraping sound, like the one he'd heard at the fork, though now that it was closer, Zed could hear a layer to the noise that he'd missed before. The sound was ... wet. Like a foot dragging through mud.

Zed pressed against the wall. Whatever the noise was, it was coming toward him. He tried to calm himself, but his heart was beating so quickly he worried the pounding could be felt through the stones.

It can't see you. Be calm. Move slowly.

Zed waited for the creature. The squelching noises of its movements were agonizingly slow. He watched the far corner intently, warning himself not to run at the first sight of the beast.

But it wasn't a beast at all. It was something far worse.

A large shape broached the edge, slow as a slug. At first Zed couldn't make sense of what he was seeing. It looked like a second wall had emerged from the corner. Its mass filled the entire space of the corridor—floor to ceiling, wall to wall. But it wasn't made of stone, or earth, or even vegetation. The entire body of the thing was wet and viscous, as if it were a giant glob of mucus.

The mass slurped forward, lazily rounding the corner. And then Zed saw what was inside it.

Bones. Possibly hundreds of them. And not just bones. The carcasses of half a dozen animals were suspended within its body, each in various states of decay. The largest of them was a bear—Zed recognized the creature from an old storybook he'd once used while learning to read. The bear was almost twice as tall as Zed himself, and had likely once been *more* than twice as strong.

Now, what was left of the poor animal's face was twisted into a gruesome expression of pain and terror. Whatever this thing was, it had digested the bear alive.

Zed took a step back. The mass continued to advance unhurriedly. Panic shot through him. He searched for a way through—a way past it—but the gelatinous mound filled every corner of the tunnel, like pudding in a cup.

As it edged closer, Zed was forced to fall back around the corner he'd just come from. He glanced behind him and realized the dead end was only a dozen feet away. Zed's eyes landed on the scoured mural. Suddenly he had an idea what had eroded it.

The shape of the mass appeared around the corner's edge. The huge, lidless eye of the half-digested bear stared right at Zed. He scrambled backward until his shoulder blades made contact with the wasted mural.

Zed tried to scream for help, but the cry produced no sound. The hall was silent except for the sloshing, sucking movements of the approaching horror.

He pressed as far back against the mural as he could.

No, Zed thought. No, this can't be happening.

Abandoning any intention of stealth, he pulled his small knife from its leather sheath and threw it forcefully at the mound. It struck with a sickening squelch. Immediately the side of the creature burst open like a pustule and enveloped the blade. Zed heard the leather grip hiss briefly as it made contact with the mucous wall. Then the knife was completely swallowed, and the hall was quiet again.

The mass slurped forward, ever forward. The knife's leather grip sagged and melted as it began to dissolve inside the creature.

Not like this. Fear clawed at Zed's thoughts. He opened his mouth and cried out for help again and again, all in vain.

Soon the ooze was near enough that he could reach out and touch it. With a slosh, it crept toward him. The bear's terrified gaze followed him the whole way.

The corpses inside *all* watched Zed. Their skeletal faces grinned in anticipation.

Not like this!

His mother's expression at the Guildculling. Her fingers pressed against her mouth. Tears running down her face.

NOT LIKE THIS!

Zed held out his hand. Tears burned hot against his own cheeks, and his vision blurred. Everything around him became cloudy, suffused with a sudden fog. The gelatinous mass lurched forward, inches away. Zed could see the other end of the corridor through its horrible body.

And then, with a pop in his ears and a distant sound like a small explosion, Zed was there.

The tunnel swayed and his head spun. Zed nearly collapsed, but fought to regain his balance. Looking around him, he was shocked to find he had somehow covered the distance of the corridor in a second. The mass was now behind him, pressed flat against the mural wall, right where he'd been standing.

A strange, unearthly mist clung for a moment to Zed's body, then evaporated slowly away.

Hexam. This must have been one of the wizard's protections.

But then why did Zed suddenly feel so tired? Whatever had just happened, it had exhausted him.

He fought through the fatigue. Who knew how long that awful creature would be content to dally at the end of the tunnel?

Putting one foot in front of the other, Zed took a wobbly step forward, and then another, and then before long he was galloping through the corridor, pushing himself off walls for extra support.

Belatedly Zed realized he had lost the invisible shroud. The otherwordly gauze had disappeared. He didn't care. Brock was right—he needed to get out of this place.

Soon he arrived at the crossroads with the pile of bones, and the way out.

Zed paused. He glanced down the other fork, the one he hadn't taken.

The one that must lead to the focus.

He muttered a long string of terrible words, none of them audible, then dashed at full speed down the untraveled corridor.

This tunnel was longer than the other, much longer, with many more twists and corners. Zed's mind was clanging like an alarm bell the whole way as he sprinted through it.

Turn back!

It's coming right now, you fool!

Still he plunged forward.

Finally, the tunnel opened up into a small chamber. At its center was a pool of dark, glistening water.

Perhaps once this had been a placid reflecting pool for the druids, a place of contemplation and serenity. Now it was a mass grave. A mountain of bones rose up from the depths of the water, ten times as high as the one that waited at the shrine's entrance. And these were not just rat skeletons. Zed recognized cracked humanoid skulls sneering at him from the pile. Were these . . . the elves?

His eyes darted around the small chamber, desperate to find the focus. What had Frond said? It was some sort of gem. It should be obvious. It should be—

And then he saw it.

On a raised altar, just behind the pool, a shattered crystal lay in pieces.

No . . . Zed scrambled across the room, around the sluice. On a simple stone plinth, an enormous gem had been smashed into glittering fragments.

Zed picked up the largest of the pieces, biting back a useless sob. The shard was cool and heavy in his hand.

But the wards . . . the wards don't work without a focus. Then how . . . ? Zed thought back to their journey to the shrine, and the conversations outside.

No one had checked to make sure the wards were intact.

He wanted to scream. In fact, that would likely be the first thing he did when his magical protections wore off. But for now he needed to get out of this awful, cramped space.

Zed slipped the chunk of broken crystal into the small

satchel at his waist, then swept the rest of the fragments in as well. He took a step away from the plinth.

"I *see you.*"

A voice echoed in the chamber. Zed jumped and yelped silently. He searched around the shrine, but saw nothing.

"You came for the stone," the voice drawled. "Didn't you?"

Zed couldn't answer even if he'd wanted to. He backed away from the altar, his eyes darting around the room. The space was so small . . . where could the speaker possibly be hiding?

"I came for it, too. I was ordered to take the stone far away. But its magic was already gone—just a few drops left. So I smashed it to be sure. Now . . . *what* was the second order?"

Zed's eyes fell on the glistening surface of the water. Glistening with . . . light. Finally, with growing dread, he thought to look up. And in that moment he realized the chamber wasn't cramped at all.

It was enormous.

Huge tree branches extended upwards for what must have been hundreds of yards, linked by the crumbling remains of bridges and stairs into a spiraling tower. Though now a ruin, Zed could still see the wonder this structure had once been. *This* had been the home of the druids—a whole temple built vertically into the twin trees, twisting endlessly into the sky.

Light poured in from broken arches like reams of cloth, draping over dozens of handsome statues of figures with long, elegantly pointed ears. A city full of elves looked down upon Zed, their stone faces kind and contemplative.

And there, watching him from amid the statuary, was the owner of the voice.

"Ah yes," the figure said with a cheerful chirp. "Now I remember. *Kill anyone* who comes after the focus."

At first, the intruder appeared to be human. He was clothed, albeit in dirty, threadbare rags. Two bulging eyes and a thin-lipped smile watched Zed from a hooded face. He had two arms that were perched forward, supporting his crouched legs, and bare hands and feet that were filthy with grime.

Then the figure's face split open.

It divided from the top of its head to the chin, as if tearing along a vertical seam. Within this grisly cleft were rows and rows of pointed barbs, extending down into a puckered gullet.

Zed discovered he was running only after the fact.

He'd just scrambled past the pool of bones when he heard a crash from behind him as the figure landed within the pile. Femurs and fingers whizzed past Zed, and he had to skip to avoid a waterlogged skull that rolled into his path.

"Run, run, run, little adventurer," the man-shaped monster warbled from behind him. "Creeper is always just behind you!"

Zed did. He ran as he'd never run before. Fear pounded through his head like a drum. He sprinted down the long, narrow tunnel, not daring to look back, scrabbling around every corner. And then, after what felt like an eternity, he saw the fork in the tunnel and the small pile of bones—and on the other side was the gelatinous mass, slowly closing the gap that led out.

"He-he-he-he-he."

The voice sounded so close that Zed imagined he could feel its breath on his neck. He screamed noiselessly, forcing himself to run faster despite his burning legs and flagging energy.

"Can't outcreep *old Creeper*," the monster hissed in Zed's ear.

And Zed realized it was right. The lurching ooze ahead of him was halfway through the fork. He'd never make it. Either he would slam into the jelly and die a slow, agonizing death, or his pursuer would catch him in that gruesome maw.

He tried to think, to form some plan. But he had nothing. No way out. Panic clouded his thoughts like a choking mist, obscuring his vision.

A mist.

Zed remembered the strange magic that had gotten him past the gelatinous mass earlier. He'd thought the spell was Hexam's, but somehow using it had drained Zed himself, like . . . like he had used his *own* mana.

Could he have . . . ?

Zed squinted his eyes and tried to remember what the effect had felt like. Tried to picture the odd swirling mist that had come with it.

And then, unbelievably, the mist was there, clinging to his arms, filling the edges of his vision.

Zed cast his eyes desperately to the exit tunnel, to the pile of bones that marked the path to freedom.

His ears popped. There was a sick careening sensation as his viewpoint exploded with silvery fog, then lurched suddenly forward. He heard a soft plop from behind him, and a high-pitched scream.

Zed crashed forward, falling face-first into the mound of bones. Instantly he twisted around, and was met with a horrifying sight.

The man-shaped creature that had been chasing him was caught by the jelly. He howled as he fought to escape, but whatever substance the ooze was made of, it wasn't letting go.

"It hurts! It *hurts*!" the creature shrieked, writhing his body in an effort to break free. His red, bulging eyes looked ready to pop out from their sockets. "*Mother, help, IT HURTS!*"

Zed heard hissing and sizzling sounds as Creeper was dragged farther and farther inside. After several agonizing moments, his pursuer was entirely subsumed, and the corridor became silent once more.

Zed was grateful when the mass continued slowly away down the tunnel. He didn't want to see any more of what would follow.

Breathing heavily, more dazed and sickened and suddenly *hungrier* than he'd ever been in his life, Zed finally found the strength to stand. Bones clattered away as he righted himself.

His hands were shaking uncontrollably. It took all of his

resolve not to break down and weep right there. Zed squeezed his eyes closed for a moment and fought back against stinging tears.

Finally, summoning what was left of his willpower, he opened his eyes.

He was about to turn and head back up the exit, when something caught his attention. A small pendant lay on the floor of the tunnel, right where the monster had been struggling against the ooze. Zed bent over and picked it up with trembling fingers.

It was a wooden charm, carved into the shape of a grinning mouth full of sharp teeth.

Zed had seen charms like these before, of course. Hundreds of them.

They were carved by Old Makiva.

Chapter Ten

Brock

B rock paced the tree line, unable to remain still, though his eyes did not move once from the pitch-black entrance to the shrine. He wasn't sure he even blinked in all the time Zed was gone.

He could feel the fury like an aching heat behind his eyes. He could taste it at the back of his throat. It made him feel dangerous, like a thousand sharp edges piled together in the shape of a boy. Anyone who got close to him now would be sliced to ribbons.

He wouldn't look at them, but he could feel the others hovering about the clearing, pretending not to worry but steadfastly ignoring one another. His companions were good at looking tough, but for all the confidence they had on display, Brock could see the chinks in their armor, just big enough for a dagger to slip through. A dagger, or a barbed word.

It was something thugs like Alabasel Frond would never understand: Hurting people was easy. Choosing not to— sometimes that took real self-control.

Brock rubbed his cheeks, remembering when she'd struck him. This was why she'd brought the apprentices along, endangering them once again—so that she could use Zed. It was probably why she'd drafted him in the first place. The longer Zed remained out of sight, the more Brock felt his control slipping away.

His friend hadn't even said good-bye.

Despite the fact that Brock cast his glare down the tunnel like a lifeline, it was Frond who saw Zed first. She leaped into action, fast and silent as a snake, darting to the shrine's entrance and beyond, into the dark, where Brock saw Zed teeter and fall into her arms. Brock and Liza both ran to the opening, but Hexam shooed them away so that Frond could pass, carrying Zed in her arms as if he weighed nothing. His arm hung limp.

Liza gripped Brock's shoulder in a way that might have been supportive—or might have been an attempt to hold him back. "What's wrong with him?" she asked.

Frond ignored the question. "Syd, Fife, guard that doorway," she said, wincing as she placed Zed upon the ground with great care. Hexam dropped to his knees beside the boy and put his fingers to Zed's neck. Then, quick as a snare, he pulled away once more, shaking his hand furiously as if stung.

"Fie," he said. Then he chuckled to himself. "Well, whatever he found in there, it didn't set off Gestalt's Lightning Nettle." He made a precise gesture, dispelling whatever protective spell had caused him pain, and Zed stirred.

"I'm all right," he said. "I'm just . . . really tired."

Hexam produced a water skin and held it to Zed's lips. "Drink your fill, son," he said, and Zed gulped eagerly at its contents. The color came back to his cheeks almost instantly.

Brock exhaled deeply. The knot of anger in his chest uncoiled, his sharp edges eroded by the passing storm of anxiety and dread and finally relief.

He realized Liza was still gripping him, leaning her body against his, and he quickly detached himself, rubbing his hand over his hair.

"You're famished," Hexam said, eyeing Zed like a curious hound. "What did you cast?"

Zed wiped his lips with the back of his hand, then licked them, then licked the back of his hand. "Yum. Uh, I don't know. I sort of . . . moved down the corridor just by looking."

"You elf-stepped?" Hexam asked, helping Zed to his feet.

Brock frowned. "Is that a dance? Or a racial slur?"

"It's a spell," Hexam answered. "And not an easy one. Its proper name is *hel'andora moor*, which would translate to something like 'the long stride through mists,' although elven conjugation being the quagmire that it is, you might just as easily say *veil walker* or even, yes, *dancer*, which only goes to show—"

"Zed, you cast a spell? Without a staff or anything?" Brock gripped his friend by the shoulders and shook. "You cast a spell!"

A shy smile spread across Zed's face. "It's no big deal," he said. "Hexam cast, like, twelve spells."

"Hexam's been studying magic for sixty years," Brock countered. "You're a natural!"

Hexam cleared his throat. "I am thirty-nine years old." He turned to Frond. "And yes, you missed my birthday, Alabasel. It was last week."

Frond was unmoved. "Enough," she said, and Brock turned to look at her but didn't stop jostling Zed until Zed ducked out of his grip. "I assume the fact that I was able to enter the shrine means you have the focus."

The smile fell from Zed's face. "Sort of," he said, and he pulled a crystalline shard from the pouch on his belt. "It was in a dozen pieces. I grabbed them all, but—"

"That shouldn't happen." Hexam appeared stricken as all eyes turned toward him. "A focus is all but indestructible when charged. And even if the focus ran out of magic, it wouldn't just—"

"It was sabotage," Zed explained. "I . . . met the thing that did it. It called itself Creeper."

"It spoke?" Frond demanded. "A Danger?"

Fife gulped audibly, and he and Syd both held their blades higher.

"Yes," Zed said. "It looked like a person, but then its head sort of . . . split open. It's dead now," he added darkly, and Brock felt a little chill. "It wasn't acting alone. It said it was following orders."

"Then there's another one lurking about," Hexam said, casting an anxious look into the trees.

"Maybe," said Zed. He opened his hand to reveal a wooden charm in a style Brock instantly recognized. "Or maybe its master is a human. Maybe it's someone we know."

✳

They left for Freestone immediately, moving at a pace Brock suspected they couldn't keep up. Yet as the sun dipped lower and the darkness between the forest's trees grew deeper, the adventurers moved ever more swiftly. Brock felt sweat trickling down his back and a blooming ache in his feet, but he didn't complain. He couldn't spare the breath.

Liza evidently had some breath to spare, though.

"What happens if we're outside the walls after dark?" she asked.

"Maybe nothing," Frond said. "But night is when the worst of the Dangers grow bold."

Zed shuddered, and Brock found himself wondering just

what his friend had experienced within the shrine. He grasped about for that familiar feeling of righteous anger, hoping to dispel the roiling anxiety in his stomach, but all he could manage at the moment was irritation.

"I guess the Dangers are pretty bashful in the daytime, then?" he said.

"It is a little troubling we've seen no sign of anything," Hexam said, even as he kept his eyes on the overgrown trail that had once been a thoroughfare, before being mostly reclaimed by nature. He was leading the party, with Frond bringing up the rear this time. "Not unheard of, but usually the forest is only this quiet when a, well, when an apex predator of some sort has moved into the area. That tends to spook the rivals."

"Dangers get spooked?" Brock asked. "By . . . bigger Dangers?"

"Most are no more than wild animals," Hexam explained. "Dangers follow their instincts, look for food, protect their territory. Most are just intelligent enough to avoid bands of armed humans. They are deadly, certainly, but they aren't *evil*."

Zed shuddered again. "That thing in the shrine . . . it taunted me," he said. "It laughed."

"There are notable exceptions," Hexam added.

Brock, walking alongside Zed, gripped his friend's shoulder. "It can't hurt you now."

"I know it can't," Zed said. He turned his dark brown eyes on Brock. "Because I killed it."

Brock hesitated, then nodded, unsure what to say. Suddenly he remembered how Hexam had recoiled from contact with Zed after he'd emerged from the shrine. The boy's skin had been electrified. But Frond had carried him, hadn't she?

He turned to look at her and saw for the first time the new pink welts running along her bare arms. She hadn't been immune to the spell. She must have been in agony, holding Zed the way she had.

Before Brock could fully process the thought, a howl rose up from deep within the woods.

"What was that?" Syd and Fife asked at the same time, and then Fife quickly added, "Jinx."

"Let's pick up the pace, people," Frond said, and though Brock could have argued that they were already hurrying, he had no trouble moving even faster than before.

✳

The sun's descent seemed to speed up, too, as if it were itself a Danger and intent on keeping pace with them. The trees crowded in and the shadows grew long, grasping at their ankles as they hurried down the uneven path, and when Brock stumbled on a root, he felt a momentary flash of panic that something had gripped him.

Strange sounds rang out with increasing frequency—screams and bursts of a sort of wordless yipping. The noises originated from some ways off in the distance, but no matter how quickly the adventurers moved, they weren't able to leave them behind.

And now the sounds came from both sides of the path.

"Are they following us?" Zed asked, breathless.

"They know we're here, and they're keeping tabs on us," Hexam answered. "But they won't be so bold—"

"Unless they're hungry," said Frond. "Or bored. Or don't especially like the look of us."

"I guess we won't stop for a game of cards, then," Brock said, but it came out as a wheeze. They'd been moving briskly for more than an hour, propelled along by new bursts of adrenaline with each howl.

Brock realized he could no longer see the sun. It had sunk beneath the canopy to their left, and to their right, the sky had deepened to a blue-black bruise.

Another ten minutes passed, and the intermittent howls stopped, replaced by an excited, alien jabbering noise.

"Are they . . . laughing?" Liza asked.

"Don't listen to them, Liza," Brock said. "Your hair looks great."

"Ha-ha," she said flatly.

The jabbering sounded out from one side of the trail, then the other, then back again.

"They're communicating," Hexam said.

"They're coordinating," Frond said. "We have to run." She slapped Fife, who was closest, across the shoulders. "Run! Now! Keep to the path!"

Brock ran, glad he'd chosen light, supple armor. Syd and Fife, who both wore chain mail, were showing the strain of running within moments, and Liza appeared to be struggling with the shield strapped to her back. Brock and Zed caught up to her, and just as Brock wondered whether they should slow for her, she picked up her pace, spurred on by the sight of them.

Brock no longer heard any of the menacing chatter over his own rasping breath, but he didn't for a moment think that meant they were safe.

He let himself hope, however, when they crested a hill, and above the treetops was Freestone's wall rising up in the middle distance, torches lit along its crenulations.

That was when the first of the creatures attacked.

Syd cried out in pain from behind them, and without slowing Brock cast a glance back over his shoulder in time to see a dark figure darting back into the trees. Syd's face was twisted in a grimace, but he didn't slow down, and that was good enough for Brock.

"There!" Frond cried in warning as a second creature dashed from the woods, cutting right through the group and taking a swipe at Hexam. The archivist flung up his arms to repel the clawed attack in a sudden burst of blue light.

The creature was humanoid, but not—like a man who was fraying at the edges, or a moving mound of tattered rags. Whatever it was made of, the Danger had arms, and its digits were sharp enough to produce sparks as it slashed against Hexam's magical shield. It didn't attempt a second attack, just kept moving, sweeping back into the forest in a fluid, unbroken motion. They were using hit-and-run tactics, leaving the safety of the trees just long enough to slash at them.

Eventually they'd strike something vital.

Hexam went on the offensive, blasting a stream of fire into the trees as he ran.

"We can outrun them!" Frond cried from somewhere behind them, and Brock heard the sound of her throwing stars thudding into the trees. "Keep moving!"

Liza had taken the shield from her back and held it between her and Zed; she'd be able to fend off an attack on either of them if she reacted quickly enough. Sticking to Zed's other side, Brock drew his daggers, holding them out so that they might stick anything that got too close, even if he *didn't* react quickly.

Dark figures continued to harass them, leaping out of cover, swiping, and disappearing again before they could be targeted. But the group was wise to the tactic, and the creatures' slashing attacks were kept at bay time and again. And all the while, Freestone's great wall drew closer.

We're going to make it, Brock thought.

And then he saw the figure standing ahead of them in the middle of the path, right where the narrow passage opened onto the treeless plain that circled the city. It was a natural chokepoint, and blocking it was a man. His features were obscured in shadow, but his eyes shone red.

They were the strange compound eyes of an insect.

"Don't stop!" Frond called from behind them. And then she was beside them, overtaking them, running ever faster and making directly for the creature blocking their path.

"Don't stop!" she cried once more, and then she hurled herself at the man-shaped thing, throwing her full weight at it and bringing it down in a brutal tackle. Brock didn't dare look down as he and Zed and Liza ran past, leaving the forest behind at last and breaking out into the open air. The sky above seemed huge, stars appearing by the hundreds as the sunlight was forgotten. A series of mournful howls went up from the trees, but their enemies did not pursue them.

"The gate!" Hexam cried in the direction of town. "Open the gate!" Then, with the wall mere yards away, he stopped running, spun on his heel, and released a series of crackling starbursts from his hands.

Hexam collapsed to the grass, but the magical motes of light found their mark, streaking across the plain to strike the creature still scuffling with Frond. She took the opportunity to run while the thing appeared dazed.

"We have to help Hexam!" Liza cried. She grabbed the unconscious man's wrist and pulled.

"Open the gate!" Fife called up to the Stone Sons atop the wall.

"They're not opening the gate," Zed hissed as he joined Liza, taking Hexam's other hand and dragging him toward the closed portal.

"They won't," Syd said through gritted teeth. "It's illegal to open the gate when a Danger is in view. They won't risk it."

Brock's heart clenched as he saw the creature regain its feet on the far side of the field. It was missing pieces now. An arm had split open, and the long, segmented leg of an insect poked from the torn flesh, a barbed point at its end where a hand should be. Brock was pretty sure it had lost an ear, too, and there was a strange clicking sound coming from deep within its throat, as if something inside were twisting around, forcing its way up.

He couldn't look away. Frond was running full tilt for them, her scarred face a picture of fury and determination. But the beast hurtled toward her, moving far faster than its ruined body should have allowed. It scuttled more than it ran, hunched over, using its strange, barbed limb to propel itself. Liquid frothed from its jagged mouth, too dark to be saliva or even blood. Once in striking distance, it rose to its full height without breaking stride, and it brought its spear-like arm back.

Brock screamed—"*Frond!*"—as the barbed limb shot forward.

There was a sudden flash of light at Frond's back, and she was wreathed in a glowing, crackling spectrum of colors. The creature was hurled backward, and Brock realized what had happened—it had struck the wards full in the face.

Frond realized it, too. She stopped running. She gasped for breath, the fury still etched upon her features. Turning to consider the Danger writhing upon the grass, she grinned an evil grin.

She stepped out from the safety of the wards.

"Wait!" Liza cried, and Syd and Fife stepped forward, but Frond waved them off, back to safety.

She grabbed the creature by the scruff of its neck and hurled it toward Brock and the others. Light flared again, and this time Brock saw it took the shape of small symbols, flickering into view and then gone again, as if this unfamiliar alphabet were the stones and mortar that formed the invisible wall.

If it *had* been built of stone, the creature could not have hit it with greater impact. A crack rang out as its face bounced off the wards, and it crumpled to the ground once more.

"What is it?" Brock asked Hexam.

Hexam shook his head mutely.

Brock turned to Fife. "Have you ever seen one of these?"

"I have never, in all my life," said Fife, "seen a Danger wearing tailored pants."

Brock, to his horror, realized it was true: The Danger wore fitted leather pants, and the tatters around its torso were the remains of a homespun cotton shirt. The clothing was not fine, but it was a far cry from the rough-stitched pelts the kobolds had worn.

This creature did not just look like a man. It was dressed like a citizen of Freestone.

Frond didn't stop to ask questions. She bared her teeth, grabbing the creature again by the back of its head and slamming it once, twice, three times into the wards. Finally she let the creature fall at her feet.

"Wards are working fine tonight," she said as she marched past them, back to the safety of the city, her hands dripping with black ichor.

✳

The Stone Sons charged with guarding the wall had evidently called for reinforcements. By the time the massive gate finally swung open, there were a dozen knights on the other side, weapons at the ready. Each and every one of them took a wary step back as Frond marched over the threshold and into the city.

Brock had always considered the armored Sons as tough as they came, but seeing them shrink away from Frond now, they seemed small and meek. They didn't brandish their weapons so much as they hid behind them.

The Sons were equipped to deal with trouble inside the city, but they had never faced a naga, never fought a kobold.

Or encountered whatever that crumbling nightmare had been.

Frond was bleeding from a dozen shallow cuts, and Syd had a gash across his back, and Hexam, though he'd regained his senses, was weak with exhaustion and barely able to walk in a straight line. For his part Brock was undamaged, but his legs burned and his entire body was slick with sweat.

Only Frond returned the knights' stares directly. "I need you to come with me to the market. To Makiva's tent." She wiped her dripping hands upon her leathers. "I want to talk to the woman, and there might be some trouble."

The knights exchanged a look.

"Well?" she growled. "What in the infernal realm are you waiting for?"

"There's . . . been an incident in the market," one of them said.

"I think you'll want to see it for yourself," said the other.

Brock wanted to weep as Frond took off at a clip, but they all managed to follow, even Hexam. As they neared the market, the crowd grew thick. It was unusual for so many people to be out at this hour, when the market would be closing up for the day.

And then he smelled the smoke.

Once they'd pushed to the front of the crowd, it was only too obvious what had happened. One of the marketplace's most prominent tents was gone. It had been a lush purple tent filled to the rafters with wooden trinkets and charms.

Those same charms must have served as excellent kindling.

All that remained of Makiva's tent was a pile of ash.

✳

After the traumas of the day, Brock thought it would be difficult to sneak out of the guildhall. He imagined Zed would want to talk late into the night, that Liza would insist on speculating what the fortune-teller's ruin might mean.

In the end, though, it couldn't have been easier to slip away. Frond, Hexam, and Lotte had barricaded themselves away to discuss matters in private. Liza, showing no sign of the exhaustion she must have felt, hurled herself at the practice dummies in the yard. Zed, in a failed attempt at furtiveness, pulled an old tome from where he'd hidden it beneath his mattress and snuck away to read it in some dark corner of the hall. The rest of the adventurers found noisier ways to entertain themselves; Brock was almost flattened when the woman he'd previously seen wrecking the chandelier careened around a hallway corner, howling with laughter as she pushed a wheelbarrow loaded with a wooden keg, Hank the physician, and a squealing piglet.

Brock sighed heavily at the sight, but he was glad he didn't have to worry about stealth or excuses. He simply walked out the side door and into the night.

The town was silent, most of its people evidently determined to stay behind closed doors while the Stone Sons investigated what had become of Old Makiva. Brock found the quiet deeply unsettling. He liked energy and noise. He'd spent his entire childhood sneaking out of his parents' quiet, clean, austere home to run wild in the streets at every opportunity. Tonight, though, all of Freestone seemed to be holding its breath. The empty streets felt alien, and the darkness carried a sense of threat.

Or maybe Brock had just seen too much these last few days.

He retraced their steps from the previous day, heading in the direction of the castle. The Adventurers Guild was situated near the gate, along with stables, tanneries, and housing for the poor. The deeper he went into Freestone's interior—the farther he got from the wall and the Dangers it represented—the more affluent the neighborhoods became.

Brock realized for the first time what that meant. If the wall were ever breached—if the wards did in fact fall—the underprivileged of Freestone were a wall of another sort, standing between the monsters and the king.

He passed his own house, closer to Freestone's center than to its perimeter. He spared it only a glimpse and kept walking. Soon he came to the mansion he'd been looking for. He briefly considered going up to the front door and knocking, but he thought better of it. Doing things the proper way meant you could be denied.

He went around to the side of the house and walked right through the servants' entrance. There was an apron hanging on a peg by the door. He put it on and took a deep breath. He wasn't particularly convincing as a member of the staff, but with luck he would be able to make his way to the inner chambers before coming under any scrutiny.

As soon as he stepped out from the small foyer, however, he encountered a young woman. He sized her up quickly. She was only a few years older than him, wearing the same style of apron and holding a sterling silver tray of drinks. She startled for a moment when she realized he was there and opened her mouth to ask a question, but he spoke over her.

"Are those for the master?" he asked sweetly, raising his

eyebrows a bit, hoping the girl saw a young and overeager apprentice before her.

"Uh, yes," she said, momentarily distracted from her skepticism.

"I'm to bring them," Brock said, and he smiled bashfully. "I've never gotten to do it before. I promise I'll do a good job. Is he in the dining room?"

"Uh, the study," she corrected, handing him the tray.

"Oh, right, the study," Brock said. "They said you can take the rest of the night off. I'll see to Master Quilby."

✳

Quilby's mansion was the picture of decadence. The size of the place was itself obscene—in Freestone, there was no greater commodity than space, and Quilby was one of the few who had enough of it to waste. Seeking the study, Brock found a closet the size of Zed's home, a dining room table long enough to seat twenty, and an entire room dedicated to books.

At last he came upon the study, a high-ceilinged, wood-paneled chamber with portraits hanging from its walls and a stone hearth at its center. Quilby sat in a cushioned chair near the fire, beside two men Brock didn't recognize. They were all admiring the shine of Quilby's dress shoes.

None of them acknowledged Brock's entrance. They didn't even look up as he circulated among them, allowing them to grab the glasses from his tray. It wasn't until Brock stood at attention on the far side of the room, pointedly refusing to exit, that Quilby finally seemed to sense that something was out of place and looked up from his shiny new shoes.

His eyes went big when he saw it was Brock.

Brock tapped his own nose theatrically, in an imitation of Quilby's favorite gesture.

Quilby's eyes went even bigger.

"If you'll excuse me, gentlemen," he shrilled. "I've just remembered . . . something requires my attention."

Quilby hurried from the room. He didn't spare Brock another glance, but Brock knew he was to follow. They went a short ways down the hall, ending up in the library.

"Messere Dunderfel," Quilby began, his composure back in place, "while it's always good to see you, I really must insist that I dictate the time and place of our meetings. This level of impropriety is not called for, surely?"

Brock felt it then: the tiny flare of anger at the core of his being, like a smoldering coal fanned once by the bellows.

"I'll tell you what's not called for," he said evenly. "My friends and I almost got eaten by monsters today—again! And this time, it's because your little cabal sent us on a lousy dead-end errand."

Quilby chortled as if Brock's lack of respect amused him. "If you recall, Messere, we sent Frond on that errand—or mission, rather. That she chose to endanger her young charges once more only reaffirms—"

"With respect, Messere," Brock said with a marked lack of respect, "stuff it."

Quilby was less amused by that. "Ex—*excuse* me?" he sputtered.

"I agreed to be your eyes and ears," Brock said. "Don't you want to know what I've seen and heard? I think it might interest you."

Quilby only glowered at him.

"It struck me when I was standing over the ashes of Old Makiva's tent. It got me thinking about the last time I'd been there, and that got me thinking about the perfumer. Remember when we met in his tent?"

"I remember," Quilby said coldly.

"I was really impressed with the perfumer, you know. You think you've seen it all, and then somebody comes along with a whole new use for familiar ingredients. It's good for you, too, right? The Merchants Guild gets a cut of everything he sells."

"Get to the point, please. Time is money, young Dunderfel."

"Everything's money to some people. Which is why I didn't understand why you'd want a man inside the Adventurers Guild. By all accounts, they're broke. No money coming in. No money going out." Brock tapped his nose again. "But that doesn't mean they don't have anything of value. After all, where does a perfumer get his chemicals? Where did Makiva get all that extra wood? I've seen a balm made of Danger gristle that can protect skin from burning. I've seen armed men on a mission of crucial importance stop to pick flowers—flowers that could be used to create the dyes for a lady's scarf." Brock looked down meaningfully. "And your shoes are very shiny, my lord. Just where did the wax come from? The Adventurers Guild supplies it all, don't they?"

Quilby continued to scowl for one beat, two beats. Then his face broke out into a wide smile. "You are a smart one, Brock. My faith in you wasn't misplaced, was it?"

"But you knew all this already," Brock said. "So why do you really want me there?"

"I suppose I've had enough of Frond's nonsense," Quilby answered. "Her people are the only ones allowed outside the walls for any reason. They have access to all the wonderful resources the world has to offer. And Frond refuses to take money for any of it!" He wiped spittle from his chin. "She insists on a barter system. On *fair trade*. It's positively primitive."

"And it makes it impossible for you to take a cut," Brock added.

The man shrugged. "There is that."

"It sounds like you think Frond is the problem. Not the guild."

"Of course. The guild itself provides an invaluable service. And I have reason to believe Frond's replacement would be much more agreeable. Her second-in-command was once a noble, from what I understand. And those of noble backgrounds do tend to speak my language." He made a gesture with his fingers as if jiggling coins.

Brock leveled a serious look at the man. "How far would you go to get rid of her? Would you send her into harm's way?"

Quilby's look of incredulity made his innocence in the matter easier to believe than any words he could say.

"Did you have anything to do with Makiva's tent burning down?"

"Come now. Nothing could be worse for business than that."

"Is Makiva dead?"

"We don't believe so." Quilby shrugged again. "No body was found. Ser Brent's men are looking for her now."

"The woman with you in the perfumer's tent. Who is she?"

"Ah, our dear Lady Gray. Don't mind her—she's a trusted associate. Goes where I can't and watches my back when I need her." He looked over his shoulder absently, licked his lips. "Think of her as my shadow."

Brock stood in silence for a moment, mulling everything over. He knew that Quilby was neither honorable nor trustworthy. But neither did the man seem especially complicated. It was easy to see what motivated him, and thus easy to believe he had nothing to do with magical focuses or failing wards or whatever Makiva might or might not be up to.

"I'd like to revise the terms of our deal," he said.

Quilby laughed once, a short, sharp bark. "You do amuse

me, Messere Dunderfel. I suppose you see the opportunity to make some money here."

"No," Brock answered. "Don't presume we have the same motivations, Lord Quilby, even if we want the same thing."

"Meaning?"

"Meaning I'll help you take down the Basilisk. But then I want a way out. For me and my friend."

"The young sorcerer?"

"His name is Zed," Brock answered. "And he's earned a place in the Mages Guild."

Quilby sighed. "Would that you only asked for riches. What you want is nearly impossible." He licked his lips. "You, of course, have a place here. We laid the groundwork for that before the Guildculling. But your friend . . . The rules of selection are quite inviolate."

"I'll bet the rules about targeting other guild leaders are pretty strict, too," Brock said. He flashed a smile. "Lord Quilby doesn't let *rules* get in the way. Does he?"

It was half praise and half threat. Quilby narrowed his eyes, wondering which half to respond to. In the end, he threw up his arms. "Very well. You and your friend will be reassigned to the guilds of your liking. *After* Frond is taken down." He fixed Brock with a stare. "There will be another council tomorrow. I will need you to speak up against her then. Anything you can say to make her look incompetent or untrustworthy. To convince the king that she is a danger to the people of Freestone."

Brock took a moment to consider it. *Was* she endangering the town? That wasn't really why Quilby was after her, of course. But wasn't it true?

He remembered the welts on her arms when she'd carried Zed from that ruin.

And he remembered she'd sent Zed there in the first place.

In the end, it didn't matter what Brock thought about Frond. The only thing he knew for certain was that if things remained as they were—if he and Zed didn't get out of there any way they could—it was only a matter of time before they found trouble they couldn't walk, run, or elf-step away from.

"You have a deal," Brock said, and he shook Quilby's clammy hand.

Frond had told him to take his best shot, after all.

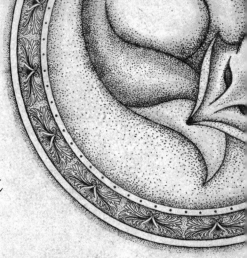

Chapter Eleven

Zed

Zed opened his eyes and stared at the ceiling. It was early—too early, he could tell by the lack of light peeking from under his door—but his churning thoughts wouldn't let him return to sleep.

Every time he closed his eyes he saw . . . terrible things. Ghastly blobs and grinning faces splitting in two. Fanged Dangers striking out at his friends, and the inhuman eyes of the very human-looking monster that Frond had crushed against the wards.

And Old Makiva's tent, still smoldering in the market.

What had happened to the charm seller? Why had the

monster who destroyed the focus been carrying one of her charms? None of it made any sense.

Zed gently pushed himself up into a seated position. Every part of his body ached, a dull but constant grumbling from muscles unused to the strains of these past few days.

He glanced at the book lying closed at his bedside. *Bonds of Blood and Fire* . . . Whatever Hexam had hoped Zed would learn from it, the truth was he could barely understand the rambling text. The rites within didn't make any kind of sense.

Walk a path to its third crossroads, turn left and greet the stranger you meet there.

Watch the first star of evening from a north-facing window until you hear a dog's howl, then open the door.

And so on.

A month ago if Zed had found this book on the street, he'd have tossed it right back. It seemed full of nonsense.

And yet . . .

As he lay alone in his bedroom the previous evening, there had been . . . something. A moment. He was reading an explanation of covens: gatherings where warlocks and witches discussed assorted fiendish topics. The book described a shadowed trail that carved itself slowly through the woods, guiding the witch to her coven like a knife slicing through leather.

Zed hadn't felt himself falling asleep. He hadn't even been particularly tired. But he dreamed that he himself was walking down that trail. He smelled the scent of the trees, and saw winking lights flitting between their trunks. Zed heard the creaks of the branches and the unnerving gekker of what he instinctively understood was a fox in the distance. He watched as the carpet of leaves parted before him, a trail drawing itself with every step he took.

Zed had felt a presence in the dream—like eyes watching him—and he knew that this presence was what waited at the end of the trail. With it came a new smell, spoiling the pristine scent of the woods.

Sulfur.

He woke a moment later, with Hexam's book splayed over his chest, his hand clasped around the elven chain.

The strange dream had unnerved Zed, but somewhere deep down it also excited him. And that unnerved him even more.

Zed now tore his eyes away from the dark leather-bound cover. Enough of dreams. It was time to greet the morning.

He slipped out from his room and found the barracks hallway was still dim with predawn light. There was time, then, before they had to appear before king and council and admit that they had failed. That Zed had failed.

Zed crept to Brock's door and opened it carefully, peering inside. His friend was fast asleep, splayed out on his bed still fully dressed.

Zed wished he could just unload his worries on Brock, like

he had before they'd joined the Sea of Stars. Tell him about the nightmares, and the strange book, and his nagging worry that something was wrong in Freestone. Perhaps *terribly* wrong.

But Zed wasn't the only one suffering. Brock had been through just as much these past few days, including the wrath of Frond herself.

Zed closed the door. He would let Brock sleep a while longer.

He padded silently down the corridor, exiting into the guildhall's common room. He saw a figure standing rigid in the center of the hall, arm raised, and gasped aloud before he realized it was the petrified apprentice.

Zed shook his head and exhaled. The stone boy watched him with a frozen look of horror.

BOOM!

A loud thud sent Zed scrambling backward with a yelp. He scanned the dark room for its source.

After a moment a second *BOOM!* sounded, this time accompanied by a girl's shout. Zed realized it was coming from the training yard.

✹

He found Liza alone, her shield gleaming blue and pink in the early dawn. Her dark hair was matted against her olive skin.

"Do nobles not sleep?" Zed called out with a smile. "Is *that* what makes them so noble?"

Liza glanced at Zed and wiped the sweat from her forehead. "Oh, Micah sleeps plenty."

"What about you?"

Liza shrugged, letting the shield fall to her side. "Mother filled my days with etiquette lessons, but early mornings were always mine. Plus, I like the quiet. Practice dummies don't make wisecracks."

Zed glanced at the beleaguered dummy beside Liza. It was painted with a red target on its chest and a dripping frown on its face. Better him than Brock, Zed thought.

"Am I bothering you?" he asked.

Liza shook her head. She stuck her sword into the ground and rested a hand on her hip, looking for all the world like a younger version of Frond herself—not that Zed could truly imagine such a thing. "What about you?" she asked. "Couldn't sleep?"

"Everything hurts," Zed admitted with a whine.

Liza smirked. "You're out of shape. The ache goes away as you exercise more."

"And what about the nightmares?" Zed had asked the question before he could stop himself. Liza's smirk fell, and his ears began to burn.

"I don't know," Liza said gently. "But I hope so. Was it bad . . . in the shrine?"

"No worse than what came after. Or before." Zed glanced up.

The sun hadn't yet scaled Freestone's walls, but its light leaked over—the trickle before the flood. "If I hadn't cast that spell, I'd be dead."

Liza tilted her head thoughtfully. "Could you do it again, do you think?"

Zed shrugged. "Not sure."

Liza's face split into a grin. "Let's *make* sure." She lifted her shield arm, positioning the already scratched and dented emblem so it pointed right at Zed. "I'll run at you. See if you can . . . what did Hexam call it?"

"Elf-step," Zed said nervously.

"Right. See if you can *elf-step* out of the way."

"Liza, I don't know. What if I can't do it?"

The girl's eyes gleamed with a wild light. "Then you get hit," she said cheerily.

"You and your brother are more alike than I realized," Zed mumbled.

Liza didn't answer. Instead, she dug her foot back, preparing to charge. Zed searched the yard, trying to remember how the magic had felt.

But suddenly Liza's shape filled his line of sight. Shield held high, she rushed at him with a warrior's scream.

Zed screamed, too, but less warlike. He cast his eyes to the practice dummy and wished desperately to be anywhere but in front of the girl barreling in his direction.

A puff, a pop, a twist of air.

Zed landed heavily against the dummy, then spun on one leg and went sprawling to the ground on his rump. The yard swiveled dizzily. All around him, silvery mist was already dissipating like morning fog. Zed looked up to find Liza watching him from a dozen feet away, grinning madly, as a cloud of the same mist evaporated from where he'd been standing a moment before.

"You did it," she said with a laugh. "Zed, you're a mage!"

✴

The two sat together in the yard, enjoying what was left of the morning. After the first bell struck, Zed heard the sounds of people rousing from within the guildhall. His stomach growled. He hoped there would be time for breakfast before they visited the king.

Beside him, Liza was unbuckling the shield from her arm. "Are you angry with Frond?" she asked almost absently. Almost. "For sending you into the shrine? Or for drafting you in the first place?"

Zed thought about it a moment, staring up into the blooming dawn. The sky was the color of the timber lots in spring, when Freestone's tracts of lumber and fruit trees blossomed into soft clouds of pink and white.

Was he mad? He certainly had been when this all started. His eyes left the lightening sky, falling back into the shadowed courtyard. "You know, the funny thing is, I'm not. Even after everything that's happened to us . . . to *Jett.*" He swallowed. "Do you remember when Frond told the king she thought something was going on?"

Liza's face became serious. "You believe her." She spoke softly.

"The things that attacked us looked human. And the one in the shrine had Makiva's charm," Zed said.

"It could have found it somewhere," Liza countered. "No doubt other adventurers have bought charms from Old Makiva. Maybe someone lost it, or died with it outside the wall."

Zed shook his head. "But then her tent mysteriously burns down on the same day? It's too much of a coincidence."

Liza nodded, standing with a grunt. "I agree. I've been thinking about it all morning. You said this . . . Creeper had been sent to sabotage us, right? Why now? The focus has been there for hundreds of years."

Zed remembered the creature's taunting voice as it called down from the ruined temple. It said it had been *ordered* to kill anyone who came for the stone. "It knew we were coming for it," Zed said with a frown. "So whoever commanded it must have known that *our* focus was failing."

"Exactly," Liza said, pacing back and forth. "So unless there's someone living outside the walls—sewing leather pants and sniffing the wards for weaknesses—the saboteur is working from *inside* Freestone." She paused and turned to Zed. "Actually, is that possible?"

He sighed. "I'd be willing to believe anything at this point, unless Fife said it. But it just seems unlikely that someone beyond the city would know exactly where to find the replacement crystal, so they could destroy it right when we needed it." Zed frowned. "Makiva's the most likely suspect. But why would she want the wards to fail?" he asked. "Why would *anyone*? It doesn't make sense."

Liza paused and shook her head. "I don't know," she said, looking down at him. "If the wards fall, then all of Freestone falls. The walls wouldn't protect us forever on their own. Fie, a single dragon could probably take down this whole city. I can't think of why anyone would want that. But there's one thing I do know . . . Frond was right. Something weird is going on."

Zed nodded slowly. "Frond was right," he repeated.

"Tell me I'm still asleep and this is just a nightmare." Brock's voice cut through the yard. Zed turned and saw his friend padding through the open doorway, his short hair a disheveled mess. "Those are not the words I wanted to hear first thing in the morning."

"Is it still morning?" Liza said breezily, tossing her shield to the side.

Brock opened his mouth to respond, but bit it back. He glanced at his feet. "Uh, listen, you guys might want to come inside. Especially you, Liza. Someone's just arrived."

"*Someone?*" Zed asked.

Brock let out a long, slow exhale. "It's probably better that you see for yourselves," he said. "Don't want anyone pummeling the messenger." His eyes flicked up nervously to Liza, then back down to his feet.

"Why do I have a bad feeling about this?" Liza grumbled, striding forward.

✳

The guildhall was still quiet when they entered, but Zed was surprised to find it was actually full of people. Pockets of guild members stood together, gawking at the entrance door and snickering among themselves. Zed couldn't see much over their heads.

They found Jett near the back, carefully laid out on what must have been the guildhall's most undamaged chair. The sight of the dwarf out of bed nearly took the breath from Zed. His bitten leg was carefully wrapped in rolls of linen, and the boy looked thinner than Zed had ever seen him, but he was smiling with the rest of the guild, shaking his head at whatever was going on.

When Jett caught sight of the three, though, his smile dropped fast.

"I can't believe you're up already!" Zed gushed, springing to Jett's side. It was all he could do to restrain himself from grabbing him up out of the chair for a gigantic hug.

"Dwarven constitution," said Jett, puffing his chest a little. "Also, dwarven boredom. Hank set me up here, but don't tell

Frond. I'm not technically supposed to be out of bed until . . . well, not yet."

"What's happening?" Liza whispered, tilting her head toward the front of the room.

"Lotte's talking with a visitor," Jett mumbled, suddenly shy. His face pinkened a shade. "A recruit."

"Who?" asked Liza.

Jett's face reddened even further. Unable or unwilling to answer, he just pointed toward the door with his thumb and looked away.

Liza, Zed, and Brock wormed through the crowd, peering between bodies to get a better look. Zed spotted Jayna standing alone in a far corner, but when he raised his eyebrows questioningly, the girl simply ignored him. Then he heard Lotte's clear voice rise above the whispers.

"And why should *we* take you, then?" the quartermaster asked wryly.

"Because you have to!" demanded a familiar voice. "That's your deal, isn't it?"

"Oh, *Fie*," Liza cursed, just as a clump of journeywomen parted to reveal Micah, formerly of the Guerras, standing in the open doorway. He was carrying nothing and wearing the shabbiest set of Golden Way robes Zed had ever seen. They were faded and threadbare, the once-vibrant sunburst blanched from gold to beige.

The former noble's hair had been shorn since Zed had last seen him, cropped close to the skull. His face was dirty—had he been sleeping outside? Despite it all, though, he was still as handsome and arrogant as ever, and the full force of that aristocratic gaze was now leveled at Lotte.

To the quartermaster's credit, she didn't seem ruffled.

The woman shrugged. "We certainly *can* take anyone. Whether we *have to* is another matter."

Micah's eyes narrowed. "Don't play games with me, you fey-brained dolt. I know the laws of this city."

Lotte just smirked. "'Fey-brained,' is it? Perhaps my mind *has* gone to Fey. Tell me again why the Healers Guild would relinquish such a promising young novice into the streets?"

"That hag Brenner has it out for me!" Micah barked. "I didn't even do anything."

"Ah, perhaps that was the problem, then," Lotte said, clapping her hands. "Most guilds expect you to *do* a thing or two."

Micah's eyes burned. Zed saw desperation creeping in behind the boy's bluster. It was the same look he'd had at the Guildculling, when he'd begged Ser Brent in front of practically the whole city. Zed had never heard of a guildless noble before, but then he'd never heard of *anyone* getting kicked out of the kind and tolerant Healers Guild. There was more to Micah's expulsion than he was saying.

Micah searched the faces of the assembled guild. Zed steeled himself as the boy's gaze passed over him, but it didn't linger long. Micah soon caught sight of his sister, and his face brightened with recognition.

"Liza!" He practically shouted the name. "Tell this idiot the Adventurers Guild has to accept me!"

Every eye in the guildhall turned to Liza. The girl's cheeks flushed and she pinched the bridge of her nose. "Oh, Micah," she sighed. "What have you done now?"

"*Nothing!*" Micah insisted. "I was just walking around after curfew. Two nights ago I ran into Brenner and some guildless guy who came in for healing, and I said he stunk—*which was true.*"

"Ah, then that must be irony I smell wafting up from your robes," Lotte cracked.

A door crashed open above them. Frond stood at the top of a stairway leading up to the guildmistress's private chambers, buckling her glove. She took a long, stony look at the proceedings.

"What's this?" she asked, her eyes landing on Lotte.

The quartermaster's smirk was gone. She nodded toward Micah. "This one's newly guildless, dropped by the Golden Way."

Frond studied the visitor, no doubt also remembering the events of the Guildculling. Micah's face would be a hard one to forget. "Can he heal?" she asked.

Lotte snorted and shook her head. "He's been a novice for less than—"

"I can heal!" Micah spoke over her, staring imploringly up at Frond. "I healed a bird on my second day—Sister Maeve said I was a natural at tapping into my anima."

"And yet here he is, guildless at our doorstep," Lotte marveled. "The most talented young bird healer that the Golden Way has ever seen."

Frond finished buckling her glove and crossed her arms. She glared down at Micah for a moment.

"He's in," she said finally. "Set him to work with Hank, and see that he does whatever healers have to do to get their power. Meditation, starvation, flagellation—I don't care. Within a moon, I want him healing more than pigeons."

Micah let out a celebratory howl that had most of the guild hooting and cackling after him.

"We're out of apprentice quarters," Lotte said officiously, calling over the laughter. She pointedly ignored the smug face Micah was making right beside her. "He'll need to double up until one opens."

Zed was already sinking into the crowd when Frond said, "Give him a cot and put him with Zed."

She began walking briskly down the stairs. "In the meantime, I'll need Hexam, Zed, Liza, Brock, Syd, and Fife. Get dressed fast, people. We're leaving for the castle before second bell."

✷

Zed held the copy of *Bonds of Blood and Fire* to his chest, frowning over his already cramped room.

Where could he possibly hide the book from Micah?

Hexam had said that members of the Adventurers Guild had freedoms that others didn't, but he didn't *exactly* say that witchcraft was permitted. And somehow Zed doubted Micah would be very understanding if he discovered his elf-blooded roommate was squirreling away forbidden tomes.

Zed thought about hiding it under his mattress again, but decided that was too obvious. For all he knew, the first thing Micah would do was snoop around.

Eventually he wrapped the book inside a clean bit of linen, then placed the bundle under his dirty laundry. If there was anywhere Micah was likely to avoid, this would be it.

When Zed was satisfied that the book was as safe as he could make it, he pulled open the drawer to his bedside table, where his small collection of keepsakes blinked up at him: the wooden fox on the silvery chain and his Adventurers Guild token. He scooped up the chain, fastening it around his neck and tucking the charm underneath his shirt—better to keep it on him for now—then glanced down at the remaining token.

Scuffed and dull, the Adventurers Guild coin looked pretty drab. The blue and white paint depicting the Sea of Stars emblem had faded long before Zed ever held the thing. His mind flashed briefly to the pristine token he'd been forced to return to the mages when he was drafted, still literally glowing with promise.

Zed closed the drawer and left the room.

He paused in the hall. A pair of hushed voices crested and fell in quiet conversation. They weren't whispering, exactly, but the low tones indicated a private conversation.

He started down the corridor toward the barracks' exit. The others would be waiting—and besides, his mother had taught him better than to eavesdrop.

"You shouldn't be out there." Frond's voice cut through the hall.

Zed snapped around, an apology already on his lips, when the guildmistress spoke again.

"You aren't well enough, Jett. With what's to come . . . your body needs rest."

Zed realized the voice was coming from Jett's room. Frond's tone held a softness that Zed had never heard the woman produce. She didn't sound angry or scolding. If he didn't know any better, he'd say that she sounded worried.

"It was only the main hall," Jett grumbled. "Hardly a dangerous journey. Yesterday you took the others out past the wards."

A long moment of silence passed between the two.

"Once I return, I'll have Hank look you over," Frond said coolly. "In the meantime, stay in bed. That's an order, Jett."

The door creaked as Frond moved to depart. Zed nearly scrambled away, but Jett's voice brought him up short.

"An order?"

The dwarf's usually sturdy voice cracked with naked despair. In all the time Zed had known Jett, he'd never once heard the boy so much as whimper or whine.

"Why am I even still *here*?" Jett continued. "I'm no use to the guild anymore. I'm *broken*."

The last word echoed through the hall like shattering glass. Zed's shoulders slumped and his arms went limp.

Jett. All that confidence and optimism. All the dwarven bluster. Was this what he'd really been feeling this whole time?

Zed saw Frond's shadow pause at the door. He heard the shift and scuffle of boots as she turned around.

"Jett, I don't ever want to hear you say anything like that again."

The boy's voice broke into a sob. "It's *true*! Just send me to the Golden Way and give my room to Micah. At least then it can go to someone useful—someone who's whole!"

Frond's shadow disappeared from the door. A moment later, Zed heard Jett's bed creak as the guildmistress sat down.

When she spoke, her voice was gentler than Zed had ever imagined it could be.

"I'm going to tell you something, dwarfson," Frond said. "Something my guildmaster told me when *I* was first drafted into this infernal guild. The truth is, not a single member of the Sea of Stars is whole. And I'm not talking about our injuries.

Or our scars. These . . ." Frond paused and let out a husky sigh. "These are *nothing*.

"Every one of us," she continued. "Liza, Brock, Zed, me, and you—we are all just small points of light, burning desperately against the darkness that surrounds this city. Separately, none of us could ever hope to survive that much darkness for long. But together . . . together those points of light can become something more. Something truly whole. A handful of stars working together can make a constellation to guide the lost. A skyful could illuminate the world."

The bed groaned as Frond rose again. "You acted to protect your friend and fellow guild member," she said kindly. "You did it without hesitation, and may very well have saved his life. *Nothing* is broken in you, Jett. You are the *heart* of this guild, and I have never been more proud to call someone my apprentice."

The door creaked open as Frond exited Jett's room. She closed it gently, muffling the sounds of the dwarf's quiet weeping. Frond turned and her eyes found Zed's, which were wet with tears of his own.

She passed by him without a word, but as she did the guildmistress rested a hand on Zed's shoulder and gave it a single squeeze. Then she strode briskly into the main hall.

Chapter Twelve

Brock

"Frond is *wrong*," Brock whispered.

He squinted into a mirror that the guild kept tucked away in a low-ceilinged dressing room under the stairs. It was tarnished and warped, but it gave him a clear enough view of himself. His eyes were bloodshot, and he'd slept in his clothes—briefly, and fitfully. But looking bedraggled would only help with his performance before the king.

He considered the mirror as he ran his hand over his hair, which he kept short. Sheets of reflective glass were not easy to come by, and this was a large one. Where had the guild come across it? The answer was likely gruesome and terrible. Maybe it was plundered from the dungeon hoard of some creature with worms where its eyes should be. Maybe it wasn't glass at all, but the coagulated gore of a hundred silver-blooded goblins. Maybe it was the scale of some tremendous reptilian beast that glowed like a furnace in the sunlight and all but disappeared in the dark.

Brock shuddered. There might or might not be a mirror-scaled monstrosity lurking outside Freestone, but there were certainly plenty of things out there to fear.

When he turned back to the mirror and saw a pair of dark brown eyes glaring out at him, he took a startled step backward—and collided with Liza.

"I wasn't scared!" he yelped.

Liza shoved him aside. "Get off of me! And stop hogging the mirror."

Brock crossed his arms and pointedly avoided looking back at his reflection. "I wasn't hogging anything. I was spending a perfectly acceptable amount of time with it."

"I don't know, Brock," she said, stepping forward to consider her own reflection. "I've seen some scary things the last few days, but your ego might be top of the list."

The dressing room was small, barely large enough for a three-legged table with a bowl of water for washing, and Liza had positioned herself between Brock and the door. She undid her ponytail and her dark hair fell loose to her shoulders. The effect was extraordinary—immediately she looked less like a soldier and more like a noble. He could see the evidence of her former life in a half-dozen features he'd overlooked before. He saw it in the manicured arch of her eyebrows, the whiteness of her teeth, and the little dimples in her earlobes where jewelry would go.

But she didn't have the floral scent of most noble girls. She smelled like oiled leather and whetstone. It was an honest scent. Brock found himself leaning subtly toward her.

Liza clucked her tongue at the mirror as she ran a comb through her hair, forcing it through a tangle. "I should cut this off," she said.

Brock opened his mouth to tell her not to—that she should keep it just as it was.

But then she added, "I see why Frond keeps hers short."

Brock bit back the compliment on his lips and made a rude sound in the back of his throat instead. Their eyes met in the mirror.

"Speaking of Frond," Brock said. "I keep forgetting to mention how she's a delusional, despotic nightmare who's going to get us all killed."

Liza threw her hands up as if surprised. "Is that what you think? Well, thank goodness you said something. You're so civil, I never would have guessed what you were thinking."

They glared at each other a moment more, and then Liza resumed her combing. "Zed disagrees, you know."

Brock pinched the bridge of his nose and sighed. "I wish you'd leave him out of it."

"We're all 'in it,' Brock! Everybody in Freestone is in danger."

"That's funny. I'm pretty sure the rest of Freestone got to stay home while Zed went all alone down into a crumbling death trap. And for what?"

Liza shook her head sadly. "I didn't like it, either. But it was the right call. And you know who else thinks so?"

Brock sullenly refused to answer.

"You and Zed have been friends a long time, haven't you?" she asked.

"Yeah," Brock said. He kicked absently at the baseboard. "His mom used to work on my block. She wasn't very . . . popular, I guess. I heard stuff as a kid. She had a hard time finding work, for a while. I think my mom had something to do with it."

"Your mom?"

Brock shrugged, his eyes on his boots. "My mom had something against her. Against Zed. She'd never even met him, and she had all these opinions. I think I . . . I think maybe I sought him out just to get on her nerves." He bit his lip. "Just at the beginning."

Liza didn't say anything for a moment.

"Zed doesn't really know any of that," he added.

"Well, I think it's sweet," Liza said. "You've been looking out for him for years now. But he's really capable, Brock." She laughed. "He's a mage! And he's measured up to every challenge he's faced since I've met him." Her voice softened a bit. "Take it from someone who knows: There's a very fine line between protective and *over*protective. Even if your heart's in the right place—after a while, it's insulting."

She appeared momentarily lost in thought, then found his eyes in the mirror again as she gathered her hair and pulled it back. "I know you mean well. I know you hate seeing him in danger." She fastened her ponytail in place with a bright red ribbon. "But Frond is looking out for *everybody*. She puts herself between Freestone and a hundred Dangers every single day."

Brock tried to look defiant, but he felt his certainty cracking. "Even if it's all true," he said at last, searching for the right words. "Even if there's some sort of conspiracy afoot and not just bad luck . . . why do we have to be the ones who deal with it?"

Liza shrugged. Her ponytail made her features sharper, but the hardness had gone from her eyes.

"Who else, Brock?"

✳

Zed was waiting for them in the common room, perched upon the edge of a table. He had put on a fresh shirt, but his hair was a disaster, reaching in a dozen directions at once. As Brock watched his friend, trying to imagine him as a font of magical skill, the boy swatted at a fly, lost his balance, and nearly toppled off the table.

Brock sighed.

Frond stormed into the room a moment later, dressed for

war in dark leathers studded with metal. "We're due to see the king," she said. "He's not going to like what we have to tell him." She turned toward the door.

"Good pep talk," Brock grumbled.

Frond threw open the front door—and took a step back in surprise when she saw a steward standing there, poised to knock.

"Ugh," Brock said under his breath, recognizing Peter Magniole from their trip to the palace. "Not that kid."

"What? He seems nice," Zed said.

Brock rolled his eyes. "Don't you start, too." He pointedly avoided looking at Liza, who had probably gone all weak in the knees.

"The king requests an audience," Peter said, his perfect cheekbones infuriating Brock.

"We know that," Frond said. "We're on our way now."

"You misunderstand," the steward said. "The king requests an audience . . . now." He stepped aside, and there in the small courtyard beyond the door stood a full complement of knights, all four High Guild guildmasters, and King Freestone himself.

Even at a distance, his eyes blazed with anger.

It was immediately obvious to all that the guildhall was no place for royalty. A pair of stewards stepped past Frond and began to fuss about the common room, but there was clutter everywhere and precious little space.

Brock quailed at the thought of bringing the leaders of the town down below. The only room large enough to accommodate the full party was lined with gruesome weapons and the severed heads and limbs of a score of monsters.

In the end, they convened in the training yard, with the knights stationing themselves in a broad semicircle. Shoulder to shoulder, they made a wall of flesh and steel that afforded some privacy for those within the yard.

Brock couldn't help but feel trapped.

He had been in awe of the king at the castle, but it had been a natural sort of awe, like when he saw a particularly bright harvest moon glowing orange in the night sky. A rare sight, but not completely unexpected.

Seeing the king here was like finding a bright harvest moon inside an outhouse. Strange and ominous and wrong.

The king looked around the sad little training yard as if contemplating where his throne had gone. Finally he chose to stand at the far end, by the dummies used in archery practice, where he could have a good view of the entire yard. He planted his feet in the dirt, placed his hands on his hips, and radiated his displeasure.

The guildmasters—Ser Brent, Archmagus Grima, Mother Brenner, and Lord Quilby—took up positions on each side of the king, their expressions severe, save for Grima, who looked on placidly.

Frond stepped to the center of the field, Hexam and Lotte right behind her. The quartermaster ushered the apprentices forward, and Zed cast Brock an uncertain look as they and Liza took their places beside the leaders of the guild. The rest of the adventurers filed out from the guildhall in a steady stream, filling the yard. They were uncharacteristically quiet, but Brock could feel them at his back.

"Alabasel Frond," Peter announced formally. "With her young charges, apprentices of—"

"That's fine, Peter," the king said coldly. "We're all acquainted." He turned his gaze back to Frond. "Alabasel. How nice to see you haven't maimed any of your apprentices since last we spoke."

Frond's body went taut, and for a moment Brock wondered if he would even have to say or do anything after all. But she kept her mouth shut.

"I'd like to know why you didn't come directly to the castle on your return last night from a mission of critical importance."

Frond waited a moment to see if he would continue. When he didn't, she answered, "It was very late, Majesty."

The king barked a brief laugh. "So, decorum? That must be a first."

Frond grimaced. "It was also not a successful mission." She gestured for Hexam to step forward. He did, reaching into his satchel to produce the splintered remains of the focus.

The king looked down his nose at the shards and waved Hexam over to Archmagus Grima. The mistress of the Mages Guild reached to take the crystals, oblivious to Hexam's scowl. Brock sensed bad blood there, at least on Hexam's end.

The king spoke. "This is unfortunate, Frond, and it does not bode well."

"We are agreed on that, Majesty."

The king sighed heavily. "I mean it does not bode well for you, Alabasel." He said her name in a tone of mixed reprimand and regret. "There are those who have questioned whether you're fit to lead this guild." Purposely or not, he inclined his head toward Quilby, who squirmed a bit to find himself under Frond's scrutiny.

"There have always been those who questioned," Frond said, eyeing the merchant lord. "And I have ever said to them—come here and do the job yourself."

Brock heard grumbling coming from the adventurers at his back while the king regarded Frond coldly, contemplating whether to take her response as a challenge.

Mother Brenner spoke first. "All respect and deference to Your Majesty," she said, "but is now the time for this? It's surely not in question whether placing another at the head of the guild would have made any difference here." She gestured at the fragment of crystal in Grima's hands. "Frond didn't do this."

"Indeed not," the archmagus said. She turned the crystal to catch the morning light. "No human hand could shatter a focus crystal."

"Oh, for Fie's sake," Brent said. "What about a human hand holding a large hammer? Honestly."

"You misunderstand," she replied. "A focus full of mana

cannot simply be hammered into pieces. It would need to be emptied first."

"It wasn't Frond," Zed said, as forcefully as he'd ever said anything. "It was a Danger. It bragged about it."

"You . . . spoke to a Danger?" the king said.

Zed didn't blush. He held his head high and said, "Yes, Your Majesty. It claimed to know we were coming."

"You specifically?" the king asked.

Zed hesitated.

"Think carefully, son. This is important."

Zed shook his head. "It was expecting someone to come. It didn't say who."

"Your Majesty," Frond said. She paused, tapping at the sharp points of a throwing star on her belt as she considered her words. "How many people knew about the focus in the shrine? Who knew that we sought it?"

Silence was her answer. The guildmasters looked from one to the other. The king remained very still.

"There's still time, Your Majesty. We can fix this. But we must pursue the truth, however uncomfortable—"

"And there it is." The king glowered at her. "You can't have a single conversation without sowing discontent—"

"That's because you don't listen!" Frond shouted, and Brock wasn't the only one who flinched at the sound.

"The enemy is out *there*, Alabasel!" the king shouted back, gesturing at the wall that loomed above them. "Perhaps you've been looking at monsters too long, and now you see them everywhere." He sighed, deep and mournful. "I know well the service you have done, and I honor it. But in times of trouble, nothing is more important than stability and discretion and trust among the leadership.

"The wards are failing. We must find a solution. If that solution is out there somewhere"—he gestured once more at the wall—"then your guild will be notified. Until then . . ."

"Until then *what*?"

The king frowned. "The Adventurers Guild is not to leave the guildhall outside of scheduled patrols." Grousing and grumbling sounded at Brock's back. The king raised his voice. "You're not to speak of anything to do with wards, focuses, or anything else we've discussed here. I will summon you when the current crisis is past, and we will decide then what sort of leadership the Sea of Stars requires."

Brock held his breath. The men and women behind him had gone silent, scarily so, and he could feel Frond's barely contained rage coming off of her like a static charge in the air. The king held her eyes, willing her to stay silent—to accept his judgment. And Quilby . . .

Quilby was looking at Brock expectantly.

Brock had hoped that he might not have to say anything. Frond had built her own pyre, after all. But she had stopped shy of lighting it.

That task, it seemed, would fall to him.

He thought about everything he'd heard here—everything they'd learned in the last few days. And he knew that she might not be right about everything, or even about much . . . but Frond wasn't wrong about this. One broken focus was bad luck, but two . . .

It didn't matter. There was nothing he or Zed could do to fix things. The most they could hope for was to be far from the trouble when it all boiled over.

Quilby was their best chance for that.

"Frond is right," Brock said, breaking the silence. The words felt strange on his tongue, so he said them again, willing himself to believe what he said. "Frond is right. She . . . she puts herself between our town and a hundred Dangers. Every single day."

Out of the corner of his eye, he could see Liza turn to him and smile. He felt his heart ache a little, and kept his eyes on the king.

"Go ahead," he continued. "Tell her to look the other way when the town's in peril. Tell her to ignore her gut when it's telling her something is wrong. Tell her to be *discreet*.

"It won't stop her," Brock said. "She's going to save us all . . . whether you like it or not."

The king cast a dark look at Frond. "I do believe you're right, boy," he said sadly. "Brent. Take her in."

At a sign from Ser Brent, the knights stepped forward.

"No!" Liza shouted, and her voice was echoed in two dozen calls of protest.

Then she drew her sword.

"Liza," Brock warned, holding out a calming hand as the knights closed in. He looked over his shoulder to see the entire guild on the verge of action, and he wondered, if it came down to it, were these people loyal to their king or to Frond?

Armed, dangerous, and potentially treasonous. No wonder Quilby wanted Frond ousted.

"Enough!" Frond said, holding out her hands, turning her back on the king to address her guild. "Everyone stand down immediately."

Liza hesitated. "But—"

"That's an order," she said, addressing Liza directly now.

Liza slowly lowered her sword. She nodded, a dazed look in her eye.

The knights surrounded Frond then, binding her hands and taking care to remove the dozen blades she had affixed to her leathers. It was a long and awkward process, and though the adventurers made no move to interfere, they booed and hissed at the knights, making obscene gestures and talking loudly about their mothers. Brock shifted his weight nervously from foot to foot, his eyes flitting about the training yard.

He saw Quilby trying not to smile; Brenner shaking her head sadly; Grima running a finger over the shard of crystal.

He saw Brent and the king speaking in low voices, their faces grim.

He saw the blade of Liza's sword drooping into the dirt, and

Zed watching the assembled guildmasters with suspicion, his nose crinkled up as if in distaste.

And though he tried to look away, his gaze came inevitably back to Frond. Set within her scarred and stony face, her eyes were hard and hateful. They struck him breathless with their fury.

She knew exactly what he'd done.

Chapter Thirteen

Zed

"They can't do this," Liza said. "How can they do this?"

Zed, Liza, and Brock watched from the second-floor window as a retinue of knights took up posts outside the guildhall.

Apparently word was getting around that Frond had been arrested and the Adventurers Guild imprisoned within their own hall. A crowd had congregated nearby, pointing and whispering. Some had amused expressions, but most looked worried and even a little scandalized.

Whatever they think of us, they know how important we are to the city, Zed thought.

Boards had been nailed across the guildhall's front door, along with a vellum sign bearing the royal seal. Zed had only caught a glimpse of the notice before it was hammered to the door, but the words KEEP AWAY were written large and clear.

Beside him, Brock groaned. "Zed, you may not want to see this . . ." he said.

But it was too late.

Zed spotted his mother as she pushed her way through the crowd, her face frantic. Considering the time of day, she must have run straight from her noble patron's home. She was still wearing her uniform, and her hair—usually twisted into a neat bun during work hours—had slipped out into several ribbonlike strands.

Zed's mother squeezed between two gawkers, then rushed for the guild's doors. A knight immediately stepped into her path, shoving her back roughly with a gauntleted hand.

"Mom . . ." Zed rasped. *"Mom!"* He shouted it this time, pounding his hand against the window.

His mother couldn't hear him, of course. She was arguing with the knight, though Zed couldn't make out any of the exchange. After a few moments of heated dispute, the knight seemed to lose patience; he glowered and placed a hand on the hilt of his sword. The gesture was undeniably a threat.

Zed's mother narrowed her eyes at the man.

"No, no, no," Zed moaned. "I'm all right, Mom. Just back off. . . ."

Another figure emerged from the crowd. A second woman rested a hand protectively on Zed's mother's arm, then stepped between her and the knight.

"No way . . ." Brock breathed.

It was Brock's mother. Zed had only ever spoken to the Mistress Dunderfel a handful of times in the marketplace—and a sharp, prickly handful at that. Brock would never say so, but Zed had long suspected that she didn't approve of him or his family. As usual, the woman was dressed finely—a much more impressive sight than Zed's mother in her gray Servants Guild smock—and she leveled a look of such scorn at the Stone Son that the guard's hand immediately fell away from his sword.

The knight's stern expression melted. His palms rose apologetically into the air as he spoke. But he still blocked their path. In the end, Brock's mother led Zed's back into the crowd, supporting her with an arm around her shoulder.

"Did . . . did Fie just freeze over?" Brock asked. "I can't have just seen what I think I saw."

Zed watched the two go, a tightness slowly unknotting in his chest.

"I wonder if my parents or brother have heard by now . . ." Liza said softly. "Or if they know about Micah."

"Oh, they know." Micah's voice spoke up from behind them, dripping with contempt. "But don't expect *them* to come throwing themselves at the doors anytime soon."

Zed felt a shudder run up his back. He'd nearly forgotten about Micah.

The three turned around to find the boy leaning against the doorway. His face was scrubbed clean, and he'd traded his tattered robes for an unsoiled jerkin and trousers. "The dolt from the door is calling a meeting." Micah scowled. "I guess *she's* in charge now? I have got to be the most unlucky scud in this whole city."

Liza frowned at her brother. "I still can't believe you're here," she said, shaking her head. "How does someone possibly get kicked out of the Golden Way?"

Micah rolled his eyes. "Spare me, Liza. Brenner's a hag. She's had it out for me since my first day."

"I can't imagine why," Liza replied innocently. "Oh, wait. Do you think it could have to do with the time you practically screamed 'Please don't put me in the Healers Guild!' in front of the whole city?"

The boy crossed his arms and shrugged. "I've lost my title and my name, and I've been publicly humiliated more times this week than I can count on one hand, so you should all be very happy." His eyes flicked to Zed. "Except maybe for you, sorcerer. Just so you know, I snore."

"For crying out loud—his name is Zed!" Brock said. "*Sorcerer* is not a name."

Micah shrugged again. "I'm going downstairs. Come if you want. The dolt is already in over her head, so at least there's some entertainment."

Liza sighed, but she followed her brother out. After a moment, Brock trailed after her, leaving Zed hanging behind.

Zed frowned at his feet.

He had a secret.

Well, a few of them.

There was something he needed to tell his friends. He knew he should have said it already—probably should have screamed it out in the training yard—but he just wasn't sure how people would react. Would his friends turn against him? Would the city?

As bad as things were now, Zed had a feeling they were going to get a lot worse.

✳

Lotte *was* in over her head, literally. Guild members crowded around her in the main hall, most towering over the woman. Nearly all were shouting.

As he entered, Zed spotted Jayna standing near the back beside Hexam, nervously biting her lip. Her eyes caught Zed's for a moment, but then she quickly looked away.

"Everybody *CALM DOWN*!" Lotte shouted, finally cutting through the noise.

The guild members quieted, though Zed definitely heard Fife's voice finish ". . . should set carnivorous pixies on 'em!"

Lotte cleared her throat, then stood a little straighter. "For now, no one will be allowed in or out of the guildhall, except as part of our routine patrols outside the wall. I've been told this is a temporary lockdown. Once the king has deemed that the guild is truly penitent, our probation will end."

"Penitent for *what*?" a voice demanded and was joined by others in agreement.

"Frond is charged by the king's council with recklessness and insubordination," Lotte said. "And her actions reflect on all of us. As bad as this sounds, it could have been worse. A sword was drawn this morning in the presence of the king. Under normal circumstances, that would be called treason."

Lotte didn't look at Liza, but Zed felt her stiffen beside him. *Treason?* Liza had just been trying to protect Frond!

"King Freestone is showing us a mercy," Lotte continued, "and to earn back our place in the city, we must show *him* that we are still prepared to protect it. Patrols will resume outside the city as normal, but only through the guild's private wall access door. Our mission is the same as always. Nothing has changed."

Except that Frond is shackled away somewhere, Zed thought bitterly.

"What about the hole in the wards?" a deep voice called out. Every eye in the room turned to Hexam. Zed had never heard the wizard speak up in a full guildhall before, but the rest of the guild members seemed to defer to him. "What about the focus, and the evidence of foul play? The council can't just ignore our warnings."

Murmurs of agreement rose from the other guild members. Everyone had seen the pieces handed to Grima, and heard Frond's accusation. *They* were the only citizens of Freestone who knew that the wards were in danger, and now they'd been separated from the rest of the population.

"They trapped us here to shut us up!"

"The whole city's coming down around us!"

Lotte raised a hand. "*Thank you*, Hexam," she said testily. "The council is looking into this, and a bounty has been put out for Old Makiva's arrest."

"The mystic?" Hexam asked. "On what grounds?"

"On the charge of witchcraft. Several items survived the fire that indicate she was in fact a practicing witch. Apparently she had quite a few focuses of her own, made from carved bones. The bones of what, I don't know, but after seeing the token that you brought back, the council believes she may be connected to—"

"Makiva didn't know where we were heading," Hexam interrupted. "Not even the scribes were told what their map was *for*. Only the council knew. Frond said as much, Lotte." Beside the archivist, Jayna wrung her hands.

Lotte sighed as the guildhall fell into silence, awaiting her response. "We don't know anything for sure," she said. "And there's nothing we can do about this now. The king has heard our side. If we continue to agitate, we could *all* end up like Frond."

Suddenly the guildhall was filled with dozens of shouting voices—some demanding action, some urging prudence. Others simply shouted. Lotte's voice was swallowed up in the chaos.

Zed was dumbfounded. Makiva truly *was* a witch? He brought his fingers nervously to the elven chain tucked under his tunic. For years people had been saying as much about the charm seller, though no one actually believed it. There hadn't been a real witch or warlock in the city for decades.

Except . . .

Except Zed knew something the others didn't. Something he'd been keeping to himself. It was time to come clean.

About everything.

He turned to Brock and Liza, and was surprised to find Micah standing just behind them. Brock was watching Lotte with a strange expression on his face. He looked anxious and fidgety.

"I need to talk to you guys about something," Zed said. "But . . . only you. For now."

Liza looked around the crowded room. "Let's go back to the apprentice quarters," she suggested.

Zed nodded.

"We can meet in Jett's room," he said. "I want him there for this."

Jett looked confused.

"Um?" he said.

"Hey," said Micah, nodding to the dwarf. "How's it going?"

Zed wasn't thrilled that Micah had followed them to Jett's room, but he also didn't have the courage to tell him to leave. Micah would probably discover the truth before long anyway.

Jett frowned at Micah from his bed. Then he glanced toward Zed and the others. "Can someone tell me what's going on?"

"Don't look at me," said Brock. "I stopped paying attention hours ago."

Zed sighed. Once, when he was younger, he'd been stung by a bee while out playing in the streets. His friends had crowded around him that day, watching the welt on his arm swell and redden.

"You've got to scrape it out, or you'll release more venom," one girl had said.

"No!" a boy countered. "You're supposed to squeeze the stinger and pull, or the barb will scratch you."

Zed had sat there, paralyzed with indecision, until his mother finally found him an hour later. With quick efficiency she removed the stinger—Zed didn't even see how—and scolded him for leaving it in so long.

"It doesn't matter how you get it out, Zed," she'd told him, "just that you *do*. The longer the poison's there, the worse it'll be."

Zed's welt had lasted for days.

He glanced over at Jett, who had sacrificed so much for Brock without even a second thought. Why couldn't Zed do the same for the whole city?

"There's a warlock in the council." He blurted it out quickly, before his fear could stop him.

His friends stared at him, stunned.

"That's not possible," Brock said quietly.

Zed shook his head, and his eyes fell to the floor. "I'm sure of it."

"How?" Liza said.

He took a deep breath. "Because I can sense dark magic. It has a . . . a smell. Hexam says it's because I'm a sorcerer. I can notice magic without casting a spell. Wizards' mana comes from Fey—*that's* the minty one—but the mana of a witch or warlock is connected to"—his ears began to burn—"to Fie."

His friends were quiet while this sunk in.

"I know the smell because I've sensed it before," Zed continued. "When we were in the woods on our first day. The magic I cast against the kobolds—the spell inside that staff—it was fiendish magic.

"I didn't know until after," he added weakly.

Zed's hands were slick with sweat. He paused, waiting for someone to say something, but the silence stretched on.

It was Micah who finally broke it. "Really dramatic," he said, rolling his eyes. "Now get on with it."

Zed looked up, shocked. His friends were waiting for him expectantly. He'd anticipated reactions more like Jayna's, but no one seemed especially disturbed by his confession.

"I'm telling you I used dark magic!" Zed said. "On accident, but still..."

Brock shook his head. "I'm more surprised you managed to keep a secret for this long. What's it been, two days? This might be a new record."

"Zed," Jett spoke up from the bed. "You're saying that you sensed dark magic from someone in the council?"

Zed nodded. "It was after Frond was arrested. I couldn't tell who it was coming from, but I *definitely* smelled sulfur. Hexam says that's the scent of Fie."

"But what does this mean?" Liza asked.

Zed shook his head. "I don't know. But if someone in the council really did betray us, then maybe it's related."

"It's even worse than that."

The door to Jett's room creaked open. Zed swung around to find Jayna watching them from outside.

"I'm sorry," she said, tucking nervously into the room and closing the door behind her. "But I saw you all leaving together, and..."

She looked over to Zed, and this time when their eyes met, she didn't look away.

"A witch or warlock would be capable of corrupting the wards," she said. "*If* they had access to the city's focus. Since the energies of Fie and Fey are like oil and water, fiendish magic could be used to crowd out the mana put there by the Mages

Guild. If it were done slowly, the Silverglows wouldn't have any idea it was happening until it was too late. Then, with the two types of mana warring inside, the focus would be weakened enough to destroy completely—like the one you found."

"This is crazy," Brock said, shaking his head. "No one on the council would mess with the wards. Who even *could* do it?"

"Grima has access to the focus chamber," Jayna said. "But so does everyone else on the king's council, in case of emergencies. Apprentice mages meet the whole council down there as part of our yearly inauguration. King Freestone gives a speech."

Brock glanced at Zed. "Well, you missed the focus chamber, but you also got to skip the speech. That's one upside to getting drafted."

"And the truth is that anyone can become a warlock," Jayna added darkly. "Which is exactly why the Mages Guild restricts arcane knowledge from the public. All it takes is a pact with a patron, usually a powerful fiend or another warlock."

Brock's smirk fell, and his eyes found Zed's once more. "*You* haven't accidentally made any pacts . . . right?"

"No!" Zed answered hurriedly.

"A sorcerer's magic is innate," said Jayna. "Which is why Zed could use that wicked staff. He'd need a real patron to cast warlock spells of his own."

"How do you know all this?" Jett asked from the bed.

"These are the *basics* of a mage's education," Jayna said, turning to him. "Or at least they should be. The wards, the focus, the perils of dark magic—every apprentice is taught this much in her first month."

"We have to tell Hexam about this," Liza said. "King Freestone needs to be warned."

Zed frowned. "The king could be the warlock, though," he said. "As crazy as that sounds, he was with the rest of the council. We can't rule him out."

"There is no possible way that the *King of Freestone* is a warlock," Liza said. "It's got to be Grima. She barely seemed to care that the wards were failing."

Jayna bristled. "The archmagus hates dark magic," she said. "The first lecture she gives to new mages is a warning against it."

"All the better to throw suspicion away from her," Liza said.

"It's probably Brenner," Micah piped up, scrunching his nose. "The hag."

"The truth is we don't know who it is," Jett interrupted. "And if we tell Hexam and he goes to the king without proof, he might end up like Frond—or worse, if the witch or warlock decides he's a threat."

Liza sighed and threw up her hands. "So what *do* we do?"

Jayna shuffled from foot to foot. "Well," she said. "That's the thing. I know where the focus is. If we saw who was corrupting the wards, we'd know who to accuse. I can't get us into the chamber without a key, though. The door is locked from the outside."

Liza turned to Zed. "But not from the inside?" she asked.

Zed slowly realized what Liza meant. "If there's a keyhole to see through, I *could* elf-step inside the door, then open it," he said. "We could hide out and see who the traitor is."

"*What?*" Brock yelped. "No. Zed, come on. That's crazy. Even if all of this is true, there could be more to it that we aren't seeing. If we get caught—"

"Then we're just a bunch of dumb kids who snuck out," Liza said. "Better *we* end up in trouble than Hexam, or the whole guild."

Brock's eyes widened. "Not better for *us*!" he said. "These are our lives!" He glanced from Liza to Zed. "Please, Zed. Let's just wait until this lockdown blows over. I'm sure that . . . *someone* will help us once they can actually listen to your story. We just have to be patient."

Zed frowned at his friend. "We may not have time to wait," he said. "What if the wards fail before we're freed? What if nobody listens, or we tell the wrong person? Liza's right. This is the best way."

Brock was silent after that, but it felt as if his eyes were burning a hole into Zed. It seemed like he wanted to say more, but didn't know how.

"You were right in the yard," Liza said gently, placing her hand on Brock's arm. "Frond would stop at nothing to protect this city. How can we do any less?"

Brock coughed out a hard, humorless laugh, then glared

down at his feet. He took a long, deep breath. In and out. When he looked back up, his expression was resolved.

"Fine," he said. "But I'm going, too. No more solo trips into danger."

"Me, too," said Liza. "And we'll need Jayna."

"I'm coming, too," Micah said.

Everyone turned and looked at the boy.

"What?" he challenged.

"Micah," Liza sighed. "The more people there are sneaking around, the better chance we have of getting caught."

"Then leave the merchant kid behind," Micah seethed. "At least *I* can heal."

"We're not going to a pigeon coop, you know," Brock said. "The birds might need you elsewhere."

"I'm telling you, I'm a good healer!"

"Enough," Liza groaned, raising her hand from Brock's arm. "Fine, you can come. Just don't get in the way."

Jett cleared his throat. Zed and the others turned back to him, and it felt like the room deflated a little.

"I know I can't go with you," Jett said with a strained smile. "And that's all right. But if you do run into trouble, then we need to have a plan, yeah?"

"We should leave tonight," Liza said, her tone apologetic. "The Stone Sons only sealed the front and side doors, so we might be able to sneak out from the door to the training yard. If we aren't back by breakfast, Jett, tell Hexam everything. Either we've been arrested, or . . ." She faltered, her eyes flicking to Brock.

"Or the warlock got us," he finished with a shrug. "And murdered us all."

Chapter Fourteen

Brock

"The secret to sneaking out," Brock said firmly, "is to not look like you're sneaking out."

Zed nodded sagely, glanced over his shoulder, and then realized Brock was singling him out. "Me?" he said, pointing to his own chest.

"You," Brock confirmed.

They'd gathered in the small antechamber that led to the guild's outdoor training area. Liza and Micah, Jayna and Zed. And Brock . . . who now found himself sneaking out for the second night in a row. He was counting on a rush of adrenaline to keep him awake, but hoped he wouldn't find that rush on the business end of a Stone Son's sword.

Zed looked down at his clothing. He was dressed entirely in black—black cloak, black canvas trousers, black shoelaces in black boots. "I'm going for 'incognito,'" he explained.

"That's the problem," Brock said. "Look, anybody who sees you will know you're up to something. We should just look casual. Like a bunch of kids out for a walk."

"Leave him be, Brock," Liza said. She was lacing up her own boots. "He's fine. And it's not like we've never snuck out at night before."

"I haven't," Jayna said, raising her hand primly. "My mom always said that any business that can't take place in the light of day is no business worth doing." She quailed a bit as the others turned to look at her. "Uh, not that I'm judging anyone. I'm sure any reason you'd have for sneaking out seemed perfectly legitimate at the time. Like now!" She realized her hand was still raised, and she quickly brought it down again.

"Wait, *you've* snuck out before?" Micah asked, his dull eyes suddenly sharp on his sister. "Like, back home? Why would you sneak out? You were Daddy's princess."

"Exactly," Liza said with a note of finality, though Micah didn't seem satisfied with her response. "A prison with drapes and comfortable chairs is still a prison, Micah."

"Spoken like someone who's never seen the inside of a prison," Brock grumbled.

"Spoken like someone who's about to see the inside of the healers' hall!" she countered.

"Oh, for— Can we get on with this?" Micah said.

"Fine," Brock said, sliding his hostile glare from one sibling to the other. "Just follow my lead, everybody." He turned, opening the door to the training yard.

Standing just on the other side, blocking their way, was a grim-looking knight.

It struck Brock in that moment just how appropriate the term *Stone Son* really was. The man's posture was rigid, the line of his jaw sharp and severe. His arms were crossed, so his rock-hard biceps bulged from beneath his slate-gray tunic. The man looked carved from granite.

His eyes, too, were hard and cold as rock.

"Doors are to remain closed," he said, but made no move to close it himself. He stood there, absolutely still, expecting to be obeyed without debate.

"But we need your help with something, good knight," Brock said, and he opened the door wider. Then he took a small object from his pocket and tossed it to the Stone Son, who had to move then, and fumbled a bit as he caught the item by pressing it to his chest.

The knight held the object up to the light. It was a carved figurine of a badger.

"This is Old Makiva's work," he said darkly.

"That's what I thought!" said Brock. "We just found it in the common room. I think . . . I think she's inside the guildhall. I think she's come for us!"

The knight cursed under his breath, then turned to bark orders to any ally in earshot: "On me! Now!" He drew his sword and took a step forward, over the threshold.

"Uh," said Brock, shuffling out of the way, "the sword's probably not technically . . ."

The knight took off, running past them and out the ante-chamber into the guildhall proper.

". . . necessary," he concluded, and three more Stone Sons ran by.

"Oh, Lotte is not going to like that," Jayna said.

"Lotte can handle it," Liza said. "But if they do a sweep of the place, it won't be long before they realize we're gone." She was the first one out the door. "So let's get gone."

There weren't any more Sons in sight of the training yard, and though Brock braced for it, no call went up as they crossed the yard and stepped through the gate to the dirt road beyond.

"Jayna, lead the way," Liza said. "Let's walk briskly."

"So I'm guessing 'kids on a casual stroll after dark' is out the window," Zed put in as he fell into step behind Jayna.

"Right," Liza said. "But Plan B is fine. Plan B is good."

"Plan B?" Brock said. "Plan B involved pantsing the guard, actually, but he didn't seem the bashful type. Plan C was a bribe. 'Distract everybody with a trinket and then run for it' is a D plan at best."

"And where exactly," grumbled Micah, "did you get that trinket?"

"Oh, Micah," Liza said. "Please don't badger him." She giggled at her own joke, her laughter surprisingly light and carefree, and Brock couldn't bring himself to shush her for the sake of their mission.

✳

Jayna led them through the winding streets. Though she seemed somewhat unfamiliar with the area, it was easy enough for her to find her way. Their destination was Silverglow Tower, which rose above all of Freestone from the very center of town. The precariously stacked multifamily homes along their route occasionally blocked their view of the tower, but it always reappeared around the next bend.

Brock had long felt more at home in outtown than in his own neighborhood. It was rougher here, true, than where he had been raised. But the rowdy laughter coming from the taverns spoke of warmth and joy and liveliness. He could feel a pulse thrumming in the outtown air, like the night was a living thing he could tame, or try to tame. And he wondered, really wondered for the first time, what he'd be doing right now if he were with the Merchants Guild.

Sleeping, probably. Or staring at ledgers wishing he could sleep.

As they traveled inward, the dirt streets became cobblestone and the ramshackle taverns, lively with voices and music, were replaced by darkened market stalls and then shuttered homes.

Rather than bring them directly to the tower, Jayna eventually took a sharp turn down a side alley.

"Aren't we going to the tower?" Zed asked.

"Yes and no," she answered. "The focus is beneath the tower, but it would be too obvious to have access to it there. The entrance is in a shop."

They finally arrived at a small, nondescript building. The sign outside identified it as a chandler's shop.

"Candles? Really?" Liza said.

"It's kind of poetic," Zed said. "Lights in the darkness? Like Freestone itself."

"Archmagus Grima does like her metaphors," Jayna confirmed. "I still think of mana as a clear, cool lake fed by a mountain stream in a verdant valley, untouched by man and Danger alike . . . even if that description made Hexam laugh so hard he wept." She shrugged. "But on the other hand, they do actually sell candles here. They just also happen to have a back room that opens onto a tunnel that leads to the focus."

The door was locked, and Zed made to squint through the keyhole.

"Hold on," Brock said, waving him back. "Save your verdant stream or whatever." He tried a window, and it slid open smoothly. "Someone give me a boost?"

Inside, the structure was just as anyone would expect. Wax candles of varied length and girth adorned every surface.

There were baskets full of them, and hanging from the rafters were dried spices, herbs, and flowers that would be used for the scents. Now that Brock knew what to look for, it was so obvious to him that only a small fraction of the plants here could have come from within Freestone. Even humble candlemakers must have dealings with the adventurers.

He unlocked the door and let the others in. "Look who's not totally useless," he said to Micah, who ignored him.

"It's empty?" Liza asked as she entered. "Totally unguarded?"

"The store is," Jayna said. She led the way into the back room and to a trapdoor in the floor. "But there will be at least one mage on duty below."

"What's our plan for dealing with them?" Brock asked.

Jayna looked mildly horrified. "I'm sure we can reason with them. They're not thugs."

"Of course. You're right," Liza said soothingly, but then behind Jayna's back she touched her sword's pommel and cast a hard look at the others. Brock read her expression easily enough: *Be ready for a fight.*

While Micah tugged on the trapdoor's ring to pull it open, Brock put his hand on Zed's shoulder. "Zed, whatever happens in there," he whispered, "stick close to me, all right?" He frowned a bit. "Except I guess for the part where you blink out of existence and reappear on the other side of a locked door. We might have to split up for that."

Zed smiled, totally unconcerned. It was the smile of a kid who'd always been chosen last for neighborhood games, or left out entirely—and now found himself the star of the team.

"Don't worry, buddy," he said, and wrapped his arm around Brock's shoulder. "I've got your back." Then they turned to see the dark hole beyond the open trapdoor, and Zed said, "I'll go first."

If a hole in the ground of a candle shop's storeroom felt unimpressive to Brock, the tunnel beyond made up for it. The long subterranean corridor was lit by a series of softly glowing orbs, each set high into the wall and pulsing with colored light. Since no two orbs emitted the same color, the effect was eerie, but much easier to see by than torch or candle.

"I haven't seen these for sale in the marketplace," Brock noted.

"The lamps need to be maintained pretty regularly," Jayna explained. "Unless you had a mage coming by to charge them, they wouldn't give off light for more than a day or two."

The tunnel ended in a tight wood-paneled room outfitted with a bookcase and a large wooden desk. The man at the desk stood immediately, although the alarm on his face faded when he realized the group was composed entirely of kids.

"I hope you have a good reason for being down here," he said. Brock thought he felt the temperature in the room rising and saw the man was making a small, repetitive gesture with the fingers of his right hand.

"A very good reason," Jayna said. "I'm with the Sea of Stars now, but I was a Silverglow first, and I'm concerned something may be wrong with the focus."

The man didn't seem convinced. "Sorry, who are you again?" he asked. "I don't think you're allowed down here."

"I'm begging you to be reasonable," Jayna continued. "Your job is to protect the focus, right? What harm could it do to let us check, just to be absolutely certain?"

The mage seemed to think about it. He nodded. "You're right."

Jayna visibly relaxed. "Oh, thank you. You wouldn't believe how difficult—"

"Let's just get the archmagus first," the mage said. "You can explain the whole situation to *her*."

"No, we . . . we don't need to bother the archmagus," Jayna said.

Now the mage was outright suspicious. He narrowed his eyes and looked from one of them to another, his gaze lingering over their weapons.

"Let's just get the archmagus," he said again, continuing the subtle motion of his hand. Brock felt the hair on his arms stand on end. It might have been a trick of the light, but he thought he saw a brief flash of lightning arc between the mage's fingertips.

"Wait!" Zed shouted, and he pulled a glittering chain from

beneath his shirt and held it out to the mage. Dangling from the chain was a small carved figure of a fox.

"What is that?" the man asked. "A dog—?"

"It's a fox," Zed answered, sounding mildly offended. "More important: It's Old Makiva's work! We think she's here!"

The mage gave him a puzzled look. "So?"

Zed blinked, confused. "Oh, you've probably been down here and didn't hear about it. See, there's a bounty because—well, actually, first her tent burned down and—"

Liza slammed the mage across the back of his head with a massive leather-bound book.

Zed yipped and leaped backward as the man crumpled atop his desk.

"Ha! I knew books had to be good for something," Micah said.

"Nice job distracting him, pal," Brock said, patting Zed like a puppy.

Zed chuckled awkwardly. "Distracting him, right!"

"Was that really necessary, Liza?" Jayna asked, hands on her hips.

"We tried it your way and got nowhere," she answered, unconcerned. "My way, he wakes up with a headache and the wards intact. He'll get over it. Micah, what are you doing?"

Micah was running a quill over the open ledger on the man's desk. "Signing the guest book."

"Guest book?" Brock leaned over to see Micah put the

finishing touches on an obscene drawing beneath the list of handwritten names. "Jayna, do you know these names?"

Jayna looked at the open book and blushed furiously, looking quickly away.

"Jayna, this is important," Brock insisted. "I see Grima, Brenner, Brent, the king, and a whole bunch of names I don't know."

"They're mages," Jayna said, taking furtive peeks. "They're the ones charged with maintaining the focus. Nothing suspicious on the surface, but any one of them could be dabbling in something they shouldn't."

The wood-paneled office led to a long, low room of stone. There were no orbs lit here, and the light from the office at their backs cast their shadows along the entire length of the room. At the far end was an imposing steel door.

"This is it," Jayna said. "The focus is on the other side of that door."

"Zed, you're up," said Liza. "Get us in there."

Zed nodded, stepping forward and bending down on his knee before the door. He peered through the keyhole. "I can see it," he said. "All right. Here goes." He took a breath, threw back his shoulders, and disappeared in a faint wisp of silvery mist.

Brock felt completely disoriented seeing it, as if the room were tilting. His mind groped for a logical explanation—Zed had fallen in a hole, Zed had slipped into deep shadow—even though he knew the explanation perfectly well: magic.

But this wasn't the magic of lit globes or invisible walls or even hurtling fireballs. This wasn't just moving energy around—this was something older and weirder and somehow unsettling. He didn't fully trust it.

The sudden rush of doubt and distaste felt like a betrayal of Zed, though, and he quashed it down. But he couldn't deny that he'd felt it.

The hair on the back of his neck rose. He was terribly uneasy waiting for Zed to get that door open, their five long shadows cast upon the wall like specters caught between life and death, unable to act, waiting for judgment. And then Brock thought:

Five shadows . . . ?

He turned, expecting to find that Zed was back or had never actually left at all. Instead he saw Mother Brenner standing in the open doorway.

"Oh, great," Micah said.

Liza elbowed him in the ribs. "Shush!"

"Mother Brenner," Brock began, "we can explain . . ."

"Please do," she said primly. She stepped forward into the room and crossed her arms, but with the light at her back, her features were lost to shadow. "This area is *beyond* off-limits."

"We're here as representatives of the Sea of Stars," Liza said. Her voice was clear and firm. "One of the oldest and most storied guilds of Freestone, and the guild with the most authority concerning matters beyond the wall. Luminous Mother, please listen to us. We have every reason to believe that Frond was right. If you'll listen . . ."

"Frond," Brenner said, and it sounded like a sigh of exhaustion. "Always Frond. But very well, let's talk. Come along, and we can discuss this in my sanctuary."

"Oh, no," Micah said. "No way. Forget it."

"Micah!" Liza warned.

"That's where she takes all the guildless weirdos," he hissed under his breath. "You can smell something foul's in there, even through the door."

"I'm sure the *four* of us can handle a bit of old-lady smell," Brock whispered. "We should go with the Luminous Mother. All four of us."

"Right," Liza said slowly, realization dawning in her eyes. If they left now, Zed at least would be able to carry on with the plan. Even if Brenner proved useless, if she refused to listen, Zed's stakeout could uncover the proof they needed.

Unfortunately, just at that moment, the door behind them opened, filling the room with the otherworldly purple-blue light of the focus.

"Oh, man, it's worse than we thought," Zed said. "There's definitely a warlock—er. Good evening, Mother Brenner."

Mother Brenner didn't return the greeting, and the placid smile was gone from her face. In the shifting purplish light she appeared menacing, the lines of age on her face deepening and twisting into a scowl. Her eyes were flat. Rather than catching the light of the focus, they remained deep pools of shadow.

"I so love children," she said, her tone mournful.

Brock took a step back and pressed his shoulder against Zed. Something wasn't right.

"They wouldn't let me have any of my own, you know. I joined the Golden Way as a little girl. I didn't grasp then what was being asked of me—didn't fully understand my vows. By the time I did, it was too late. . . ."

"We . . . we all must make sacrifices for the good of Freestone," Liza said, reciting a pledge they'd all known since they were old enough to speak. She stood at the front of the group, and though her hand had gone to her sword, she seemed reluctant to draw it.

"Indeed we must," said Brenner. "And we do. But I found a . . . loophole. Or I suppose it found me. Now I have . . . so many children . . ." She took a shuffling step forward and smiled a purple smile. "So many mouths to feed."

"Mother Brenner, please," Liza said. "Let's all go back upstairs. Like you said."

Brenner took another step forward. Liza drew her sword, slowly. "Please."

The others gathered tightly behind Liza.

"I can . . . smell her," Zed whispered hoarsely.

"You," Jayna said. "You're the witch."

"Witch?" Brenner laughed, but it was a hollow sound. "No, no. Witches and warlocks beg and barter for power, child. I've had power thrust upon me." She held her hands out in an exaggerated shrug. "But I like it."

"I'll ask you one more time," Liza said pleadingly. "Mother Brenner, please, remember who you are."

"Who I am?" Brenner continued her shrugging motion. She rolled her shoulders back, and her head tilted to one side, then the other. "You know," she said thoughtfully. "I don't think I *am* Luminous Mother Brenner anymore." Her head tilted to a wholly unnatural angle. "I don't think I have been for some time."

There was a popping sound, and then a wet smacking noise, and Brock felt a wave of horror and revulsion as he realized the woman's head was coming apart from her body. In the seam that appeared across her neck, a small worm appeared, poking tentatively at the air. It was a tentacle, and it was followed by a second, a third, a half dozen tentacles and a series of spindly, bone-like legs, all pressing forth from the woman's neck as the rest of her body went limp and slumped lifelessly to the floor.

They screamed—all five of them—but Liza's scream was fueled not by terror, but by rage. She launched herself forward, arcing her sword through the air. But the creature batted her sword aside with a tentacle, all ropy muscle and slick with mucus.

The sword wasn't just deflected—it was shattered.

Liza fell back, and Brock caught her, taking just a step forward—but now he was standing between the beast and his friends as it reared back with several tentacles, preparing to strike.

One of those tentacles had broken steel. What would several do to flesh and blood?

Zed pulled a knife from Brock's belt.

"Zed," Brock said, not taking his eyes from the creature before them. "Zed, get behind me."

Zed put a reassuring hand on Brock's shoulder. "Not this time," he said, and suddenly the pressure of his hand was gone. Brock saw silver mist at the edge of his vision.

The monster twisted, lashing out with its murderous tentacles.

Brock winced, closing his eyes.

There was a flash of light. A roar of pain.

Brock opened his eyes to see Jayna standing before him, her arms raised and fingers outstretched. "Wizard's Shield!" she beamed. "It worked!"

Jayna had thrown up a large enough barrier to protect herself and everyone behind her, Brock realized.

But then he realized not all of them had been behind her when the beast had whirled and attacked.

Zed must have elf-stepped. He must have decided to get on the other side of it. To strike from behind.

Instead, he'd been struck by the creature and hurled across the room. Brock saw him crumpled in a heap against the far stone wall. He was bleeding, and small, and utterly still.

And the beast that had been Brenner remained standing.

Chapter Fifteen

Zed

Darkness.

That was all Zed saw, as silent and empty as a starless sky. He felt no pain or fear, no worry for his friends or shock at Brenner's horrific transformation. He felt nothing at all—a peaceful nothing that covered him like a blanket in sleep.

So it was with a small twinge of annoyance that he awoke to the sound of birds chirping.

Zed opened his eyes. Dim light fell through a canopy of leaves, draping gently to the ground like glimmering threads. The trill of birdsong surrounded him. He was in a forest, nestled against the trunk of an enormous tree. More trees stretched on for as far as he could see.

I must have fallen asleep, Zed thought groggily. He rubbed his eyes and stretched. Brock will be worried.

Brock.

It came back to him then. The focus chamber, and Brenner, and the thing she had become. Zed scrambled to his feet, searching the landscape around him. This wasn't right. Where was he? Where were *his friends*?

"Hello?" he called out, not even sure whom he was calling *to*. "Is anyone there?"

Only the birds answered him.

Zed took a step forward. Was he outside the wall? How was this possible? Just a minute ago he'd been standing with his friends, and then . . .

And then the creature that had been Brenner struck. Zed remembered the moment of incredible pain when the tentacle hit him—pain so intense that his body seemed to scream with it, drowning out the rest of the world—and then nothing.

I'm dead, he decided numbly. Brenner killed me, and she'll kill my friends next. I failed everyone. I failed the whole city.

But if he had died, then where was *this*?

Glancing around, Zed began to realize the forest was oddly familiar. Had he been here before? These trees didn't look like the ones outside Freestone. They were too large, and their smell was different. Instead, they reminded him of . . . of a dream he'd had once.

He took another careful step forward. The ground was covered in a layer of leaves as thick as a carpet. An eerie mewling cry sounded from far away.

Another step. Strange lights flitted between the trees in the distance, like tongues of green fire.

One more, and the leaves beneath Zed's feet began to part.

It was as if the air itself were cutting a trail along the forest floor, one that snaked forward into the woods. Zed gasped and stopped, but the path continued undeterred, winding into the trees until he could no longer see the end.

He *had* been here before—or at least he'd dreamed he had, while reading the book that Hexam had given him. He remembered the eerie path that unfolded as he walked it, and the sensation of being watched.

So was he dreaming again? There didn't seem to be any other explanation. Zed tried not to imagine himself broken and near death, hallucinating a forest that wasn't there.

He rubbed his eyes, but the trail still stretched before him, untroubled by his doubt. Not knowing what else to do, Zed followed it.

The path continued far into the trees, carving a twisted route. Zed wasn't sure how long he walked it. His thoughts were thick and strange, and the green lights in the distance were distracting.

He didn't notice as the forest became darker, but he could hardly ignore the smell of sulfur that crept from between the trees, growing stronger the farther he walked.

And when Zed finally reached the end of the trail—and discovered what waited there—he found that he wasn't surprised. It felt as if he'd been walking this path since that first day in the market.

Old Makiva greeted him with a smile. "Zed," she said.

"Makiva..." Zed cleared his throat, which was suddenly dry. A long beat of silence passed between them. Makiva looked just the same as he remembered. Kind and pretty, and far too young for her name. "You disappeared," Zed whispered. "They—they said you were a witch."

The charm seller nodded at him. "They've said so for many years," she answered. "Many more than you've been alive."

His gaze wandered around the copse. The flashes of green light were closer here, and more frequent. He looked up and was mildly startled to discover that the branches of these trees were filled with glowing orbs, floating like ghostly lanterns. The green wisps were so thick in places that Zed could hardly make out the leaves among them. Hundreds of the lights dipped lazily from the trees, low enough that he could reach out and grab one if he wished.

"Where did you go?" Zed asked, slowly drawing his attention back down from the lights. "Are we outside the wall?"

"A safe place," Old Makiva said. "Outside many walls." She

tilted her head and frowned. "I sensed what Brenner had become too late, I'm afraid. And *she* sensed *me*. I knew she would come for me, so I left for a time."

Zed was almost too afraid to ask the question. "What *has* she become?"

"A fiend," Makiva said plainly, her eyes flashing. "There are worse things than witches in the world, Zed. There are some monsters that spread like disease, carving out what you are from the inside. Brenner has preyed on the guildless for months, sowing the same corruption that claimed her. Some she consumed and some she infected, sending her new *children* outside the wards before they transformed and were discovered."

The woman sighed sadly. "I'm sorry, Zed. But she *will* destroy the city unless you stop her. She'll devour your friends and destroy the focus. Then she and her brood can feed in earnest. There is nothing left of the Luminous Mother. There's only her hunger now."

Zed felt a sob catch in his throat. "How are we supposed to stop that?" he said. "She's too powerful."

Makiva's eyes glinted. "Then you'll need power, too." The charm seller held her hand out, and a curl of green flame unfolded within her palm, burning with an unnatural light. "I can help you, Zed."

Zed watched the flame dance in her hand. "How?" he asked suspiciously.

"The same way I've helped countless others just like you,"

Makiva answered. "I'm part of a tradition of magic that stretches back long past even Freestone's history. Once my students lived all across Terryn. They shaped *the world* with their spells."

Zed shook his head. "How old *are* you?" he asked.

Makiva smiled mischievously. "You remind me very much of my last student—so kind and bright . . . and lost. He was around your age when we first met. And he wanted to help so badly."

Zed felt a prickling dread crawl up his arms. "Who was he?" he rasped.

Makiva sighed. "I think perhaps that's where things went wrong. The desire to be valuable got all twisted up inside him. It became a craving for power. Poor Foster . . ."

"Foster . . ." The name sent a wave of fear and revulsion coursing through Zed. "You want me to make a pact."

Makiva smiled, her face sharpened by the green glow in her hand. "You could be better than he was, Zed," she said. "You already have a fire in you. I sensed it the morning of the Guildculling. I can help you unlock it."

"And what do you want in return?"

"Nothing," the charm seller murmured. "Nothing for now. Save your friends. Save the city. Once you've made your way, we can speak again."

Zed shook his head. His hands were shaking.

"Make no mistake," Makiva continued. "If you don't act now, then you and your friends will die. Micah, Jayna, Liza, and Brock—Brenner will slaughter them all. And then she and her children will devour the city. One of the last lights in Terryn will be gone forever."

She was right. What choice did Zed have? "Fine," he croaked. "I'll do it."

Makiva smiled at him, and though it was the same coy smile she'd worn when she gave him the elven chain, it looked ghastly behind the green light. "Hold out your hand," she said gently.

Zed did as he was told, slowly raising his palm.

Something small began to burn in Zed's hand. A red ember flared to life in his cupped palm. Zed stared at it with wonder. Was *he* doing this? The flame grew slowly, uncoiling as if waking from a nap.

Makiva moved before Zed had a chance to react. There was only a glint of metal and a sudden sting as she lashed out with a small knife—the same curved dagger she'd used to whittle his charm—slicing a thin line down his thumb. Zed hissed in pain. He tried to pull his hand away, but Makiva caught his wrist with her free hand. She held it in place with alarming strength.

She brought the knife down, its edge streaked with Zed's blood, until the tip of the metal had sunk beneath the curl of flame in his palm. Zed gasped. As it burned through blood and blade, the color of the fire changed, green eating through the red, downward from the point of the dagger.

Soon the flame in his hand was entirely green. Zed no longer felt any heat coming from it.

"Back in my time, they called them will-o'-the-wisps," Makiva said, smiling down at the glow. "Or fox fire. Though I doubt they remember that name nowadays."

As he stared down at the flickering emerald flame, voices began to call out from the woods—voices that Zed recognized.

"Zed! *ZED!* Wake up—*please*!"

"Just hold on, and keep that thing away from me!"

"Oh, no, no, no. It's coming back!"

Zed glanced up, searching the trees for some sign of his friends, but he couldn't see anything beyond the flickering lights—lights the same green as the fire in his hand.

Pain began to bloom in his chest—the same pain he'd felt after Brenner struck him. But even as the pain returned, it was ebbing away, soothed by a new warmth.

"It's time to go, I think," Old Makiva said, though she didn't release his wrist. "Be careful, Zed. Use this gift wisely, and keep your ears held high."

"Wait!" Zed said frantically, turning back to her. "The green fire—how do I use it? What does it do?"

This time when she smiled, the charm seller's eyes flared with the same eerie light as the fire.

"It burns, Zed."

✷

"Please wake up. Please, please, please."

Warm honey-colored light bled through Zed's eyelids. There was a sharp pain in his chest, but it was quickly fading.

Zed took a gasping breath. It felt like the first he'd taken in a while. He swallowed more air, and began coughing violently.

"Take it slow," said a voice from right above him. "You're all right."

Zed opened his eyes.

Micah was kneeling over him, his dark eyes intense with concentration. His hands were pressed against Zed's chest and gold light spilled from his downturned palms, as if he were holding a tiny window that opened out onto a warm spring day.

"He's alive," Micah called, keeping his gaze focused on his work.

"You did it." Brock's voice was astonished. "You *actually* healed him."

Micah rolled his eyes. Zed couldn't breathe well enough to laugh, but he grinned at Micah, and the boy smirked back at him.

"Brock!" Liza's voice shouted. "It's coming back again! We need you!"

Zed took in his surroundings. He and his friends were inside the focus chamber—they must have dragged him in here. It was a large, empty room layered in stone tiles. At the center of the room the focus floated over a raised plinth, glowing with purple-blue light. Zed remembered the eerie mix of mint and sulfur when he'd first found it—two smells that did *not* work well together.

Liza and Jayna were pressed against the door, barricading them inside. Brock leaped up to join them, and just in time.

There was an enormous crash from the other side, and all three were nearly thrown to the floor.

Liza recovered first, her eyes studying the door. "It won't hold," she said finally, suppressing the panic Zed was sure lay just beneath that statement. "Those tentacles can shatter steel. All we can do is be ready." She glanced to her brother. "How is he?"

Micah scowled. "He got hit with a steel-shattering tentacle—how do you think he is?"

"I'm all right, actually," Zed said. The pain was almost entirely gone, and his breathing had returned to normal. Zed tried to sit up, but Micah's hand was firm on his chest.

"Like Fie you are," he said. "I'm not finished showing up your mouthy friend."

"Micah," Liza said. "So help me, if you pass out because you were too stubborn to quit *healing* . . ."

There was a horrible screeching on the other side of the door, then the sound of tearing metal. Jayna screamed and scrambled away from it, ducking behind Liza just as a slick, ropy tentacle ripped through the door as if through parchment.

"Behind me, now!" Liza shouted, motioning with her hand. She raised her shield, as if it would do any better against the creature than a reinforced steel door.

Micah cursed, but he finally took his hand away from Zed's chest. He and Brock helped Zed to his feet, and they all crowded behind Liza's raised shield.

The creature that had been Brenner shredded the metal door apart in moments. Spindly, bone-white legs cracked as the monster ducked its awful head through the opening it had created, tentacles writhing around it like a halo of worms.

Brenner's eyes were wide and wild and hungry as it forced its way inside. Zed no longer saw the Luminous Mother there. Watching the creature pull itself through such a tiny space, he only barely suppressed a wave of nausea.

Liza gestured her friends back as the creature rose to its full height, towering over them like a gigantic harvestman spider. Its bony legs clicked against the stone floor.

"Brenner," she said nervously. "If you're still in there . . . if you can hear me—"

The tentacle struck amazingly fast. It shot forward, but Jayna's hands were already raised, and a glowing semitransparent barrier blossomed just in time to intercept the blow.

"Yeah," Micah said, "I don't think the monstrous severed head is listening."

"I'm almost out of mana," Jayna whispered. When Brenner's grinning face tilted curiously to take in her prey, Zed worried that she *could* still understand them after all.

"Just—just stay close," Brock said, pointing a dagger up at the creature. "Everyone stay together and we'll be all right."

Brock was a good liar, but no one was *that* good. The situation was hopeless, and all of them knew it. Zed saw Liza reach back and grip Brock's hand with her free one.

Zed looked down at his own hands and caught sight of something glinting beneath his shirt. The elven chain twinkled with an eerie green light that seemed almost to be coming from the metal itself.

Then he remembered the dream. And Makiva's burning eyes. And her promise. *It burns, Zed.*

"It *will* be all right," he murmured. "I can protect everyone."

"Zed . . ." Brock said warningly.

Zed knew Brock would argue. Or try to stop him. Brock had been protecting him for as long as he could remember—from bullies, and nobles, and even Dangers. But Brock couldn't protect him from *this*.

So Zed didn't give him the chance to try. He bolted away from the group without another word, his friends gasping and shouting at him as he went.

The monster's wild eyes turned from the others, following him. Brenner's smile opened into a mangled cavern of teeth and she bayed out an inhuman scream. The creature's skeletal legs tore forward, skittering across the stone tiles with disturbing speed.

Zed dashed to the side, his palms raised and pointed right at it. He just needed to put some distance between it and his friends. He just needed—

He tripped.

It seemed to happen in slow motion. His foot caught behind

him—he wasn't even sure on what. Zed tried to right himself, but his balance was already thrown, and his other foot slid out from under him. He pitched forward, his hands braced out, and realized as he fell that he was going to die.

Zed's shoulder hit the floor of the chamber with an audible crack and a shock of pain. Above him, the creature screeched excitedly.

He waited for it to strike, remembering with terror how intense the pain had been.

But the blow never came. Instead, Zed heard Brock shouting, "Hey! *Hey!*"

He glanced up just in time to see his friend standing below Brenner's head, plunging his dagger upward from beneath it.

The creature shrieked as the blade struck. Brenner's distended eyes rolled from Zed to Brock, and her tentacles all moved suddenly as one, stabbing downward together.

Brock released the dagger and covered his head.

Liza dashed forward, her mouth open in a shout.

Zed threw his hands up, and he thought of fire.

And there was fire. It surged from his palms in an enormous green funnel, casting the entire chamber in emerald light. In an instant, the monster was swallowed by the flames, only a dull smudge visible from within the inferno. It screamed, but soon even that was consumed by the blaze.

Liza reached Brock a second later, tackling him away just

as the creature's legs gave out from beneath it. It crashed to the floor in a plume of green flame, right where Brock had been standing.

The blast guttered out quickly from Zed's hands, but the Danger was still covered with green fire. Its legs clattered frantically against the tiles, and its tentacles lashed out in every direction. It managed to lift off the ground, hurtling across the length of the chamber and nearly smashing right into the focus.

Then, with a sickening snap, one of its legs split in half, and it toppled again to the floor.

The creature's tentacles thrashed from beneath it, as if trying to escape the fate of the rest of its body. But the flames that consumed it didn't behave like normal fire. They spread hungrily along the entire length of the beast's form, burning with unnatural speed.

In a matter of moments, there was nothing left of the creature but a charred and smoking frame.

Zed watched it all numbly, as exhaustion took hold. The spell had eaten every bit of his mana. Darkness pressed against the edges of his vision.

That was when the adults showed up.

There was a clamor of shouting and thudding feet from outside. The shredded steel door burst open with a metallic shriek, and Zed saw Lotte's blond curls and stunned face emerge into the chamber. She was followed by Hexam and several Stone Sons, their weapons drawn.

All of them took in the scene, gaping at the charred pile still smoldering with green embers.

The knights pulled away and circled the Danger, cautiously pointing their swords at it.

Liza and Brock had crashed into a groaning pile several feet away. Jayna was pressed against the far wall, sobbing into her hands. Micah just stared blankly at the smoking lump of what had once been his guildmistress.

"What—what *is* this?" Lotte rasped. Her eyes found Zed, still laid out where he'd tripped.

We just saved the city, Zed realized.

He opened his mouth to say so, but the world faded to blackness as he fainted instead.

Chapter Sixteen
Brock

I t was a beautiful late-summer day in Freestone. A cooling breeze blew in from outside the walls, bringing with it the music of birdsong and the scents of flowering plants from somewhere deep within the unseen forest beyond the wards.

Sounds and smells, light and wind. These things and nothing more were able to pass through the rejuvenated wards. Another day of peace had dawned in Freestone, and it was all thanks to the Adventurers Guild.

And so the guild was throwing itself a party.

Brock stepped outside to find the training yard transformed. Swaths of colorful fabric had been draped over the fence and hung from the adjacent rooftop, but messily, as if a basket matched linens had blown away and landed there. The armor table had been swept clear of tools and now was laden with small cakes and a bowl of punch. Festive hats had been placed upon the yard's many training dummies.

But it was the dwarf standing in the yard who brought an immediate smile to Brock's face.

"Jett!" he cried, and he nearly tackled him in a hug.

"Easy," Jett said, laughing. "I've not quite got the hang of balancing yet."

Brock pulled back to get a good look at his friend. He'd propped himself up on an ornate wooden crutch, and though he'd grown somewhat pale, he was out of bed at last and he looked healthy and strong.

"Something's different about you," Brock said, narrowing his eyes.

Jett gave him a condescending look, then lifted his left leg, which ended just below the knee. His trousers had been pinned carefully closed. "Aye, something's different," he said, his tone playful. "I can't quite put my foot on what."

Brock frowned, unsure how to respond, and Jett laughed at his discomfort. "It's all right, Brock. I lost a leg, and I wish I hadn't." He gripped Brock's shoulder. "But that's all I lost, and in the end, it's not all that much. Do you get my meaning?"

"I think so, yeah," he said, and the knot in his stomach came loose at the sight of the good humor in Jett's eyes.

"Good." Jett nodded. "Because it only takes one foot to kick butt, and I aim to prove it."

The yard was slowly filling with their guildmates, some of whom helped themselves to the refreshments, all of whom gave Brock and Jett knowing smiles or slaps on the back. The party was meant to celebrate the fact that King Freestone had promised to issue a public statement about the recent threat to the wards and the young apprentices who had put a stop to that threat. Some weeks had passed, and their scrapes and bruises had healed, and now, today, their heroism would finally be acknowledged.

Brock couldn't help but feel some thrill in knowing his actions had kept Freestone safe—and if the thrill doubled at the thought of getting credit for those actions, well, he didn't feel the need to apologize for it.

Zed certainly deserved some recognition. He emerged from the guildhall wearing his finest tunic—it was the very one he'd worn during the Guildculling, and Brock marveled at how little had outwardly changed about his friend since that time. Who would ever have guessed that the short, slight elf-blooded boy with the goofy smile would prove so capable in the face of Dangers?

Zed stumbled momentarily in his eagerness to approach them, almost tripping, but quickly righted himself. "Jett!" he said. "You shaved your beard!"

Brock laughed, realizing that was what had struck him as different. The few straggly strands of peach fuzz that had recently adorned Jett's chin were gone.

Jett shrugged lazily. "Hank promised that shorn hair comes back twice as strong."

Zed looped his arm around Jett's shoulders and pulled him close. "You could say the same thing about dwarves. It's good to see you up. Liza's crutch really suits you."

"Liza made that?" Brock asked, failing to mask the astonishment in his voice. The crutch was masterfully carved in the design of a dragon, the mythical source of the dwarves' great forge fires.

"I know!" Zed said. "Is there anything she can't do?"

But it wasn't Liza's talent for woodworking that made Brock feel a sudden pang of jealousy.

The yard was getting full, and Brock spotted her across the way, Micah fussing over a minor bruise she had picked up while training. It was a familiar argument by now: Micah had turned out to be quite protective of his sister—and perhaps overeager to put his healing talents on display. Liza, for her part, didn't care to be fussed over.

She spotted Brock watching and raised her hand in greeting, but just then Frond strode into the yard and Brock went still. As she crossed to a lopsided plywood platform that somewhat resembled a stage, the guildmistress's eyes trailed coldly across the crowd, lingering ever so slightly on Brock.

In the weeks since she'd returned from her night in the king's dungeon, she hadn't said a word about Brock's role in sending her there. But she kept looking at him as if she might. Brock felt there was an ax hovering above his head at all times, one that would inevitably fall when he least expected it. He hadn't slept peacefully in weeks.

Then again, few of them had. The horror that had befallen Mother Brenner would stay with them a long time. As Hexam had explained it, she had been the victim of a penanggalan— a sort of fiendish parasite that had hollowed out her body and warped her mind. There was no way of knowing how much of the true Brenner had remained in the end, but in the dark of night Brock imagined the kindly woman looking out from alien eyes, screaming in silent despair as she watched herself—her body—performing acts of horror against her will.

In a rare display of collaboration, the Stone Sons, Silverglows, and Adventurers Guild had worked together in the days following Brenner's death. While the mages put each member of the Golden Way through a rigorous screening process devised by Hexam, knights scoured the streets to take a census of the guildless, aided by those adventurers who had once been among them. While the healers were untainted, it became clear that some untold dozens of guildless men and women had disappeared over the course of a year. Brock supposed they'd never know precisely how many of Freestone's poor had been preyed upon, infected, and cast out to live among the Dangers, waiting for the day the wards came down.

A day, thanks to the Sea of Stars, that should never come.

Frond took to the rickety stage, scowling down upon it as if daring it to crumble beneath her weight. Once she had her balance, she looked around the yard, from the gaudy fabrics to the party hats. "Who's responsible for this?" she said gruffly.

"Ah, yes," Lotte said, walking toward the stage but thinking twice before actually stepping upon it. "Let's have a round of applause for our party planners, Syd and Fife." She gave Frond a meaningful look over the halfhearted applause that followed. "They were the only ones who volunteered and did a fine job with limited resources."

Frond glared at Syd and Fife, who were giving small curtsies from the edge of the crowd. "Well done," she said stiffly. "I am impressed and grateful for your work." She bared her teeth in a forced smile, and the effect was terrifying.

"She looks like she wants to eat them," Jett whispered.

"I think she's trying to be nicer," Zed whispered back. "I heard Lotte lecturing her on the importance of keeping morale up."

"It's working," Brock put in. "If she smiles at me like that, I'll be the first one to volunteer for patrol outside the wall. Anything to get away from her."

"We have much to celebrate," Frond said, addressing the crowd. "The king has just released a decree acknowledging our role in averting the recent crisis. It is to be posted all over the city later today." She unrolled a small parchment scroll emblazoned with the king's own seal, cleared her throat, and read: "'Let it be known that King Freestone this day thanks the Adventurers Guild for its service to the city.'"

There was a long silence while the crowd waited for Frond to continue. Finally, some brave soul called out: "That's it?"

"That's it," Frond said.

A low muttering broke out. Brock frowned at Zed, who shrugged.

But all eyes returned to Frond when she brought the parchment to her face—and blew her nose, loudly and messily. As they watched, she crumpled up the now soggy scroll and dropped it to her feet. Lotte rubbed her forehead as if a headache were coming on, but said nothing.

"We don't do it for the glory," she said. "And we don't do it for a pat on the head. We do it because it needs to be done." She scanned the crowd. "And we're good at it. But you don't need me to tell you that, and you don't need the king to, either."

Frond stepped off the platform, just as Brock thought she was getting warmed up. But her terse speech had been enough for the assembled men and women. They lifted their cups, their fists, their swords, and uttered a hoarse cheer. Zed hurled his voice in with the rest, and he clapped Brock hard on the shoulder. Brock clapped him back.

The party began in earnest then. Syd and Fife had somehow lured a bard to the guildhall, and she got the crowd clapping along to a popular tune about the splendor of the faraway elven city, Llethanyl, last of its kind and staunch ally to Freestone.

Brock scanned the crowd for Liza, determined to tease her about Jett's cane. But as he peered through the bodies of the assembled warriors, some of whom were near twice his height, his eyes fell upon a sight that put all other thoughts from his mind.

It was the Lady Gray. She was here, weaving among the men and women with the careless grace of a housecat. No one seemed to notice her. Brock was tempted to grip Zed, to point to her, to ask whether she was even really there.

Somehow he felt that was the worst thing he could do.

Her eyes met his, and he shivered as if the sun weren't shining full on his back.

Still, when she beckoned, he followed her indoors without a second thought.

✳

The woman seemed as at ease in the cramped and dirty guildhall kitchen as she had in the council chamber. She was straightening up the mess Syd and Fife had left behind in their frenzied preparations.

"Stop that," Brock said. "I know you're no servant."

The woman shrugged, putting a final dirty mug beside the sink. "But you'd be amazed the doors that open to a person wearing servant's grays. Haven't you used this very trick?"

"Our guild doesn't even have any servants," Brock said. "So how does that work here, exactly?"

She shrugged again, a carefree motion, graceful as a practiced dance step. "It so happens luck is on my side today. Yours, too."

She withdrew a rolled parchment from her gray sleeve and held it out. Brock snatched it, eyeing her as he unrolled it. "What is this?"

She didn't answer, and as he scanned the parchment, he felt the blood drain from his face. "This isn't . . . This is impossible."

"Is it?" she said. "Odd, you'd struck me as the sort of boy who was used to getting what he wanted."

She was right. It was exactly what he'd wanted. Exactly what he'd asked for. This fragile piece of parchment, curled and crumpled, was a royal decree nullifying the Adventurers Guild's claim on him—and on Zed. It laid out their new assignments in plain language, making no apologies and offering no explanations. It was signed by the king himself.

Brock fought to keep his face impassive. He blinked. He took a breath. And then he tore the parchment right down the middle.

"Oh, ho ho," the woman chuckled.

"I've reconsidered things," Brock said boldly. He rolled his shoulders back. "The Adventurers Guild is our home. We make a difference here. And Frond is . . . Frond is crass. She's rude, stubborn, and terrifying. But I'm beginning to think she's exactly the leader this town needs." When the woman didn't respond, he added, "I may not ever like her, but I respect her and—"

The woman held up a silencing hand, and Brock stammered to a halt reflexively.

"You've chosen the right words," she said. "But your tone needs more conviction. Rehearse a little more before anyone else asks, hm?"

Brock flushed, that old coal of anger sparking again.

"*Who* are you, exactly?"

"I represent the true power behind the Merchants Guild. I am first among Shadows."

"Never heard of you."

"Ah, that's the trick," she said. "Hidden in plain sight, and there from the beginning. We don't call Dox Eural the Moneylender, do we? It's not Dox the Shopkeeper."

"It's Dox . . . the Assassin," Brock offered.

She nodded. "He never really changed his ways, our Dox. It's true he founded the Merchants Guild as a way to keep Freestone viable and self-sufficient. But he understood better than most that there is necessary work that must happen . . . behind the scenes. So Dox's Shadows do the work that can't be done by the light of day. We see to it that Freestone survives, no matter how unsavory the details."

"Unsavory," echoed Brock. "You . . . kill people?"

She held up her hands. "Very rarely. Assassinations shove society in a particular direction. I much prefer to . . . nudge. Mostly, I gather secrets. And among the secrets I have recently acquired is this: Your elf-blooded friend has shown an affinity for forbidden magics. Hasn't he? The sort of . . . talent that the Mages Guild would recognize in an instant. An instant later, they'd throw him to the Dangers." She gestured at the torn decree in his hands. "I can see why you'd turn your back on *that* particular deal now."

Brock felt his stomach twist. "How . . . ?" he said, and his throat closed on his words like a fist. He took a moment just to breathe.

"You can't tell anyone," he said at last. He didn't even try to hide his despair. In his mind's eye, he saw the fury of the town—saw how quickly they would turn against Zed if they knew what he could do, that he could sense fiendish magic—could access it, as he had with the staff. They would drag him from his bed and tear him to pieces.

As awful as the thought was, it led inevitably to another, darker imagining:

What might Zed be capable of if forced to defend himself?

What might he unleash?

"Fine," he told her, clamping down with his teeth as if he could bite his fear off at the root. "Tell me what you want, and I'll do it."

She didn't smile. She showed no pleasure at the news. The woman simply nodded as if Brock had said something she'd already known, and known well.

"You needn't worry, Brock," she said. "It isn't anything as dire as you might think. I only want to learn the truth of what happened to Mother Brenner."

"I can help you there," Brock said, smirking grimly. "Tentacles grew out of her head. It was a whole thing. Stop me if you've heard this one before."

The woman fairly radiated her lack of amusement. "Think about it. When would the leader of the Golden Way have possibly been infected by a fiendish seed?" She tapped her own chin. "Here's a hint: I can assure you she never, in all her years, set foot outside the wards."

"So she was infected in Freestone. But . . . but the wards couldn't have weakened until after she was infected. So how . . . ?"

Brock thought back to his very first night with the guild. He remembered the hideous naga laid out on the slab in Hexam's workshop. He knew why they'd brought it in. They'd been able to distill an antitoxin from the thing's venom. That had saved Jett's life, and might save other lives in the future.

He knew why they'd brought it in. But he'd never stopped to ask *how*.

"The Adventurers Guild can get monsters past the wards. Pieces of them . . . trophies. They do it all the time."

The Lady Gray nodded knowingly. "Someone smuggled in the seed that led to Brenner's corruption. Perhaps it was an accident. But I don't think so. I think there is a traitor in the Adventurers Guild." Her eyes went hard, the playfulness gone. "And I don't like not knowing who it is. Not one bit. You, Messere Dunderfel, are going to help me do something about it."

Brock knew he didn't have a choice in the matter—not if he wanted to keep Zed's secret. He sighed heavily as this new obligation settled over his shoulders like a weighty chain.

It was then that a strange sound rang out. It was a horn, but not any sort of horn Brock had ever heard before—a long, low, mournful note sounding from nearby, in the direction of the wall's main gate.

"What was that?" he asked.

When the note sounded again, it was somewhat closer.

"That is a rare thing." The lady smiled.

"You've heard it before?"

"Three times. Most recently twelve years ago. It's the sound of friends hailing friends . . . and it's coming from outside the wall."

It took Brock a moment to puzzle out her meaning. The entire guild was in the training yard. No one should be outside the wall today.

At least, no one from Freestone.

He felt a thrill as the realization struck him. He didn't even spare her a glance as he turned on his heels and ran outside. He feared Zed would already be gone, but his friends were all there in the yard as if waiting for him.

Zed looked fit to burst. He hopped from foot to foot, and his eyes held a manic gleam. "Brock! Did you hear?"

Brock nodded.

Zed said it anyway. "The elves are here!"

"They're at least a few months early," Jayna said.

"Yeah," Micah said. "But they probably tell time by watching the swaying of the grass upon the tallest hill on the night of the full moon, so you've gotta cut them some slack."

Liza slapped him across the shoulder, but her heart wasn't in it. "I have no idea what the elven calendar is like," she said happily. "But get this: We can ask actual elves! Today!"

"Should we . . . ?" Zed began.

"Go on," said Jett. "Get over there! We'll catch up."

Zed nodded excitedly with his whole body, took Brock's hand in his own, and ran.

Brock let himself be pulled along, out the training yard and onto the road and into the crowd of townspeople who had left their homes and begun ambling toward the nearby gate. Zed wove among them, ducked under them, never loosening his grip, and with each footfall Brock felt his worries jarring loose. The Lady Gray's words, the fearful images they'd conjured, the dreadful promise he'd made—such things did not belong in the light of day. Not this day, at least.

Zed and Brock pushed their way to the very front of the

assembled townsfolk, before a line of Stone Sons who maintained a space between crowd and gate. Zed danced on the balls of his feet as the minutes ticked by. More and more people arrived in the square, chattering nervously. Brock saw the perfumer and a dozen other merchants, all having left their stalls behind in their excitement. He saw nobles in their finery rubbing elbows with peasants in their work clothes. He saw a clutch of servants at the edge of the crowd, just arrived from intown. Zed's mother was among them, and Brock waved at her wildly.

"Zed!" she cried, and she hurried toward them.

Zed launched himself at her, throwing his arms around her, and she spun him around and, laughing, said, "Oh, Zed, your *hair . . .*"

Brock noticed there was some activity up on the wall. The Sons on guard duty there, charged with watching over the gate and its controls, seemed to be arguing. Neither of them made any attempt to activate the mechanism.

"Something's wrong," a familiar voice muttered, and Brock turned to see Frond come up from behind them and shove her way past the knights. She strode to the wooden staircase built into the wall and took the stairs two at a time.

Brock watched as she exchanged words with the guards at the top, then slapped them about their helmets in frustration. Gazing out at the horizon, past the wall, she took the controls in her hands, pulling the great crank with all the strength she could muster.

For as much haste as Frond displayed at the controls, the gates parted slowly. Agonizingly so. Brock bit his lip anxiously as the doors groaned open to reveal an elf standing past the threshold.

The elf was tall and pale, with a sheet of pale blond hair cascading about his shoulders and down his back. His eyes were a luminous green, standing out above sharp cheekbones and thin lips pressed tightly together. Brock couldn't read anything in the elf's expression, but he couldn't help smiling at the sight of his pointed ears.

Those ears put Zed's to shame.

The elf raised his hand as the gate continued to swing open, revealing a second elf at his shoulder, and a third. The gesture was weak—less a friendly greeting than a palm of supplication.

"People of Freestone," the elf called out, just loud enough to be heard above the groaning of the widening gate. "We beg of you—help us."

"Oh, no," Zed said softly, and just as Brock was about to turn toward his friend, he saw what Zed had seen.

"Oh, no," he echoed.

With the gate fully open, Brock saw not the ten or twelve elven ambassadors they'd expected. There was no wagon laden with exotic goods and unfamiliar medicines. Instead there were hundreds of elves beyond the wall, and more streaming from the distant tree line with each passing second. They were dirty, blood-streaked, and wretched, clutching only what meager possessions they had managed to carry with them. From somewhere within the throng, a baby wailed.

"Llethanyl has fallen to the Dangers," the lead elf said. "Freestone is our only hope."

Acknowledgments

I t's been a long journey getting this book published, but no adventurer campaigns alone. We are so thankful to the many talented people who have been with us through this process, and who made the book better—and possible!—with their contributions.

First, thanks to David Levithan, without whom we simply would not be where we are today. David, we are forever grateful for your guidance, encouragement, and friendship— and, of course, for the writing retreats. You are an exemplary guildmaster!

We'd like to thank our agents—Ammi-Joan Paquette for Zack, and Josh and Tracey Adams for Nick—for sticking with us over the years. It took a while for this to happen, and without your unwavering faith, it might not have ever come together. We're both so appreciative of your patience and enthusiasm.

Thank you to everyone at Disney-Hyperion who's had a hand in making this gorgeous thing. Especially Kieran Viola, our whip-smart editor, who made the manuscript better every time she touched it—as if by magic! There's no one else we'd rather have leading us on this quest. Designer Phil Caminiti, cover artist Manuel Sumberac, and map artist Virginia Allyn outfitted us expertly for a perilous marketplace. We could not be more in love with their brilliant visuals. And thanks to all the assistants, managing editors, copy editors, proofreaders, and production folks who work so hard behind the scenes; and to the rights, sales, marketing, and publicity teams who tirelessly endeavor to connect books with readers. We both work in publishing and understand that it takes a small army to get books out into the world. Thanks for sharing your creativity and your expertise with us.

We stuck this manuscript under the noses of nearly every friend we've ever made, at various stages in the writing process. Thank you to all our early readers for your feedback. Huge thanks to Rafi Mittlefehldt—who might have been our first fan, right when we needed one—and to Billy Merrell, Tony Sarkees, and our sensitivity reader, Preeti Chhibber. Thanks to Nick's fabulous writing group: Laura and Michael Bisberg, Gavin Brown, Mallory Kass, Grace Kendall, Laura Jean Ridge, and honorary members Matt and Josie. Your joyous and insightful company made this process much less daunting and much more fun. (And the pizza didn't hurt!) And thanks to Rosemary Brosnan and again to Grace, in another context; you made us feel special during a very scary moment. We're still humbled by your enthusiasm.

Thanks to our Dungeons & Dragons group, who listened patiently every week as we blathered on about this book: Travis Berklund, Scott Blair, Eddie Doherty, Lee Edwards, and Teri Yoshiuchi.

Thank you to our parents and siblings: Melanie and Terry Clark, and Matthew Collin Clark for Zack; and Lou Eliopulos, Claudia French, Jason Eliopulos, and Lindsay Eliopulos for Nick. (Plus Katie and Kayla, Cole and Luke, Kathy, John, and Amma.) Thanks for believing in us, and for reading this, for cheering us on through the inevitable ups and downs that come with being alive. We are both very lucky to have such supportive families. This book is for you.

And finally, thank you, Andrew Harwell and Zack Lewis, for being our adventuring companions. This journey has been so much more fun with you in it.

Kobold

Origin: Fiend (Fie)
Threat: Low
Resistances: None

SYD AND FIFE'S
RECENT ATTEMPT
TO ADOPT A
STRAY HATCHLING
WAS EXTREMELY
ILL-ADVISED.

These reptilian pack animals roam the woodlands
outside of Freestone. Scavengers capable of using
rudimentary tools—primarily weapons.

RARE INSTANCES OF SORCERY.
APPEAR LIMITED TO BASIC ATTACK SPELLS.

Naga

Origin: Fiend (Fie)
Threat: High
Resistances: Acid

STILL HAVEN'T SOLVED
KIDNEY VS. GALLBLADDER MYSTERY.

The naga is a solitary hunter of fiendish origin.
Paralyzes its prey with a fast-acting and potent
venom, which is produced by glands in the throat.
Natural spell-casting talent (sorcery).

Slime

Origin: Abomination (Astra)
Threat: Medium
Resistances: Physical damage

EATS ANYTHING—
INCLUDING OTHER DANGERS.
CAN WE USE THAT?

Wholly alien, utterly inscrutable.
Only encountered (so far) in cramped, dark spaces.
If it has any sort of mind, it isn't one we can fathom.

Atto la Concessione di S. Barbara del Feudo di Fucci
Sanquinetia e giusto p così 1808, quale annunciata
che Terra principiate nell'anno corrente 1758 ·②
ricevendo l'anno 1763 ⓛ 20 Aprile ·

Penanggalan

Origin: Fiend (Fie)
Threat: Highest
Resistances: Unknown.

FRODO, WE MAY NEED
A NEW SCALE of
THREAT AssEssMENT
AFTER THIS.

A monstrous infection, this creature does its dark work
slowly and insidiously, hollowing out its victim's body
and mind until all that remains is the drive to destroy...
and to infect others.

TURN THE PAGE FOR A SNEAK PEEK
AT THE NEXT BOOK IN

THE ADVENTURERS GUILD

SERIES

TWILIGHT OF THE ELVES

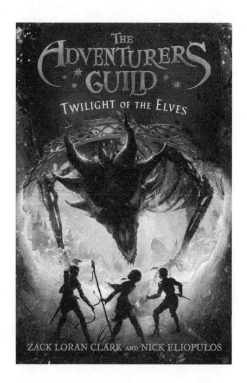

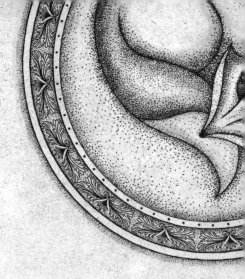

Chapter One

Zed

Zed crept through the snow-covered forest, shivering beneath his heavy cloak.

He moved quickly, cutting between the trees and following the footprints left by their leader. His friends trailed him in a staggered line, crunching noisily through the frost. Above them, the stars sparkled in a silent parade of their own.

They'd been hiking since sunup, and now, well after sundown, Zed was exhausted. His legs felt numb and ungainly, like he was walking on stilts. Ahead of him, their leader stopped midstride and raised a hand. Zed paused, huffing gratefully. His breath met the cold air as a plume of mist.

When a long moment passed and they still hadn't moved, Zed finally thought to search the woods.

"What is it?" he whispered. "A Danger?"

He quashed a kernel of panic before it had chance to take root. Still, Zed reached inward to draw upon his mana, in case he needed it. Soon he felt it there—a sensation like dipping his fingertips just below the surface of a pool of water.

Zed's *actual* fingers flickered with green pennants of flame. He was ready for anything.

But their leader turned instead, his eyes taking in the apprentices behind him.

And what a pair of eyes . . . So green and gemlike they practically glowed. The irises were huge, much larger and brighter than human eyes.

They belonged to an elf. And not just any elf: Callum was the leader of the rangers, Llethanyl's elite exploration force. He was a wood elf, the most common of the three sects. His skin was smooth and pale, with a tinge of green emerging from the hairline, and his auburn hair glistened in the moonlight like a dewy flower. Callum's ears were long and dagger thin; they made Zed's own pointed ears look practically round.

There was a crunch of snow as Brock sidled up behind him, followed by Liza, Micah, and Jett. All five of them wore deep-blue traveling cloaks.

The cloaks were new, and the fur that lined them was warm and soft. It was the finest piece of clothing that Zed had ever owned. In the last six weeks the Sea of Stars had made many friends in Freestone, friends who were excited to outfit its heroic young apprentices in luxurious, tailor-made gifts. Saving a city had that effect, Zed supposed. Recently smiths had been falling over themselves to provide the guild with the steepest discount; even Zed's mother had been given a tidy raise from her mistress.

"What's going on?" Brock flashed Zed a questioning look. "Are we there yet?"

Zed shrugged. "I'm not sure," he whispered. "Callum just—"

Behind them, Liza shushed for quiet.

"Keep moving!" Micah grunted impatiently. "It's colder than Frond's compliments out here."

Jett snorted. "Like you'd know."

"I know your mother's a—"

"*Shhhh!*" Liza hissed again, the noise buzzing through the trees.

The five were on their apprentice journey, an overnight scouting mission the guild ran to test their newest members' quest-worthiness. Any apprentices who passed would be able to join the guild on longer missions outside.

Zed knew they were headed toward some kind of shelter to bed down for the night. They had to be close now, with the sun so far beneath the trees. But he still didn't see anything resembling a man-made structure. Just mounds and mounds of white fluff.

The darker it grew, the more nervous Zed became. Night

was when most Dangers hunted, and many in Freestone believed the horrors that had driven the elves from their home might follow them. Out in the quiet forest, it was hard not to imagine monsters lurking in every shadow.

The apprentice journey was usually made with a master adventurer as a chaperone, if not Guildmistress Frond herself. That Frond trusted Callum to lead her five young recruits said much about him, and about the bond that the human adventurers and elven rangers had formed over the years.

Zed only wished that the High Ranger weren't so quiet and brooding. He had a thousand questions for Callum, only several hundred of which he'd been able to ask before the elf finally called for silence.

Jett spotted their goal. "There," he grunted. The dwarf hefted an iron maul in one hand, training it toward a particularly large snowbank.

Zed squinted at the pile that Jett was pointing to—and then suddenly he saw it. The snow parted over a tapered arch at the bottom of the mound. They weren't huddled near a snowdrift. They were standing at a doorway.

The six crept forward, congregating around the partially buried door. Liza began shoveling snow with her shield, and soon all the apprentices joined in, digging away at the pile. Callum neither helped nor commented. The elf merely watched, those bright eyes glinting in the moonlight.

Once they had dug away the pile, they saw the door itself was covered by a thick layer of ice: hoarfrost that had hardened over time. Zed could just make out a handle and lock buried under all that ice. The door appeared to be made of solid metal.

Jett pointed to his shiny new hammer, an excited gleam in his eyes. He'd been itching to use it on the mission but hadn't had a chance yet.

Micah and Liza both emphatically shook their heads no, their dark eyes and olive-skinned faces similarly grave. It was a rare moment of agreement between the twins.

Brock smirked, then raised his eyebrows at Zed. He wiggled his fingers toward the door.

"Right," Zed whispered. "Everyone stand back." He braced his feet and raised both palms toward the frozen doorway, linking his thumbs and closing his eyes. He could hear snow crunching as the other apprentices backed into a wide semicircle.

Zed glanced over his shoulder to make sure Callum was watching. The elf gave a little nod.

Silently, Zed called upon his mana.

The flames began as green ribbons snaking between his fingers, but soon they joined together and poured forth in a bright emerald torrent. In six weeks of training with Hexam, Zed had yet to match the power or precision from his first use of the spell—the blast that had destroyed the horrific monster threatening all of Freestone.

Still, anything caught within a six-foot cone in front of him would burn, and burn fast. The green flames seemed hungrier than normal fire . . . even other magical fire.

Zed opened his eyes to see that the ice was quickly boiling away. His friends' faces looked eerie, lit by the otherworldly glow. He quashed his mana with practiced care, lest it eat through the door entirely. The flames guttered out from his hands, revealing a steaming metal archway barely six feet tall.

Zed grinned, pleased with his work. After weeks of mishaps, this had been his finest spellcasting yet.

He glanced back again at Callum . . . and was dismayed to find that the elf had already turned away. Callum scraped at the ground, bringing a fistful of frozen earth to his nose. He sniffed it, his eyes narrowing as the particles sifted between his fingers.

Brock moved forward, gingerly touching the iron padlock that was fastened to the door. Apparently satisfied it wouldn't broil his palm, he lifted it in one hand and peered into the key-hole. Then he produced a pick and torsion wrench with a quick flourish, as if he'd plucked them from the keyhole instead of his sleeve.

He curtsied theatrically to Liza, who snorted. Brock had been practicing that trick for weeks.

As Brock set to work picking the lock, Zed repressed a wave of almost delirious hunger. The strain of marching all these hours without a true meal suddenly tugged at his belly. Once inside, hopefully they could stop to eat something beyond travel oats and crumbs of cheese.

"Hey look," said Jett. "A raccoon."

Zed glanced up, following Jett's finger to where a squat, catlike creature watched them curiously from the trees. Its reflective eyes shined behind a mask of black fur. Zed had learned the names of so many strange animals in the past several weeks—animals that lived only beyond the wall. Sometimes it was hard to remember which were natural and which were Dangers.

"Aren't you cold, little guy?" Jett called up.

The raccoon blinked, but was otherwise still. Zed didn't know much about such creatures, but this didn't look like a particularly healthy specimen. Its ribs jutted out, visible beneath patchy fur. A dark, unsettling wound had been clawed across its side.

In the moonlight, its shining eyes almost seemed to glow. They were a sickly shade of purple.

"Apprentices." Callum's voice was controlled, but there was an urgency behind it that sent all five of them jumping. "Inside. Now."

A low *click* followed. As he watched Brock unhook the lock from the door handle, Zed realized his jaw was clenched tight.

Liza pushed the door open, taking the lead. The hinges turned with a metallic shriek that echoed through the forest.

Micah hissed and rolled his eyes, but Liza wasn't around to see it. She'd already disappeared into the doorway.

The rest of them filed quickly inside, one after another, into the dark.

✳

"What is this place?" Zed whispered, once the door had been closed and latched behind them. Now that they were out of the woods, his shoulders slowly relaxed.

The entrance opened to a wide staircase, which descended into the earth. Zed had no sense for how deep it went. He couldn't see farther down than a handful of steps.

The walls of the structure were made of carved stone, and surprisingly well-preserved. The air here was chilly—which was actually an improvement from outside.

"A wayshelter maintained by both the rangers and your guild." Callum's lilting accent drifted musically through the dark. Zed had yet to meet an elf who *didn't* have a lovely voice. "It's one of several that mark the path between Llethanyl and Freestone. Each is stocked with weapons and supplies. My people had to bypass this shelter on our way to Freestone. It hasn't been visited in six years. Reaching here was your first goal."

"Is it safe?" Jett asked. "The door was locked and frozen over. That means there are no Dangers here, right?"

The elf laughed, and the sound was as bitter as it was

beautiful. Zed could have sworn that Callum's echoes actually harmonized with his own voice. "Dangers have a way of breaching even the tightest seals," their guardian said. "There *are* no safe places in Terryn, dwarfson. As you all know from experience."

Zed glanced nervously down the staircase. "Who has the lamp?"

Micah snorted. "Who *needs* the lamp?"

Suddenly the air came alive with a gush of warm amber light. The radiance cascaded slowly over the walls, like waves of rippling honey. Zed turned to see Micah's left hand was raised, its outline glowing as if it had been sketched from pure light.

"Don't drain your anima," Liza scolded, though there wasn't much force behind the warning. Micah could keep this up for hours. The boy was annoyingly adept at the healers' arts—but oh, did they all know it. Zed wondered if the Golden Way Temple had any idea what they'd lost when they let Mother Brenner turn their novice out on the streets.

Callum watched Micah's glowing hand for a moment, then his eyes fell to the stairs. "Your mission is to gather what supplies you can and bring them back to Freestone. Lead the way, children."

Liza shuffled to the fore. Recently she'd graduated from leathers to chain mail armor, wearing a hauberk commissioned from the Smiths Guild as a birthday gift from her father. (Micah had received a pair of socks.)

Zed truly had no idea how Liza could stand under all that metal, let alone march for hours. She might look like an average girl her age, but the noble's daughter was a force of nature.

Liza descended the stairs slowly, sword out and shield high. Micah and Brock followed just behind, with Zed and Jett behind them.

"How's your leg?" Zed whispered to the dwarf.

"Less sore than yours, I'm guessing," Jett cracked.

Zed grinned. "I think you're probably right."

Jett's left leg had been lost to a monster attack, during their very first night as apprentice adventurers. Beginning below his knee was a silvery prosthetic, a gift from the elven rangers. It was forged from a metal called mythril. "Elven steel," Jett had knowingly dubbed it. "Very impressive stuff.

"Though not as impressive as *dwarven* steel," he'd added.

The elves used mythril for all their prosthetics. It was springier than most metals, and tougher than wood. Jett's new leg ended in a long, elegantly bladed foot. With training, he had learned first to walk without a cane, and then even to run. Though he'd never been *especially* fond of running.

"If I'm honest," Jett said more seriously, "it tingles. I can still feel it there . . . literally an itch I can't scratch. And the stump aches like *Fie*."

"Micah can help with that," Zed whispered. "Once we settle in."

Jett rolled his eyes. "So it's a choice between a pain in the leg and a pain in the butt."

As they descended, Micah's light parted the curtains of darkness, revealing a second door, this one made of wood.

The door was ajar.

Zed glanced back at Callum, standing just behind him. The elf narrowed his eyes and raised his hand, hissing a short warning. The group stopped immediately.

Callum slid forward, gliding easily between the apprentices until he knelt beside the open doorway.

He peered inside.

In the silence, Zed felt a single bead of sweat trailing down his back.

"You humans are sloppy," the elf said finally. He stood and pushed the door open, revealing a spare but clean barracks. "I'll have to remind Frond to shut the inner door next time."

A chorus of relieved sighs filled the stairway. Zed and the others entered the shelter. Cots had been stacked up into neat rows, enough for a dozen travelers. There was a wooden table in the center of the room, standing over a moldy brown rug—the room's only decoration.

There were also weapon racks and stands for armor, each of them bearing equipment, and a half-dozen chests containing Fey knew what.

"How are we supposed to carry all this?" Micah groused.

"Dutifully," Callum said, glancing back at the stairway. "I would also advise quietly. But that can wait until morning. You'll bed here for the night." The ranger adjusted his gloves, tugging on the buckles. "If you children can survive without me for a moment, I'll be stepping outside."

"*Now?*" Zed protested. "But it's dark out. Shouldn't we at least eat first?"

Callum shook his head, but his face softened. "You may eat without me. Magic is hungry work, I've heard."

"Callum," Liza said. "Is everything all right?"

The High Ranger frowned. "I'm just taking a look around." He unhooked his bow from his back. "I'll return soon. If I don't, do *not* come looking for me. Wait until daybreak, then head immediately for Freestone."

"Be careful," Liza said.

Callum nodded once, then slipped out the door and up the stairs.

Micah, Jett, and Brock each threw themselves into the lower-stacked cots, while Liza set to work lighting a single dirty lantern with smudged glass panes that was hanging from the wall.

"Everything hurts," Brock moaned. "This has got to earn us a day off from drills, right?"

"I'm pretty sure the Dolt doesn't *do* days off," Micah said, using his private name for Lotte.

"Lotte *might*," Jett said. The young dwarf had rested his hammer against the cot and was massaging his residual limb, just above the prosthetic's socket. "Frond? Definitely not. Unless one of you wants to volunteer to get bit by the next monster."

"Let's not tempt fate." Lantern lit, Liza was now on the other side of the room, peering at the equipment. "Some of this stuff looks elven," she said. "Zed, there's a big wand over here. Or it might be a small staff. There's a crystal on top, anyway."

"Really?" Zed asked excitedly. He was tugging his boots off near the door. "I wonder if it's a scepter. They have a focus embedded on top to channel magic."

But Liza was already making her way down the line. "This armor looks serviceable, but we have better stuff at the guildhall."

Then she reached the chests. There were six in all. Five were the same size and make: simple wooden trunks with iron supports. The sixth looked slightly wonky. The proportions were all wrong, and it leaned almost at a tilt, as if the cooper who'd constructed it had been hitting the dwarven ale.

Liza knelt down, reaching out to open the first chest.

And then Zed saw the sixth chest, the strange chest, open its *own* lid. The inner walls of the chest transformed, its smooth wood exploding into hundreds of curling points. The interior bottom, upholstered in scarlet fabric, swelled into a fleshy, viscous blister. In the span of a moment, the chest was filled by rows of jagged teeth, leading down to an enormous, dripping tongue.

"*Liza!*" Zed screamed.

The girl turned just as the tongue lashed out, gripping her

arm like a frog snagging a fly. Liza yelped as she was jerked toward the monstrous trunk. She tried to wrestle her hand out of the tongue's grip, but it held taut, dragging her across the floor to those awful teeth.

Zed rushed forward, his hands raised, summoning up his mana as quickly as he could.

"Don't! You'll burn her!" Brock's voice brought him up short. He was right—Liza was too close to the chest. She'd be caught within the flames.

The other three boys were fumbling for their weapons, but they were too slow and too far away to help. The Danger jerked its meaty tongue one more time and Liza was yanked from her feet. Her arm fell into the gaping mouth of the chest.

It snapped shut. Liza screamed as all those teeth closed down upon her arm.

Brock appeared behind the Danger as if from nowhere. He raised his two pointed daggers high above his head, then stabbed them into the lid of the transformed chest. It let out a series of distressed croaks and its body sagged, the boxy shape melting away. The monster was looking more like a giant frog by the moment.

"Aim for the tongue!" Liza shouted. "And *don't* stab my hand!"

"So many *rules*," Brock complained. "How am I supposed to remember them all?" He yanked the blades from the Danger's head and viscous, vivid yellow fluid oozed out of the twin wounds.

The chest's mouth drooped open as it croaked unhappily. Liza used the opportunity to jerk her arm out of its maw, kicking her feet out and bracing each against the rims of the trunk. Her chain mail had protected her from the worst of the creature's bite, but healing would be needed soon.

The monster's tongue held fast, though, dripping not just with saliva, but the yellow muck. Zed rushed to Liza's side, joined by Micah, and they each grabbed her entangled arm to help pull against the creature's grip. Micah's glowing hand bounced around as they strained, casting a shadow play of the struggle across the shelter's walls.

Brock moved quickly, stabbing down on the tongue with both daggers. The monster's gloomy croaking turned immediately into a blood-curdling shriek, and the deformed chest began to lurch from side to side. As its grip slackened, Liza grabbed up more of the tongue, wrapping the cord around her arm like a coil of slimy rope. Sweat dripped down her face as she locked her legs, holding the seesawing chest in place.

"Any time now would be great!" Liza shouted.

That was when Zed saw Jett—his giant hammer already raised high. The dwarf let out a bellow that echoed off the stone walls as he plunged the maul down upon the Danger's head.

The shrieking abruptly cut off, punctuated by a loud, wet

crunch. The walls, equipment, and all five apprentices were splattered by a torrent of yellow muck.

There was a moment of quiet, broken only by Zed's and the others' labored breaths.

Then the wooden door flew open, and Callum burst into the room. Three quails hung from a loop of rope in his hand. The elf's eyes widened as he took in the scene.

"We should probably wash up before dinner," Brock huffed.

✳

Freestone's walls rose high above the tree line the next evening, as Zed and the other apprentices trudged home. Zed didn't think he'd ever seen a sweeter sight in his life. Each of the apprentices carried a giant pack of equipment, and they'd taken turns dragging a makeshift sled bearing the recovered armor. Jett pulled it now, having insisted on doing his share.

Zed heard the gate horns blare, announcing their arrival. His grip tightened on the scepter in his hands. He intended to keep that particular trophy; not even Hexam could pry the magic implement from him.

The portcullis creaked open before they'd even made it through the wards, and Zed saw several figures standing within the archway.

Alabasel Frond loomed at the front, her arms crossed. Her scarred face was as still and serious as ever.

Behind the guildmistress, Lotte and Hexam looked a bit more taken aback. Zed realized he and the others must have made an interesting sight. The five apprentices were all covered in dried yellow crust, their once-beautiful blue cloaks now stained and grimy.

Only one of the younger guild members accompanied the three master adventurers to greet them. Jayna stood beside Hexam, nervously wringing her hands. The young wizard had passed her own apprentice journey the previous year, so she hadn't been allowed to accompany her friends on their trip.

A day before they left, Jayna had come about as close to Frond as Zed had ever seen her willingly go, intending to ask for special permission to join the expedition. The girl had summoned up her courage, sought Frond out in the guildhall, and approached her slowly, one step at a time. Then, just as Jayna was five feet away, Frond turned around.

Jayna had quickly scurried down a side hall.

Now, as the adventurers passed beyond the invisible boundary of the city's magic wards, Frond stepped forward to meet the party.

"How did my apprentices do, High Ranger?" she called to Callum. "Are any of them fit for questing?"

Callum quickly bypassed the five young adventurers, who were all showing the strains of their long trudge through the woods. He alone was clean of any yellow goo.

"You've trained a fine group of apprentices," Callum said, waving a hand to Zed and the others. "I would recommend all five as quest-worthy. But Frond—"

Jayna squealed happily, interrupting the ranger. She dashed forward to hug Liza. The two girls clasped hands and danced around in a circle. With the rangers having crowded into the Adventurers Guild hall, private quarters were a thing of the past. The apprentices had all been paired with roommates—Jayna with Liza, and Brock with Jett—while Zed had been stuck with Micah even before the elves arrived.

Since moving in together, Jayna and Liza had become almost inseparable friends. Zed watched them for a moment, the sting of jealousy threatening to spoil his own excitement. He glanced at Brock, who was shucking off his heavy pack. It fell to the ground with a metallic rattle.

Once, Zed and Brock would have celebrated their accomplishment together. But things had changed in the last several weeks. Zed and his once-best friend had drifted. Now Brock's gaze passed briskly over Zed as he turned toward the city gate.

"It looks like you ran into a bit of trouble," Frond said, eyeing the apprentices.

"A Danger had infested the wayshelter," Callum said. "A shapechanger. I failed to spot it hidden among the equipment. Frond, we *must*—"

"Did you know there are monsters that can disguise themselves as chests?" Brock said. "Because that's just really not fair."

"But everyone's unhurt?" Lotte said, approaching the group. Her long blond curls had been tied back into a ponytail. The quartermaster lifted Brock's pack from the ground like it weighed nothing at all.

"Liza was bitten, but the healer tended to it," Callum said. "But Frond, we have *more urgent matters* to speak of. The Lich—" Callum cut himself off. His eyes flicked to the apprentices, then up toward the knights standing over the gate. He stepped closer to Frond before continuing in hushed tones.

Frond's eyes widened.

The Lich.

Nearly two months ago, an army of undead Dangers had risen from beneath Llethanyl's own crypts, led by the mysterious conqueror. Zed didn't know much about him, except that he was once a high-ranking minister who'd defiled the elves' sacred traditions.

Because the undead had risen from within the city, Llethanyl found itself caught off guard by the attack. The elves fought back, of course, but those who fell to the horde all rose again, adding to the Lich's vile army.

In the end, all the survivors could do was flee. The elves lost their home, and Zed lost all hope of ever visiting his father's birthplace.

Hexam and Lotte joined the other two adults, the four of them speaking and gesturing animatedly.

"What's going on?" whispered Jayna. "What did you all see out there?"

"I . . . I don't know," Liza faltered. "Callum said it was nothing."

"Grown-ups lie," Micah said with a big stretch. "Or hadn't you figured that out yet, sis?"

Finally, Frond held up a hand. She turned and marched through the gates without another look at the apprentices. Callum grimaced, then followed closely at her heels.

Hexam glanced back at the others with a long sigh before departing. Zed noticed the wizard eyeing the scepter in his hands, and he clutched it closer to his chest.

"Leave the gear here," Lotte said as she returned to the apprentices. "I'll have Syd and Fife fetch it back to the guildhall."

"Lotte," Jett started, but the quartermaster just shook her head. She suddenly looked very tired.

"Later," she said. "A meal's been set, with plenty of ambrosia. I'd hurry, though—those scuds are more than happy to start a celebration without the guests of honor." Lotte smiled wearily over the apprentices, even Micah. There was enough pride in her eyes for both herself *and* Frond. "I'm sorry, kids. I'm sure this wasn't the congratulations you were hoping for. But, truly, well done."

Zed felt his ears flush. He turned to Brock with a grin. "At least we'll have a head start on Fife. You coming?"

"Mh," Brock grunted in reply. "Save a plate for me. I need to run into town." The boy unclasped his stained cloak, letting it fall to the ground, but he left his travel leathers on.

"Really?" Zed asked. "Right *now*? Where are you going?"

"Just a quick errand," Brock said. "I'll be back before last bell . . . or not too long after."

Zed frowned. "What should I tell the others if they ask about you?" he said. "Which animal cowl do you want to wear at the party?"

But Brock was already slipping away. Zed lost sight of his friend before he'd even cleared the gate.

Chapter Two

Brock

Freestone had changed since the elves had come.

Brock had spent nearly his entire life within the confines of the city's walls, and in that time he'd walked every street and alleyway, visited every plaza and market stall. He knew the best shortcuts, knew which benches enjoyed the most sunlight on an autumn afternoon. Above all, he had the great statues of the Champions of Freestone thoroughly committed to memory. These he could see with his eyes closed: the paladin's grim face glaring from within his helm; the enchantress's ornate staff raised high; the priestess with her arms outstretched; and the assassin, Dox, staring impassively ahead, his unblinking eyes forever upon the city he and his companions had saved so long ago.

Brock wondered what Dox would think of that city now.

Traveling intown, away from the wall, Brock skirted the large area that had once been the marketplace. Where craftsmen and merchants had once practiced their arts beneath a sea of brightly colored canvas, now there was a shantytown. Those same colorful tents had been repurposed to provide meager shelter to the thousands of elves who had survived the journey from the faraway city of Llethanyl.

The population of Freestone had exploded overnight. Not surprisingly, that had caused some problems.

Brock's eyes flitted among the elves, but he was really counting the human knights—the Stone Sons—among them. The Sons had always been responsible for keeping the peace in Freestone, but usually that amounted to standing guard outside important buildings, pacing the top of the wall, and breaking up the occasional tavern brawl. Brock had never seen so many of them stationed in the same area before the elves moved in.

There was no law keeping the elves within their shantytown. But the sheer number of armed men surely sent a message that this was where the elves belonged. And from what Brock had seen, they found little welcome elsewhere in Freestone. Their language, lyrical and strange, drew suspicious and even hostile looks when spoken in mixed company. Their alien features and manner of dress had become favorite subjects of mockery for Freestone's bards. Worst of all was the popular idea that the elves were somehow to blame for their own misery. As if their unfamiliar customs and talent for magic made Llethanyl's fall inevitable. As if that made it any less of a tragedy.

Brock sighed sadly and moved on.

Near the very center of town, just before the drawbridge that led to Castle Freestone, was a park—one of the city's few natural spaces. Ringing that park was a series of buildings, each large and very old and of an architectural style that spoke of a more affluent time, when stone and wood were less precious and could be molded in whimsical flourishes. Brock loved these buildings for their strangeness. Each time he visited, he attempted to find some small detail he'd missed before: some pattern or carving he'd previously overlooked.

The largest among them was the guildhall of the merchants. Brock had been coming here since childhood, and the building fairly towered in his memory. With its tall marble columns and oversize doors, it towered over him still.

The story went that Dox the Assassin had founded the Merchants Guild on the day after the Day of Dangers. His best friend and adventuring partner, Foster, had been the warlock responsible for tearing open the gateways between worlds, allowing monsters to pass over in such numbers they consumed all of Terryn. It had fallen to Dox to execute his friend, and in doing so, Dox had saved the world—or what was left of it.

Brock had always believed that Dox's establishment of the Merchants Guild was in some ways the more impressive achievement. The merchants oversaw everything. They ensured there was always enough food to eat, enough freshwater to drink, enough ore and timber for construction and repairs. There were lean seasons when everyone had to do without some luxury or another, but for the last two hundred years, the guild had provided. They had it down to a science. Or they used to, before the elves had come.

This night, however, all appeared to be business as usual within the guildhall. There was a banquet under way; three hundred candles lit the voluminous central room from a dozen chandeliers and four times as many sconces. Musicians played, servants circulated, and a lavish spread of food acted as the centerpiece for a lively gathering. Brock, in stained leathers still wet with snowmelt and his own sweat, looked severely out of place. He ducked quickly into a washroom, where the servants he'd befriended let him keep a spare set of clothes in their supply closet.

Face scrubbed clean, in a shirt and tunic smelling of lavender, Brock was less self-conscious upon his return to the grand hall. Whether or not he belonged here, he at least looked the part. He hadn't gone two steps before a servant lowered a plate of pastries before him.

His mouth watered. He took a sticky cake from the tray and brought it immediately to his mouth. It was so sweet it made his cheeks tingle. He finished it in two more bites, then licked his fingers unabashedly.

"Wow," he said to himself. "I thought we were supposed to be rationing."

"Well, elves don't eat cake, do they?" said a woman at his elbow.

"Not if they can't pay for it, they don't," a man answered, and they both chuckled.

Brock screwed up his face. Suddenly the treat seemed to have a bitter aftertaste.

He strode through the grand hall with renewed purpose. In a corner of the room, he approached a wall-mounted candelabra and, after licking his finger and thumb once more, he pinched out one of the flames.

It was only a matter of seconds before a servant appeared. "Allow me to relight that, Messere," he said.

"The light offends my eyes," Brock said. It was the secret phrase the servant was expecting, and when the man nodded and stepped away, Brock knew to follow.

As they walked along the edge of the great hall, Brock scanned the crowd for his father. He knew just where to look. These past few weeks, the elder Dunderfel had been the constant companion of Borace Quilby, guildmaster of the merchants.

Quilby stood in the very center of the room, ruddy faced and jovial, sloshing wine from his cup as he regaled those around him with some story. Brock's father stood at his elbow and laughed on cue, his status with Quilby obviously undamaged by Brock's own troubled dealings with the man.

Brock was genuinely surprised to see who else stood at Quilby's side. Ser Brent, guildmaster of the knights, tugged at the collar of his formal white tunic and attempted a smile as Quilby droned on. The false smile didn't suit him. Ser Brent was handsome and bold, and he tended to be the focus of any room he was in. Now, though, standing among Quilby's bootlickers, he looked as comfortable as a kitten in a basket of kobolds.

Brock was deeply curious. In his experience, good things rarely resulted when the town's guildmasters got together. But it wasn't as if he could elbow his way into that conversation. Quilby hadn't so much as spared Brock a glance since last season's failed attempt to oust Alabasel Frond from the Adventurers Guild. That didn't usually bother Brock, though; he knew, now, who was really in charge here.

The servant led him out of the hall, through the kitchens, and to a nondescript wooden door, which he unbolted with a key and threw open. Brock stepped within, and the servant did not follow, instead shutting and latching the door.

Brock descended a spiral staircase and walked through a long, low-ceilinged corridor lined with torches. The stone walls grew damp as he traveled beneath Castle Freestone's moat and into a space that had once been the castle's dungeon.

Freestone had no use for a dungeon now. Since the Day of Dangers, the city could spare no resources keeping criminals alive. Executions and exile had long been the norm.

And so the dungeon currently served a very different purpose. It was now the home of the Merchant Guild's Shadow, the heart of Freestone's black market—where everything had a price, and a heavy cost besides.

Before stepping through the final archway, Brock drew up his hood and pulled from his pocket a slender domino mask, a simple black figure eight, which he stuck to his face with practiced skill. As masks went, it didn't do much to conceal his identity. But it was a necessary formality—one of the few rules of the Lady Gray's court.

Brock emerged into a larger subterranean space, lit not by flame but by the incandescent orbs favored by mages. The room was carved of the same cold stone as the corridor outside, but here it had been softened by rugs and tapestries and piles of soft pillows for sitting; burning incense masked the smell of damp. Chimes softly tinkled in a pleasant arrangement from an ensorcelled cherrywood music box.